ABOUT THE AUTHOR

JASON FISCHER is a writer who lives near Adelaide, South Australia, with his wife and son. He has a passion for godawful puns, and is known to sing karaoke until the small hours.

He attended the Clarion South Writers Workshop in 2007, and has been short-listed in the Aurealis Awards, the Ditmar Awards, and the Australian Shadows Awards.

Jason won the 2009 Australian Horror Writers Association (AHWA) Short Story and the 2010 AHWA Flash Fiction Competitions, and is a winner of the Writers of the Future contest. He is the author of over thirty short stories, and *Everything is a Graveyard* is his first story collection.

His YA zombie apocalypse novel *Quiver* is now available from Black House Comics, or via tamsynwebb.com.

EVERYTHING IS
A GRAVEYARD

Also by JASON FISCHER

Quiver

EVERYTHING IS A GRAVEYARD

JASON FISCHER

T≋
þ≋ Ticonderoga
publications

to
Kate and Logan,
My Everything

Everything is a Graveyard by Jason Fischer

Published by Ticonderoga Publications

Designed and edited by Russell B. Farr
Typeset in Sabon and akaPosse

A Cataloging-in-Publications entry for this title is available from The National Library of Australia.

ISBN 978-1-921857-58-4 (limited hardcover)
     978-1-921857-91-1 (trade hardcover)
     978-1-921857-59-1 (trade paperback)
     978-1-921857-60-7 (ebook)

Ticonderoga Publications
PO Box 29 Greenwood
Western Australia 6924

www.ticonderogapublications.com

#46

10 9 8 7 6 5 4 3 2 1

ACKNOWLEDGEMENTS

Peter M. Ball, Lyn & Lee Battersby, Alan Baxter, Leigh Blackmore, Jack Dann, Gardner Dozois, Russell B. Farr, Mark Farrugia, Jason Franks, Laura Goodin, Liz Grzyb, Lisa L. Hannett, Jeff Harris, Talie Helene, Robert Hood, Baden Kirgan, Chuck McKenzie, Stuart Mayne, Jason Paulos, Tim Powers, Michael Pryor, Angela Slatter, Cat Sparks, A.J. Spedding, Dirk Strasser, Stephen Studach, K.D. Wentworth, Sean Williams, Marty Young, all my buddies from Writers of the Future and Clarion South, and anyone else I've shamefully forgotten. Finally, to my family, and my long suffering wife, Kate.

CONTENTS

FROM THE MOUTH OF AN UNDEAD CAMEL

ROBERT HOOD

When asked to write an introduction to this collection of strange and wonderful stories by Jason Fischer, I was happy to do so as I know and respect the author and have enjoyed his stories for some years now. But was it more than serendipitous that at the same time I had an encounter of a weird kind that drove home just how highly his work is regarded among certain admittedly esoteric sections of the not-entirely-human community?

In the lead-up to the recent Australian federal election, when all sorts of lunatic-fringe interest groups were spending their time stuffing promotional bumph in my letterbox, I happened to look out my study window just as one such violation was taking place. What stuck me most about this particular invasion of privacy was the fact that the guilty party appeared to be a deceased camel.

My suburb isn't known for its camel population and an undead one is even rarer. Sure, the parliamentary election had encouraged the resurrection of many formerly deceased policies and personages—but camels? No, no. This wasn't right.

"Hey!" I yelled out my window. "What do you think you're doing?"

The camel looked vaguely offended. He said nothing, however, merely standing on three legs and waving a brochure at me with his decaying right-front foot.

I headed out and took the proffered paper, which he was holding with great dexterity between his two toes. The brochure (which sported a mugshot of the camel, smiling—a frightful sight if ever there was one) was advising would-be voters of the merits of the Senate candidate for the EFED (pronounced F****D), that is, himself.

"EFED?" I queried.

"Equality For the Exceptional Dead Party," replied the camel.

"Never heard of it," I said.

He huffed, gobbed onto my driveway and muttered, "And *that* is the problem—the speciesist prejudice of the homo-sapien living! Willing to give credence to a brain-dead PM, but an undead dromedary can't get a look-in."

It turned out the camel was standing for the Senate on a platform of equality for the dead—ALL the dead, human and non-human alike.

"Equality for all zombies?" I asked.

"We prefer to call ourselves the exceptional dead," he explained. "*Zombie* is very hominid-centric. The human exceptional dead get heaps of publicity as it is, in popular culture and academic discourse, even though they're mocked, scorned and continually shot in the head by the living. But most people aren't even aware that there are many exceptional dead species out there—and surely *everything* is equal in death! Everything, my friend," he added pompously, "is a graveyard."

I couldn't argue with that,given I'd just been asked to write an introduction to a book of the same name (or didn't care to argue when faced by the rotten bloodiness of the camel's teeth).Politely I expressed an interest in learning more. So he invited himself in for a cuppa and we sat around for maybe an hour, discussing the ins-and-outs of mortality-based inequality in general and the problems of rectifying this dreadful situation through the EFED's proposed Multi-species Undead Rights Bill (MURB). In the course of the chat, I happened to mention Jason Fischer's story "Undead Camels

Ate Their Flesh" as an example of the loosening of boundaries, and his darkly opaque eyes almost lit up.

"That man is a saint!" he exclaimed.

I was, I admit, taken aback. I've heard Jason described in many ways before, but never as a saint.

"Really?" I said.

"He is the one who inspired me and my fellow Non-Human Undead to undertake political action and get F****D up and running!"

Seems that Jason's propensity to push his zombie stories beyond the pale by including zombified animals of all kinds in them had been the main catalyst for this latest bunch of loonies to go political.

I was, I must say, impressed. Clearly Jason was a writer who had Made It.

I first met Jason Fischer during a writing rehab retreat in 2007—when I was the week-one "good-cop" therapist at Clarion South. He seemed like a pleasant-enough bloke. He socialised fairly well, took criticism with appropriately suppressed disdain, critiqued the work of others with a pleasant mix of insight and grudging humility, and brought much laughter to the mournful dissection of genre clichés and careless sentence structures that comprises a good part of Clarion's raison d'être. Clearly he was well on the way to literary mental health even then.

Underneath the veneer of niceness and normality, however, there lurked an undying evil—an evil that manifested through his writing, and through his obsessive need to indulge in outlandish, groan-worth puns. His first-week story—"Starship Zamedi"—was the tale of a bunch of immortal astronauts piloting a shipload of genetic material toward a new world (the story was subsequently published in the Library of the Living Dead Press anthology *Zombonauts: Undead in the Universe*, so you can probably guess what ended up running around the ship). "Starship Zamedi" contained much humour and eccentric imaginative flourishes as well as, by his own estimate, "approximately 5,000 bad puns". A fun, enlightening read. But the evil was there for the wary to see, an undead undercurrent of fantastical literary indulgence—rough, but full of enormous potential for rattling the cages that imprison many SF and horror fantasy stories. It was replete with omens of what was to come.

What came in the intervening years was a swath of unique tales, increasingly polished to a nice putrescent shine. I couldn't have been happier for him(or myself as reader) when his successful novella series was published as the "compiled" novel *Quiver: The Tamsyn Webb Chronicles* (Black House Comics)—a terrific pulpy read, full of classic apocalyptic imagery passed through the filter of an original creative mind. I thoroughly recommend it.

Yet while *Quiver* is probably his most notable work to date, it is in the stories included in *Everything is a Graveyard* that his authorial eccentricity really shines. There are stories here like nothing you've seen before. After you've read through them, I hazard a guess there'll be parts of them you'll want to forget but won't be able to. You can't say that about too many books. When one such comes along you should (metaphorically or otherwise) clutch it to your heart with joy and wonder.

Without a doubt *Everything is a Graveyard* contains a wealth of left-field undead storytelling. But that's not the whole story. Fischer's apocalyptic obsessions cover much wider ground than that, from sheer fantasy to the realism of the ever-present threat of drop bears. If zombie tropes, and indeed all apocalypse stories, are about our personal and social attitudes to mortality (and they are), Fischer explores the personal and social absurdities and profundities like few before him. Some of the stories are older and pre-published, resurrected here for your pleasure. Others are spanking new. As you dip into it now, make sure your loins are girded and your life-insurance premiums all paid up.

Last I heard, Eric the Undead Camel's bid to gain a seat on the Senate failed, despite his sterling commitment to eating his opponents [Sorry . . . that should read "beating his opponents". Russell, can you fix that, please?] According to an email I got from him the other day, his latest plan is to convince Jason to stand for the F****D Party at the next election. [He wanted your address, Jason, and I felt obliged to give it to him. I hope you don't mind. He promised that neither he nor his mates would eat you or your loved ones, only neighbours you can't stand.] He believes Jason's unparalleled ability to utilise extreme punning as a weapon will be an enormous asset in the Party's quest for justice.

So, dear reader, one last thing before I release you into the wonders and horrors that is *Everything is a Graveyard*. Eric has a theory regarding Jason's perspicacity and insight regarding cross-species undeath. It seems the last Bunyip, whose name was Wadi Fishermann according to birth-and-death records, was killed in 2007 when a copy of Dr Elizabeth Kübler-Ross' psychological study *On Death and Dying* fell out of the sky onto his head—thrown from a passing plane, it is claimed, though Eric has his doubts. Unnaturally, Wadi Fishermann crawled out of the pothole afterwards, now undead, and, adopting a vaguely human appearance, took up writing and unsuccessfully pretending to be normal. Well, Eric reckons the author Jason Fischer is in reality Wadi Fishermann the Bunyip. "Dropping the 'mann' and sticking an S in your name doesn't fool anyone!" he stated categorically as he headed off down my street on that fateful pre-election day. "Jason Fischer is awesome because he's an undead bunyip!"

Ridiculous, sure, but it explains a lot.

Robert Hood
Wollongong Cemetery
September 2013

EVERYTHING IS
A GRAVEYARD

L'HOMBRE

For K.D. Wentworth

Coin met the other two in the lowest levels of the arcology, a musty place of calcified pipes, wheezing room-lungs, storage for objects unsuitable for reclamation. Since the sabotage of the desalination plant there had been no reason to visit the intake suite, and it was agreed on beforehand as the most suitable place to play.

L'Hombre.

This most exclusive version of the game had been played on battlefields, gentleman's clubs, the parlour-rooms of kings, even once on the sinking Titanic. Here, at the very end of things, a folding card-table had been erected in the driest corner, with packing crates pressed into service as chairs.

"This is a rather fitting finale to our grand scheme," he said, crossing the filthy tiled floor, casually flipping a coin from hand to hand. His namesake and the death of hundreds, a shining disc that arced from hand to hand. The other two stood as he approached, hands held to their hearts. Coin returned the gesture, and seated himself on the nearest crate.

"Only fools make light of the Game," said the man to his right. Coin had never met the man, a squat looking powerhouse, skin leathery beyond anything a normal lifetime could provide.

This man had already set an ancient chess-piece on the table, a tall knight carved from bone, embedded with precious stones, some of which had fallen out, leaving little pock marks in the horse's flanks. It was a dark yellow now, with a centuries-old dark stain where the man's fingers rubbed the piece absentmindedly.

One of the old Caballeros, Coin realized. *This* will *be good.*

The woman to his left said nothing, flicking the handle of an old slave knout against the edge of the table. Tap-t-t-tap-tap-tap. The thongs spilled out from the whip, running across her lap and onto the floor. Amongst the ruffles of her dress, the man with the coin spotted squid hooks, thick rings, belt-buckles and barbed wire. She'd added her own surprises to the brutal whip.

A newer stranger, a creature of reworked lace and too much mascara. Am I surprised that the last Knave be a woman?

She regarded him coldly, hair poufed into the retro-romantic style, nervously licking at her cracked lips. Her caked-on makeup did little to hide the crumbling nature of her skin, and it seemed that she needed this most of all.

Once there'd been other Houses, odd little fraternities that had fallen by the wayside as the centuries ground on. The Toothmen with their gold-plated jawbones, Flautists huffing on their ancient tin whistles. Daggermen with legendary murder weapons, each blade storied, infamous for the lives it had taken. All gone now, long used up and dust to the Game.

"We are the final three?" the Knave asked. The Caballaro nodded, eyes not leaving the newest arrival, weighing, measuring every scrap of his shadow.

"We have *game a trois* and can continue," he said. "Your token, sirrah?"

He flicked the coin onto the table and it spun lazily, resting on tails. An eagle, squatting on a cactus, snake held aloft in its beak. CINCO PESOS, the worn script read.

"What is this?" the Caballero said, eyes narrowed. "I'll not long suffer your japery." He leaned back on his seat, brushing back his long coat from his hip. The hilt of an old cavalry sabre jutted forth, the wood sallow and choked with old resin. Nicotine stained fingers danced mere inches away, but the horseman did not draw.

"Be easy," he told the Caballero. "It's bad manners to bring cutlery to a card game."

"I should spill your bowels around you," he said. "This sword was tempered in the blood of babes, and the hilt is from the spoke of a wheel which a poor sinner was broken upon. Not even such as we could resist its edge."

The Knave leaned back slightly, whip at the ready. Smiling, the newest arrival raised his hands.

"I assure you, I offer a valid token. We do not all represent ourselves with gold drachmas and denarii."

"Hmph."

"Marius Aurelius played many the game with his brass pfennig. Myfanwy the Bold favoured a tin disc, some promissory token wrenched from a Praetorian's dead hands. This," and here he brushed a hand across the pesos, "was exactly the worth of my wife's blood, and if it doesn't serve then I hope you choke on your little chess piece."

Lips set firm, the Caballero nodded, hand moving away from the sword.

"Merci, friend. You may join us, good Coin."

"Are we all fallow-crafte here?" the Knave asked, and both men supplied the sign, she the countersign. Hands were shaken, a pass-grip predating its Masonic imitation by several thousand years.

I will take it all today, Coin thought.

The Knave supplied the markers, a box of matches so old that the striker heads were crumbling, red dust in the bottom of the tray. It was unlikely they would even catch a fire now. Twenty matches each.

The Caballero pulled out a deck of cards, splaying it across the table. Not enough in this game that one party check the deck after it has been shuffled—each player was required to investigate the entirety of the cards, to determine that all was in order, the cards not tampered with nor ensorcelled.

Considering the stakes, this was a wise practice, and a long-standing custom.

Coin examined the deck, marvelling at the pictures, the artistic style indicative of early illuminated manuscripts. Each suit had the kings standing, and there were no eights, nines, or tens. The queens were replaced by the caballero card, and the suits were more tarot than Hoyle—cups, swords, coins and clubs.

The cards been treated at some point to withstand repeated handling, but underneath the fine layer of nano-weaved laminate they were original and true. These cards had to be over one thousand years old.

"This was one of the first card decks to enter Spain," the Caballero said, scooping up the cards and shuffling them. "I was a knight in the service of Bertrand du Guesclin, off to fight Peter the Cruel. I had already won five games. Even as the castle fell, I claimed my first Coin."

He set the shuffled deck onto the vinyl table-top, and opened the inside of his jacket. The lining was completely covered with coins, a coiled whip, shrivelled ears, finger-bones carved into whistles. Coin only got a glimpse before the Caballero pulled his jacket to, caught the hint of other captured tokens that he could only guess at.

"I certainly hope not to join my illustrious predecessors," Coin said. "Shall we begin?"

The cards were dealt, and the talon established. The three players sat around their paupers' table, the weight of the failing arcology pressing upon them. A fluorescent hell, with one million people living in each other's stink.

They each staked a match into the pot, and began the bidding. The Knave was declared The Man, and the other two began to exchange cards, attempting to establish tricks against her. Coin had several poor hands, and when Knave declared he'd not even come close.

She gleefully swept the matches towards her, smiling at her opponents with something approaching a predatory bliss.

The Caballero sat there calmly in the face of his own death, and finally Coin understood. As the next hand was dealt by the smirking woman, he staked a match, and threw in another just to keep things interesting.

＊

L'Hombre was popular in Guatemala, and the bridge-like game was enjoyed by young and old. While Pieter's parents preferred the card games they'd brought with them from the Netherlands, they learnt the game so as to play with their neighbours, with friends they'd made at church. Pieter learnt the game at the dinner table, and he soon became an expert at playing with the altered deck, something that his parents never truly mastered.

"I am the Man," he would declare joyfully, trapping his opponents into bad decisions with even worse cards.

As he grew into a quiet young man, Pieter fell into circles that were less than Catholic. His esoteric leanings brought him into societies that aped the old ways, and soon the rosaries and saints gave way to forgotten things, the wearing of jaguar skins in lonely places, the potions that could bring the speed of a hummingbird and the far sight.

Even as he gained the trust of the forbidden orders, rising amongst their ranks, he hungered for all the old secrets, until there was nothing left for him to learn. Pieter was not content with knowing the arts of the old places, the nameless things that would give false life in exchange for blood, the power to compel woman and beast, the dream-walking. These things lost their joy, once learnt and mastered. The obscure became the mundane for him.

There were other stone faces brooded in the jungle, half forgotten, ousted by newer idols and finally by the Christos himself. It was told that they knew forgotten secrets, mysteries lost even to the Maya of old.

With patience, Pieter plied these idols, granting them honey, flatcakes, even the heart of a young boy. Finally, an old spirit, with barely the strength of a whisper, told Pieter about the game, about L'Hombre.

"Everybody plays that game," he said with disgust. "I should snap your face off, you lying demon. I'll smear you with dung and drop you into a well."

"The older game, the true one," the spirit whispered. "The sons of the conquerors play at a mirror of the real game. It is the Game of Man, and it is the oldest game in the world."

The spirit told Pieter the true rules of L'Hombre, the houses extant, how to craft a token, and how to call to the other players.

He remembered the lessons perfectly, ignoring his wife's screams as he carved open her chest and unravelled her innards. He squeezed the blood out of her heart, spilling this vital juice onto the coin that he had chosen as his house. *He who has money has all*, he'd reasoned. He left a five peso coin underneath his wife's tongue, burying her in a mixture of sand and finely ground haematite for fourteen days and nights.

He first played L'Hombre in the back room of a hotel in Mexico City, facing a sallow-faced Knave, a Flautist, and a Toothman. In those days, the games were often four-sided, though only three were ever to play a hand at once. They tried to ply him with strong liquor and worked together, attempting to take down the new player first.

It could have been hours, or minutes, he later could not recall. Pieter was the only one to walk out of that room, three new tokens rattling together in his pocket.

He felt good. The slow throb that was inoperable liver cancer ceased to cause him nausea and pain, and to the *dottore's* amazement the tumour itself was soon gone altogether.

Lines on his face eased, vanished. He walked taller, was more virile, had more energy. This is the true magic, Pieter decided. The jaguar dance only gave a temporary respite, a vitality that needed constant rejuvenation. Rare and expensive ingredients were required, and endless begging and scraping from otherwise worthless gods.

He'd had enough of feeding the greedy old things, and decided that the occasional game of cards was much preferable. He only needed the one coin, which he gambled with over and over, for more years than anyone deserved to see.

*

The Knave was winning, and the other two were letting her. She played recklessly, sure that she would destroy her opponents in minutes, not hours. Each trick came to her with little fight, and she cackled over the ancient cards, sweat slowly destroying her thick make-up.

The Caballero simply tapped at his token, amused at her greed. He did not look at his opponents, but made the slyest of eye contact with Coin, and favoured him for several hands. This was sufficient invitation.

The Knave held three quarters of the pot now, over forty mouldering matches neatly lined in front of her. *She cuts a pathetic figure*, Coin thought. He could guess at her origins, a goth girl who'd left the posers behind and joined an actual true coven, murdering the old secrets out of her sisters and her Eldest.

She was one of the youngest players that Coin had seen in the past few centuries. Like many from the pre-arcology days, the Knave clutched onto the fashions and modes of her day. *A pointless immortality*, Coin thought, *if one does not appreciate one's new surroundings. Ignoring the banquet of life to nibble on the dried fruits of the past.*

She giggled, patting the braided handle of the whip like it was her pet. It was her turn to deal, but she put the cards down, a frown creasing her face.

"Deal, damn you," Caballero said. She stood up, unravelling her whip, and the horseman was up, sword drawn in a flash.

"Not me, you deaf old fool. We have an uninvited guest, skulking around in yonder pipes."

They suspended play, and between the three of them they flushed out the girl, a skinny thing. Under the tender ministrations of Knave's lash, the girl spoke of hiding from the criminal water-lords, of having knifed her pimp. She had nowhere else to go, begged for mercy.

"She's no threat," Coin said, already bored. "Have your fun and let her go."

"You know the rules," Caballero said. "The child saw the game. It is not even enough to put out her eyes, or even take out her tongue. The game is void with an earthly witness."

"Alexander Pope saw the Game of Man once. He wrote a bloody poem about it!"

"That's not what I heard," the Knave said, pausing to thrash the girl again. "A player took him as her lover. It's allegory, pretty words. He saw nothing."

Sighing, Coin relented, and the girl had lost her last defender. Knave wrapped the thongs of her whip around the girl's throat, and with one smooth motion drew the coils tight.

The various hooks sliced at her, and the leather coils stole her breath. In moments she gurgled, choked, bled out and then her life left her, in the dripping depths of that desperate place.

"A justice given," the Caballero said, touching his sword by way of salute. "It will be a shame to end you, witch."

"Ha! You've not enough matches to light a cigar, old one. Hurry, so I can leave this wretched place."

"Neither of you will leave," Coin said. "Deal out, Knave."

He won the next three tricks, and soon Knave's bravado turned into panic, followed by outright terror as the matches dribbled back into the pot, snatched at equally by Coin and Caballero. She had a final spurt of success, winning a handful of tricks that encouraged her to bet big, to push in everything she had. What could have been a game-ending *Vole* on the sixth trick became a bunch of worthless cards.

That's when she realized she'd been hustled.

"You are out," Coin said. "Do it."

She fell backwards over her crate, terror sweat and tears sending runnels of make-up down her face. Finding her feet, she held her knout high, ready to strike at them.

"Foolish girl. Do you think these are normal cards?" Caballero laughed. He made no move to stand, or even to draw his unearthly steel. Coin watched her with some amusement, and finally the Knave charged at them, the horrid whip whirling about her head.

She took barely two steps, and the whip itself turned on her, disobeying her control, gouging great strips from her limbs, her face. In seconds, her dress was a mess of bloody rags, her exposed flesh littered with bloody kisses.

When she'd been punished enough for her disobedience, her token reenacted the death she'd just dealt to the arcology girl, a bloody snake that wrapped tightly around her throat.

As her unnatural life bled out of her, Coin gasped. Unseen, one half of her aether crept into his flesh, the fleeing vestiges of her essence meshing with his. It felt like a hot rush, an orgasm from head to toe, the drum-beat of life unceasing. He'd been renewed.

Across the table, the Caballero shivered as he went through the same, a smile finally spreading across that dour face. Only now did he stand, and with a pocket knife he separated one leather thong from the rest of the whip, laying it onto the table.

"The trophy. For whoever of us walks out of here today."

"You deliberately lost the last bid," Coin said, and the other man lifted his hands, smiling. "Why did you work with me to kill this one?"

"Because she was harder to read than you, friend Coin," the Caballero said, already dealing out the next hand, the thin-lipped smile not touching his ancient eyes. "And I cannot stand Goths."

❋

Pieter moved through the centuries, occasionally shedding an identity like a snake-skin, until finally he was disconnected from everything but the Game of Man.

The players met in secret and gambled their lives, dealing cards as empires rose and fell. The age of oil ended, and the secret circle did nothing, did not notice it coming. They'd been captains of industry and king-makers, but recent centuries had seen them as little more than addicts, fighting for each scrap of life.

Even as the earth choked on itself and the seas rose, L'Hombre continued. Civilisation passed into its swan-song, a final huddle of arcologies honeycombed with humanity, yet the Game of Man was all that mattered.

They took to playing it in half-flooded palaces and the splintered shells of the old cities, unafraid of the radioactivity. The card duels, once the event of a decade, became a monthly or even weekly event.

Pieter tired of this. The followers of the true L'Hombre had become worse than human, sorcerers bound into a weary ritual. They were not good company, and did not want to meet save when it was time to gamble for a greedy year or two.

All he had to look forward to was the great prize, should he get down in the card-pits and scrap for it. Life everlasting, for what that was worth. He remembered a game or two where the last members of some house—Toothers? Flensers?—had given up and simply thrown the game.

He'd called them weak at the time, but he was beginning to understand.

Pieter lived in the arcologies as a normal man, hiding among the frightened survivors for as long as he could bear to. He had every opportunity to see humanity at its worst, and passed the time by playing at the usual diversions. Faction leader, warlord, even a turn as the Mayor. Then he gave up on everything, and become just one more anonymous mouth, lining up at the water pump and numb to existence.

Then one day, he received the challenge. There were just enough players left to mount one final game, a *game a trois*. Pieter had long since vanished, the last shield of a fragmented and ancient mind, but Coin gladly accepted.

✳

The Game of Man shifted into its end phase, a two-handed duel with winner takes all. The two men hunkered over the table, pushing around matches, turning over cards, bidding with the same joy as two men at a slave block. The Caballero began to play aggressively, a bold game that unnerved Coin. He bid more matches than Coin could afford to wager, and was declared The Man.

Coin eyed his cards, fighting off a rising sense of panic. He'd been dealt a series of bad hands, and could do nothing with the two of swords, the caballero of clubs, or the seven of coins. No matter what he tried with the man opposite, he outfoxed him with every new card from the *talon*.

He'd never had such a bad run, in centuries of tense encounters where each time he'd gambled no less than his own life.

"You disappoint me, friend Coin," the Caballero tutted. "This should be a roaring game, the ultimate battle of wits. Here at the end, I find myself with a novice. Shall we change the game? Go Fish? Snap?"

"I've seen more games than you, so holster your mouldy old tongue," Coin said. "Consider this. The horseman who outlives all horses is truly the saddest thing. Give over, and I'll ease your passing."

"Ha! I have seen the dawn of the Renaissance, and I shall see the last sputter of civilization as it goes dark," the Caballero said. "The final prize was always meant for me, and I am not ashamed to take it from you."

The horseman turned over the top card of the *talon*, to reveal the three of clubs. Smiling, he revealed a fistful of club cards, and made to sweep the matchsticks towards him.

"No," Coin said, his hand shooting forward like a snake, clamping down around Caballero's wrist. "Show me those cards."

"I will have your head!" the horseman roared, but as he reached for the hilt of his sabre, Coin turned over the Caballero's discarded hand.

It was a mixture of coins and swords, and not a club amongst them. The Caballero's face was white, and he gnashed his teeth as he attempted to draw his horrid blade. The sword was stuck in its sheath, no matter how he yanked at it.

"I may not have seen as many years as you, friend Caballero, but I have met many cowards who played with false decks," Coin said, backing away from the man. "It rarely ends well."

"It is my prize and I will have it!"

Still trying to draw the sword, the Caballero careened into the cheap table, knocking cards and markers to the floor. Coin saw the chess-piece fly into the man's throat, and he began to choke, clutching his throat with his left hand.

At that moment, the sword loosened in the sheath, and the Caballero had been yanking on it so hard that the blade flew up. It passed clean through his clutching fingers, slipped through his neck as if the blade was parting water instead of bone and gristle.

The Caballero's head dropped to the floor with a meaty smack. Severed fingers and blood rained upon it, and even as the horseman worked his lips silently and blinked in shock, the twitching body fell neatly beside it.

The chess-piece popped out of the Caballero's mouth, pushed by a dead tongue. It rolled across the floor until it stopped at the tip of Coin's shoe.

The immense life forces, garnered throughout centuries of false life and hoarded jealously, slammed into his body with a rush. It filled Coin to the brim with vitality and energy.

Underneath the dead man's coat, Coin found the device, a mini-comp synced with the nanoskin surrounding the cards. Each would display the image that the Caballero wanted it to. Examining the history on the computer, he was surprised to see that the Caballero had begun with an honest game. He'd only cheated when he started in on the Coin, when he realized the other man could read him like sky-writing.

The scam was elegant enough—the images could change, depending on how the Caballero rubbed at the edge of the card. While the other player's cards were inviolate, the Caballero had full control of the *talon*, and had stocked himself with winning hands time after time.

"Look who got with the times," Coin whistled. An impressive con, but L'Hombre was historically unkind to card cheats. Few had ever managed to cheat the house and live.

The new energy still pulsed throughout his body. The next time he looked into a mirror, he would appear to be perhaps twenty, maybe even younger. He could run for days and not tire. He had a century left to him, maybe two.

Enough time left to see humanity finally choke, or perhaps rise again from their own ruins. It wasn't his responsibility. These low people had nothing to offer him, nor he to them.

"It is over," Coin said, and for many long moments he simply wept. He put the blood-stained peso back into his pocket, and holding the point of the Caballero's sword to his sternum, looked for a place to brace himself. For a long moment he stood there, watching the keen point at his breast. One push, and it would all end for him.

Coin realized then that he had something left to offer this world. A reason for his existence. A broken people all around him, and he with all this unnatural life in his breast.

He lowered the sword, pulse racing. Fumbling the scabbard from the dead man's belt, he strapped the ancient sword to his own hip. Coin left that room then, left the bodies and the scattered cards to be forgotten.

Rising through the concrete tomb, he passed through a dozen gang territories. Here, lives were lost over water, and petty warlords traded slaves and access to the yeast plant as if playing at their own version of L'Hombre. Coin cut down anyone who even looked at him, dripping blood from the sabre as he stalked through the arcology. He shrugged off their knives and makeshift clubs, laughed as his flesh sealed over a gunshot wound within seconds.

"Rats, dressed as men," he muttered.

He destroyed the back-up power plants, slew those who passed for government in this broken bee-hive. The wheezing room-lungs he carved into ribbons, and whenever someone came running with tools and hand-me-down instructions, he slew them too.

The air grew foul, and the lights went out.

When he unsealed the great doors and crossed the alkaline flats, the squat bulb of the arcology was silent in his wake, a tomb in a wasteland. They would not follow him outside, knew nothing of the world but this place. He left them to choke in the dark.

"I will be the last," he said, striking out for the next enclave. "I will be the man."

＊

THE SCHOOL BUS

Nan said that Dad was at the wall tonight, keeping lookout for kangaroos. The sun was nearly at the treeline, so I rode there on my bike as quick as I could. Dad says only bloody idiots stay outside after dusk.

The wall wasn't a proper wall made out of bricks or stones. It was a junk wall—piled up truck tires and car bodies and sheets of rusty tin. Two and a half metres high, which is about how high the roos can jump. Nan says they used to jump much higher in the old days, so at least we got one thing to be thankful of.

Dad was at the lookout spot facing the main highway, and he was testing the spotlights. They had a bunch of car batteries up there, connected with bent-out coat hangers and jumper leads.

"Light," he yelled out to Mr Wenham, who was the next lookout along. I leaned my bike against a broken TV set and climbed up the ladder.

"Tom!" Dad said. "What the hell you doing here? Go home and get indoors before I tan your bloody backside."

"I got a note from school," I said, and dug the paper slip out of my pocket. "If you don't sign this, Mrs Hamilton says I'll be in even more trouble."

"Gimme that." Dad squinted at the note. "Says you didn't finish your homework."

"It's stupid and boring. An' Mrs Hamilton has only got one leg."

"You've got a bloody cheek on you. Respect your elders." Dad had a nib of a pencil in his pocket and scribbled his mark on the slip.

"We work hard to give you kids a school. If you keep mucking about in class, I'll turf you over the wall and let the roos sort you out."

The sun was starting to sink through the scrub, and all I could see out there was the cracked black ribbon—the old highway. Beats me how they spotted the roos anyway, I reckon if the lights didn't scare them off, the rifles would.

One night, Billy Wenham and I snuck out to watch a roo attack. There were dozens of them, bright eyes shining as they ran from the searchlights. We saw a roo scrabbling to the top of the wall right near our hiding spot, its face all rotten and bits of bone showing in its tail. It nearly got over but Mr Richards shot it in the face. We didn't dare sneak out again after that.

It only takes one roo getting over the wall and we're all dead meat.

"Tell your Nan that I said you get no supper," Dad said. "And you can attend to Miss Stewart on your way home."

"Aw Dad! She's really gross."

"Just feed her boy, don't go doing any of the other stuff. Understand?"

"What other stuff?" I really didn't know what he was talking about. Everyone was really weird whenever I asked about Miss Stewart.

"No backtalk. You can feed the pigs in the morning too."

I slid down the ladder and rode towards Miss Stewart's house. No supper and two extra chores. Stupid Mrs Hamilton.

By the time I got to Miss Stewart's house, it was well into dusk, and I felt a bit nervous. I should have gone to see Dad in the morning, like Nan said. But I figured he would be cranky after pulling an all-nighter.

The door was open. I'm always getting told to mind my manners, and even though Miss Stewart isn't one of the grown-ups who can get me in trouble, I knocked.

There are men coming and going all the time to see her. I guess they take pity on her on account of her situation. Sometimes they even queue out the front door, waiting to pay their respects.

"Come in," she said. Her voice was all weird and quiet. She never sounded happy or sad or anything. Dad says there's no point being miserable. He says there's no room in this town for anyone who wants to whinge and whine.

She slept in the front room of the house. There was nothing in there but an old saggy mattress and some newspapers laid out across the floor. We used to have to change the newspaper every week or so but we stopped doing that a while ago. It smelled really bad in there.

"Hello, Tom," she said, and I nodded hello. I know she can't help it, but it's really disgusting. She doesn't have arms or legs, and she's missing all of her teeth too. She's just a torso and a head.

"I'm glad you came, I'm really busting." I find the rusty saucepan that they've given her to use as a potty. The next bit's a little tricky, but I found that the best way was to sit on the edge of the mattress, resting her across my lap like a big baby. She's not allowed to wear clothes anymore, and it's weird to be able to see her boobs and everything. Some of the other boys laugh about it.

So the trick is to point her bottom end at the pan, and then she goes. The Council said all of our toilet pans are needed for the town garden, especially this year because it's heaps dry. Dad caught me peeing on the back fence once and he gave me a right belting.

When Miss Stewart is finished I help her wipe up with a bit of paper from the floor. She gets a bath twice a week, which was Nan's idea. I don't see why she's so special, I only get one bath each Sunday *and* I have to share the water with Dad and Nan.

"You're a good boy, Tom," she said, and I put her back on the mattress. It's going to be a cold night tonight, so I fetch her two blankets from a pile by the door. They don't allow Miss Stewart a fire.

There's a couple of crates of baby food in the kitchen, and a plastic tub full of rainwater. I pull out a few jars and scoop an enamel mug into the tub for her to drink out of.

"Here's your dinner, Miss Stewart," I said and sit her up on some pillows. I spoon her the apple one first, I know it's her favourite.

"How was school today?" she asked, and so I told her all about the stupid book report and how I got in trouble for not doing my homework.

"I remember reading *Picnic at Hanging Rock* when I went to school," she said, her gummy jaws working on the baby mush. "I thought it was a very boring book, but that's only because they made me read it. I tried it again, when I was all grown up, and you know what Tom?"

"What's that, Miss Stewart?"

"I still didn't like it."

Miss Stewart isn't from around here. She came in a few years ago, with a bunch of out-of-towners. Before everything went bad, she was actually a famous lady and an actress on the television. They showed us a video of her show once, but they don't play the videos anymore because all the batteries are needed for the town lights.

The grown-ups put posters of her all over the wall. It's weird to see pictures of her with arms and legs, and her hair all pretty. She's smiling in the pictures, but I can't remember ever seeing her smile. "Alison Stewart—star of Outback Glamour!" one of the posters says.

You can see wet gummy marks from where she's tried to pull down the posters on the lowest bit of the wall. I'm not sure why they put the posters there. If it's meant to cheer her up it does the opposite. I know I wouldn't want to look at my old pictures every day if I had lost my arms and legs.

Dad won't let me take the posters down, and told me not to mention it ever again.

It was getting really late, and I was so hungry I even snuck a bit of the baby food when Miss Stewart was finished eating. When she had sipped enough water I tucked her in and left.

Whoever had come here last hadn't shut the door, so I made sure it was closed. If a roo got over the wall, it could get into the house, and there would be nothing she could do to defend herself.

Someone painted the word "SLUT!" across the door, in thick red letters. I asked Nan what it meant, but she made me wash my mouth out with soap.

I got home just after dark. Nan had fallen asleep in her armchair. She'd left the oil lamp going again, and if Dad was home he would have yelled at her. There was an empty bottle of brandy on the coffee table, between her and Dad they'd polished it off within a day. That had to be the last of the grog. Dad won't be happy.

Nan must have heard me come in.

"Your dinner's in the stove," she slurred.

There were still some coals going, so I threw a few split logs into the stove to keep the house warm. Dinner was a casserole with meat and baked beans. I decided not to tell her about having to miss supper, because she was too drunk to even notice me cutting a slice of peach cobbler.

Putting a rug over her knees, I left Nan snoring in her chair. I took the oil lamp to my room, ignored *Picnic at Hanging Rock* and read my Biggles book instead. When I went to sleep, I dreamt that the town had a plane, and that I stole it and flew away forever. Everything else was dead meat, but I was safe and nothing could touch me up there.

A rifle shot woke me, and when I went back to sleep I didn't dream about anything.

✳

Nan gave me cold casserole for breakfast, and a bucket of scraps to add to the pigs' wheelbarrow. I had to hurry—school always started at 8.30 am sharp.

The piggery was just outside the town wall, so we didn't have to put up with the smell. Don't know why, but the dead things won't touch a pig. They're perfectly safe out there. They'd built the new piggery down by the creek so that when there's water in it the pigs can drink. It's just a muddy trickle most of the time, so I don't know why they bothered.

When I rolled the barrow down to the piggery, I saw Billy and Eric throwing rocks at Billy's older brother, who was in with the pigs.

Danny Wenham got bitten by a roo a couple of years ago, and the bite went bad. They knew what was coming, so Dad and Mr Wenham wired his mouth shut with barbed-wire, wrapping it around the top of his head and under his chin even while he was kicking and screaming. They wound it tight with pliers, so there's no getting the wires off. He can't open his mouth at all.

"Cut it out, guys. That's not funny," I told Billy and Eric. Billy landed a rock right in Danny's face and he looked up at us, confused as hell.

"He's dead, Tom. He doesn't know what's going on."

I told them I'll see them at school, and opened the gate to the main sty. Danny tried to bite me, his eyes all veiny and bulging out, and reached for me with fingers that looked like bruised fruit. I pushed him away, and put the shovel back into his hands. I knew he wouldn't hurt me. He was just confused.

"Stop mucking around, Danny."

He smelled worse than the pigs, and his skin had gone a rotten bluey-green colour. I know you're not meant to feel sorry for the ones that have turned, but Danny must have gotten lonely out here, night after night with nothing but pigs for company. He did what he was told though, scooping the manure out of the sty with great concentration. He worked very slowly, but he never had to rest. The town had tried to get him to do other chores, but Danny was just too simple now.

Piggery started when the Council were worried that us kids weren't getting enough protein. Some grownups got a truck working and went to the next town. That old fatty Mr Gunderson didn't come back (they never told us kids what happened to him), but Mr Wenham brought back a breeding pair—an old boar and a sow. We had trouble getting the piggery started, some disease took the first litter of piglets so they didn't let us eat those. Now there are six pigs, grown to nearly full size. If they stay healthy, folks say we could slaughter some next year.

Others say to slaughter a pig now, but Mr Wenham keeps calling them impatient fools.

Whenever we get a bit of meat we split it up, an even share for every family in town. Dad says that times are lean, but if the mother-loving-mongrels can hold their horses, we'll never run out of meat again.

*

I was heading to school on my bike when I saw the commotion. There were a bunch of people on top of the main wall, and Dad was pointing at something on the highway side of town.

I laid my bike down and climbed the ladder up the wall, but it was too packed with grownups to see. I climbed up a pile of tires till I found a gap in the tin that I could see through.

A yellow school bus was slowly navigating the cracked highway, big clouds of steam rising from the front of it. It looked in real trouble, and was moving at walking pace. The struggling sounds of the engine reached us. It sounded like someone had put a cupful of ball-bearings in that motor.

As the bus made its way towards our front gate, Dad loaded a bullet into his rifle. Since things had gone bad, we hadn't had a visitor.

Someone cried out, and I looked behind the bus. We could see them now, way back in the distance, stretched out across the dusty horizon. Hundreds of figures shuffling through the scrub, a horde of people that seemed to wriggle in the heat haze.

"Quick!" Mr Wenham yelled out. "Bring all the guns! Bring bloody everything."

Perhaps half a mile from our front gate, the yellow school bus gave a death rattle, and it stopped. I couldn't see much else till the door slid open. A man got out, waving like a crazy. Dad said a curse word, and shot at him. The bullet hit the front of the bus, and the man jumped back in, pulling the door shut.

"Dad, don't!" I said.

"Brought them zombies right to our front doorstep," Dad said, working the action open and loading another bullet. "If these morons think we're gonna shelter them, they're mistaken."

"I dunno," Mr Donaldson said. "We could do with some fresh faces in here. Some of us are getting a bit . . . bored with the entertainment."

"We've more than catered for that, you greedy old sod," Dad said. He looked real mad now. "We're not a refugee camp."

"Please," I said "They're in trouble!"

"Someone get that kid off the wall," one of the grownups said, and Dad yelled at me and told me to go to school.

I climbed down and saw Billy standing, watching us from his bike, right by where I'd dropped mine. We went to Eric's house. Mrs Hamilton was probably hiding in her cellar, the way she did every time the town was under attack. There was no point sitting in the stupid school while this was going on.

Eric took us to his room where he picked up a pair of binoculars his dad had given him, and then we rode to the old church. This was the place where we used to go to Mass, but that was before the Reverend and half the town nicked off. Mum had wanted me to leave with them, but Dad said a lot of bad words and threw all her stuff out the front door and locked her out. Then she went away and never came back.

I'd come to the church sometimes to throw rocks at the stained-glass windows, and once Danny Wenham reckoned that he dug up a body in the graveyard, though everyone knew that he was just a fat liar.

Now we laid our bikes on the dirt beside the front door. Eric hung the binoculars around his neck, and then Eric and Billy and I went into the church and climbed the stairs all the way up the bell-tower. We could see everything from up here. We were leaning out through the shutters up around the bell, and Eric was whistling through his teeth.

"Look at 'em all," he said, and let us have a go at the binoculars.

I moved the little dial till I could actually see the bus. It was packed full of people but I couldn't see much more from this far, and the windows were all dusty and scratched. The people were all sitting in their seats, perfectly still, and a couple of them were looking out the windows.

The other mob were circling the bus now, and they were definitely dead meat. You can tell because they don't walk right, and their clothes are all wrecked and rotten.

I looked at all the walking dead, and there were hundreds—broken little kids and leathery old grannies and even a mouldy old fella that looked a little bit like the old Reverend whose church we hid in.

"Give us a look!" Billy said, and I gave him the glasses. Without them you could just see the yellow brick that was the bus, and hundreds of little black dots swarming around it, kicking up plumes of red dust.

"The rotters will figure out how to get into the bus soon," Eric said. "If those folks don't run, they'll get bitten."

"But if they leave the bus, our mob will shoot them," I said.

"Deserve it," Billy said, taking his time with the binoculars. "Pretty stupid, running away from their hidey hole. There's nothing but dead things out there."

"Yep, dead things and wild pigs," Eric said. "And both will try and eat you."

"And they made a lot of noise and got the dead things worked up, brought 'em all here," Billy said. "Now we're the ones in strife."

I was angry that Billy was hogging the binoculars, but more angry that they didn't care about the people in the bus. Maybe those folks had run out of food, or their water went bad or something.

"I know that if I was in that bus," I said, "I'd want someone to help me."

Billy and Eric both turned and looked at me, like I was going soft in the head. Eventually though, I convinced them to leave the church and help the folks in the bus.

We slid the sheets of tin back to cover the gate on the piggery side, and I piled some extra rocks in front of them in case a dead man tried to get them open.

"This is really dumb. We are gonna get in so much trouble," Eric said.

"I told you, we're gonna be heroes," I told him. "Don't be such a chicken."

"Yeah, and we'll make them pay a fee to get in," Billy said, pleased with himself. "Then there'll be food for everyone."

We rode our bikes around the wall, but Billy had to show off and go over the jumps he'd made down by the creek. If he broke his stupid head open and the zombies caught us here, I don't know what we'd do. I guess we'd have two brothers shovelling s-h-i-t in the piggery then.

We stopped by the highway wall and hid behind an old washing machine. The grownups were all further along the wall, and wouldn't be able to see us so long as we didn't move forward.

"Gimme the glasses," I said to Eric, who just nodded and handed them over. He kept looking at the bus in the distance, and he turned all white. I reckoned he was about to chuck his guts.

I panned across the horde of rotters, saw them shuffling forward and kicking up dust and small stones. They were everywhere, so close now that I could see a cloud of flies buzzing around each one.

The closest one was maybe a hundred steps away from the back of the bus. He wore a butcher's coat, but the white was gone and it was all covered in black stuff now, and his knife belt was empty. He had his hands stretched forward and fingers clenched.

From what I reckoned, he was moving at a quick walk now.

"They're slow as. We can beat them!" I said. We picked up our bikes, and I made sure Eric had his and wasn't gonna chicken out.

Then we rode like hell, rode straight towards the mob of zombies. I rang my bell lots, and Billy whistled between his teeth 'cause he was really good at that.

All of the grownups were yelling at us from the wall, and if I knew my Dad, I'd be in a lot more trouble over this than any book report. They started shooting at the zombies, then I guess we were in the way and they were too scared to shoot at the rotters in case they accidentally hit one of us kids.

It worked, though. The horde began to move towards us, and we led them away from the bus, back towards the highway. Every single one of them went bug-eyed and grabby, shuffling after us.

"You're going too quick!" I yelled at Billy, when he got too far away and the zombies lost interest. He did that riding-in-slow-circles thing, but waited a bit too long before trying to take-off. Butcher Man grabbed him by the shirt and one leg.

Billy said a word that would have got him ten straps in my house, and fell off his bike. The zombie tripped over the bike, and Billy screamed and kicked and wriggled his way loose.

He ran like hell, a hundred rotting zombies shuffling after him. Our grownups started shooting from the walls, picking off the nearest zombies, but it was pointless. There were just too many of them.

I heard gunfire from the bus, and saw that someone had popped a window open to shoot at the zombies snapping at Billy.

"Stop! Stop it!" I yelled, but it was too late. Some of the zombies were moving towards the noise. Eric and I yelled and rang our bells and stopped pedalling long enough to keep most of the dead folks interested, but a few still went for the bus. They were more shots as the stupid outsiders tried to defend themselves.

"Bloody idiots!" I said, and I was glad that Nan couldn't hear me swearing. I yelled at Billy to run back to the creek side, and if it was our school's sports day he would have won the blue ribbon, he was running that quick.

The zombie mob split in three. Lots of them were interested in Billy, some of them were chasing Eric and me, and a few were hammering on the sides of the bus, trying to figure out how to get inside. What looked like a dead policeman was pushing at the folding door, so I got off my bike for just one scary second, and threw a big rock at him.

"Come on!" I yelled. "Over here!" And hopped back on my bike with the wind of dead fingers brushing against my back. Close.

Between Eric and me, we confused the zombies good, and led them around in circles for a while. When none of them were close to the bus I rode up to it, banging on the sides and pointing towards the town. I waited in front of the door, and knew that the town's grownups wouldn't shoot at anyone coming out of the bus in case I got hit.

A man cranked the partition door open, and nervously climbed out. He was a scary looking fella, covered in tatts, with a big meaty fist wrapped around a cricket bat.

"You're a brave little fella. Thanks," he said, with tears in his eye. I didn't know what to say, Dad says that a man having a sook might as well be dead so I just nodded and rode away to draw the zombies from the bus again.

We made sure those people from the bus got a clear run to the town wall. The grownups shouted at us, we shouted back, and the strangers shouted lots too.

They opened the gates though. I knew they'd do the right thing once they saw the people they'd be saving. By the time Dad was through with me I couldn't sit for a week, but it was worth it.

❋

We've had to give up the piggery. The rotters walk around our town day and night now, so many that even the dead roos have given up attacking. Danny Wenham is going berserk out there, pushing at rails and trying to join in with his new friends.

The good news is that the pigs are perfectly safe, bad news is we can't get to them, with all the rotters around. The dead folks aren't interested in our squealers. Dad says it's a waste of good meat. You can bet your biggest marble that the pigs are missing their scraps. I hope they don't suffer for long. Dad says that, in this heat, they should die of thirst in a day or two.

I heard Dad say to Mr Donaldson that the town didn't even have enough bullets left to kill all of the zombies that the outsiders brought to our gates.

But at least we have some new people in town. They're from a long way away, and they got sick from the water so I feel pretty clever for guessing right. The bus was full and there's lots of them, even a mum and a dad, and they brought a little boy called

Laurence. He's in school with us now, but he doesn't talk much and Billy says he caught him crying in the toilets. I told him not to pick on the new kid but even I think he's a bit weak.

Laurence's mum (her name is Mrs Burton) lives in Miss Stewart's house now. I asked Nan where Miss Stewart would live now, but she wouldn't say anything. I caught Mr Wenham carrying Miss Stewart out of her house, right on dusk while I was taking our toilet-pans to the garden. I left them on the ground and followed.

He hefted Miss Stewart up to the top of the wall and for a while he was saying something to her, quietly. Then he dumped her over the side, right into the reaching hands of our dead neighbours. Miss Stewart screamed for a long time before she stopped.

I'm not sure why she didn't end up in the cookpot. Nan said that she was tainted meat, but I don't understand why.

Dad and Mr Wenham gave Laurence's mum what they called "the treatment". They didn't want us kids to see, but I ran to the window when I heard the screaming. Her leg was gone by then, and Dad was cooking the bleeding stump with part of his welding kit. She was screaming her head off and thrashing around, and it was all Mr Wenham could do to hold her down.

That's when Nan started ripping her teeth out with pliers.

"You won't need these choppers, love," Nan cackled. "Can't have you biting your visitors."

Why would she bite anyone? That doesn't make sense, and it's not very fair on her. Mr Burton only had to give his left arm up for taxes.

We boiled up our share, a big reddy hunk of meat with the tatts still on the skin. I played with my food a while and tried to find the tatts, but I remembered I got maths homework due. Then, I ate up quick.

UNDEAD CAMELS ATE THEIR FLESH

With its usual efficiency, the sun blazed down on bugger-all. It was the Outback, with nothing for hundreds of miles but heat, dust and flies.

Shuffling through this wasteland was a dead man, his footprints leading back to civilisation. He'd grown in cunning since his murder, knew to avoid the roads during the day. When hunger struck, he gorged himself on roadkill, scanning the horizon cautiously as his leathery hands tore at flesh.

A truck was braving the old highway, slowly navigating the cracked asphalt. At the first sound of engines, the man fell to the ground, playing dead. The truck drove on, spluttering and backfiring as it downshifted. No-one ever stopped.

Somehow the dead man knew he was an endangered species. He had a dim memory of city streets, of walking around in a horde and smelling out the hidden fresh ones. When they caught one, it was glorious, almost communal.

Things went bad when the fresh ones fought back. There was nothing left for it but to shuffle away, hoping to escape the slaughter of his kind. Something primal told him to follow this road, and this northern exodus had taken years.

Somewhere in the centre of his dead brain certain things remained hardwired. He still knew that when things went wrong for a man, it was good to go north for a while.

For a dead bloke, he was a survivor.

❋

"I didn't mean it," Swanny said, his shaking hands still cradling the smoking sawn-off. His ears rang from the blast.

"Bloody worthless you are," Trev said, snatching the gun out of his hands. "Now we are royally stuffed. Thanks a lot."

"It went off by itself," the boy said quietly. He stepped away from the body, looking down in horror. "We killed him."

"No Swanny, you killed him. 'Coz you're a stupid twat. Now get over here and help me!"

They dragged the body into the office, bundling him up under the desk.

"We could feed him to the pigs," Swanny suggested. "Leave no trace."

"What's the point?" Trev said. "Look at all that blood and shit, all over the floor. We need to open the safe and get out of here."

Checking through the blinds, the older man made sure no-one was approaching the house. It was a big farm, and there was a chance no-one had heard the gun go off. He gestured to Swanny for the satchel, which he threw across the room.

"We could have beaten the combination out of him, but you had to blow his head off," Trev grunted, sticking the explosives to the outside of the safe. "Now every bastard is gonna hear this."

They set the fuse and ran. The explosion blew the thick metal door off its hinges, shattered the furniture, blew all the glass out of the windows. Swanny had packed the charge with his usual enthusiasm.

Coughing, Trev waded through the wreckage of Buchanan's office. He reached into the safe, beating out the flames. Half of the contents were on fire.

"I can't rely on you for anything!" Trev shouted. He opened up his bag, stuffing it full of notes.

"We're rich Trev," Swanny said with a daft grin. He'd never seen this much money.

"Ah, it's all useless," Trev said, holding up a half-charred note.

It was King Christian's face, not King William. Swanny looked confused.

"It's Danish money," Trev said with his last shred of patience. "No-one around here will take these."

They took it anyway, shovelling everything into the duffel bag and running out the back door. At least Trev's battered motorcycle was still there. Two farm-hands were yelling and running towards the house, but stopped at the sight of Trevor Flannigan with a shot-gun.

"Get back," he ordered, sweeping the gun across the frightened pair.

Swanny fell into the side-car, huddling the bag of loot on his knees. Not taking his eyes off Buchanan's men, Trev trod on the starter. Nothing.

"Mongrel of a thing," he muttered, and pushed the starter again. This time the ancient machine gave a slight cough, but did not roar into life. The silent tableau was only interrupted by the whir of the starting pedal and Trev's curses.

Just when he'd given up hope the motor-cycle roared into life, and Trev hammered the throttle, kicking up dust as he spun the machine around and shot for the gate. Swanny made sure to give the farm-hands the finger, pulling a face through his motorcycle goggles.

Trev raced through the farm district, stopping only when he caught sight of the barricade surrounding Port Augusta, a wall of old tires and broken cars. They'd picked a good time to do over Buchanan, most of his hired help were at the football final in town. At least that part had gone well.

"We can't go in there," he said over the rough chatter of the engine. "People know we went to meet with Buchanan, the cops will put two and two together."

"Can't we just spend some money?" Swanny moaned. "We're rich."

"It's Danish money, idiot. We need to get far away, right now. Those farm-hands will be riding into town."

The prospect of being hung made Swanny touch his throat gingerly, and he gulped. They had killed a man, accident or not. In the distance he could see a man on top of the barricade, gun at the ready. They'd been spotted.

"I should have shot their horses," Trev said. "I'll have to go around the town. Hopefully we'll make it to Pimba."

"Yeah, we should head north," Swanny agreed, looking at the fortified town. "North is good."

✳

Camels. A great herd of the feral beasts was coming this way. Australia turned them loose when the motor car came to conquer the interior, and they repaid this favour by breeding like mad and eating everything in sight.

The dead man could smell them downwind, and crouched to the ground. He hadn't eaten for days and was hungry. The only thing he'd found on the road were bones bleached white by the sun.

Keeping perfectly still, he lay in the spiny grass and red dust. Years of dry heat had mummified him, yet he didn't suffer from the rot or the smell that many of his companions had. With the right wind, hours of stillness could pay off in a kill.

A feral camel wandered over the rise. Oblivious to the unnatural creature that lay in wait, the first the camel knew of disaster was when something reached up and sank sharp teeth into its leg.

Squealing in terror, the beast bit back, wrenching the dead man loose. It hurled him away, the man tumbling down the sand-dunes with a mouthful of flesh. The camel spat and hissed, a terrible taste in its mouth from where its peg-teeth had broken the dead man's skin.

The herd broke into a gallop and scattered into many directions, and the bitten camel ran too. It started feeling wrong, had trouble keeping up. Frustrated, it spat and bit at the nearest camel.

This felt good, felt right. Eyes rolling and mouth foaming, it bit another one, tore through the skin this time.

✳

Trev's motorcycle started to splutter when Pimba was in sight. There was still plenty of fuel in the tank; something else was going wrong in the innards of the ancient machine. They were still several miles away when the engine gave a death-rattle and died. They rolled to a stop, engine ticking and boiling.

"I've had this bloody thing since the Plague broke out," Trev said, "Took me from Brisbane to Melbourne, and when the bloody Danes came, I got from Melbourne to Adelaide in one night. I even hit a zombie once, and it only wobbled a bit."

They sat there, Trev tight-lipped and Swanny too frightened to say anything. The older man was furious, gripping the handlebars tightly. The engine stank of burnt oil, and a cloud of flies descended on the stricken pair.

"This thing was worth ten of you," Trev said, pointing a finger at the terrified lad. "Treated me right when nothing else did. So what happens when I need it the most?"

Swanny said nothing, clutched the duffel bag tighter. Trev got handy with his fists when he was angry.

"I'll tell you what happens. The goddamn engine dies at Pimba! The arsehole of the world!"

He hopped off the bike and kicked the wheel hard, stubbing his toe. Launching into a string of curses Trev snatched the shotgun out of its holder, priming a shell and pointing it at the bike. Wailing with terror, Swanny fell out of the side-car, dragging the heavy duffle-bag behind him.

"Don't shoot it Trev!" he implored. "Tank's full of fuel!"

Glaring at the bike like a madman, Trev started to squeeze the trigger, a nervous tic causing half his face to twitch. Taking a deep breath, he pointed the weapon at the sky, when the dodgy trigger fired by itself.

"We gotta get rid of that gun, Trev. Someone's gonna get killed," Swanny said. Trev ignored him, grabbing his swag and the potato sack that housed Swanny's worldly possessions. They both landed at the lad's feet.

"Carry those," Trev said, and started walking along the cracked bitumen of the old highway. Struggling under the weight of all the bags, Swanny rushed to keep up with his mentor.

"What are we gonna do now Trev?" he puffed. "Should we stay here for a while?"

"Nah. Too close to a murder scene," Trev said. "We gotta keep moving, keep heading north. We go west, we enter what's left of civilisation. Cops, the army, jail. If we're lucky."

"Why don't we go east? We've got Danish money, why not go to New Denmark?"

"Stuff that. If I wanted to hang out with a bunch of box-head krauts, wouldn't have left in the first place would I?" Trev said. "We go there, we end up in a work-camp with everyone else, working for King Christian the fucking invader."

Swanny hefted all of the bags, wanting to stop for a rest. The road shimmered with heat-haze, and the tiny town seemed to be getting further away from them. There was nothing but the endless plodding along the cracked surface, and he could feel the heat rising through his old boots. He wondered how long the duct-tape holding them together would last.

When they reached the tiny township, it was mostly deserted. A few grubby children watched them go past, gawking at the pair that had walked out of the bush.

"Where's a mechanic?" Trev demanded, and a boy of perhaps ten pointed up the main street. They continued playing with a half-deflated football, and it was unlikely they'd ever seen a class-room.

"Arsehole of the world," Trev muttered. They found an old service station with an open workshop, an old petrol-guzzler standing over the pit with its engine pulled to pieces. The bowsers were covered in cobwebs, and there was an old sign nailed against the shop-front. NO PETROL it read, and he wasn't surprised.

"Oy!" he called out, unable to see anyone. "Anyone here?"

"Hang on," someone said, and a man clambered out of the pit, covered in grease and filth. He looked about a hundred. "What do you want?"

"Bike broke down just outside of town. I need you to fix it."

"I might have the parts," the man said, eyeing Trev's shotgun. "Do you have money, or something you can trade for it?"

"Here," Trev said, reaching for the duffel bag. He unzipped it, carefully pulling out one stack of bills. *No sense showing this arsehole how rich we are*, Trev thought. He hadn't survived this long by being stupid.

"This is Danish money," the mechanic said. "I won't take this."

"Please, we need the bike fixed," whined Swanny. "We've got more money."

"Shut up!" said Trev. "Will you fix it or not?"

"Do you have any Aussie money?" the man said. Trev shook his head.

"I lost two sons," the mechanic said. "The first was in Adelaide, and the zombies got him. Second was in the Army Reserve, and some Dane put a bullet through his head during the Invasion. When two strangers roll into town with a big stack of kraut money, I get suspicious."

"Are you calling me a box-head?" Trev yelled, priming the gun. "What are you trying to say?" The mechanic looked at him calmly, wiping his hands with an oily rag.

"Did I tell you about my other two sons?" he said, and two stocky young men stepped out of the shadows of the workshop. One held a large revolver, the other had a Rottweiler slavering on the end of a chain, a cricket bat in his free hand.

"The pair of you can just piss off," he said calmly, picking up a tire-iron. "I don't help traitors or Danes."

Trev was angry but not stupid. He would only drop one of them before the other two jumped him. He backed out of the workshop, gun levelled at the two sons. "Big mistake," he called out. "You'll regret this."

The pair of them ran from the petrol station, and ran through the dusty side-streets till they found an abandoned shack to hole up in. Trev didn't know if there was a copper in Pimba, didn't want to take any chances. After several minutes without the sound of pursuit, they peered through the broken windows, sweaty and covered in dust.

"What are we gonna do now?" Swanny said. "I'm hungry."

"I dunno idiot, how about you go to the nearest shop and buy some lunch?" Trev said. "Take as much money as you need."

Trev thought furiously, and Swanny tried to think. What passed for his look of concentration made him look constipated, and Trev only tolerated the boy because he made him feel smart. *I'd abandon him in a second if it was him or me,* he thought.

"The police force still has a working fleet of cars, and they're bound to search Pimba soon. We gotta leave now."

"Should we steal a horse?" Swanny offered, to be rewarded with a slap across the back of his head.

"The only car in this shit-hole town is in pieces, back in that tosser's workshop. We either need to steal food and wait till the heat dies down, or somehow get the bike working again."

There was a long hooting sound that cut through the air, making the broken shards of glass shake in the frame. Trev leapt to his feet, a grin from ear to ear.

"Train!" he said. Snatching up his swag, he dragged Swanny to his feet. They sprinted across the small town until they hit a train-line, and the train barrelled past them, headed towards the local siding.

"It's the Ghan!" Swanny said. "We can go right up to Darwin if we want to!"

"Train doesn't go to Darwin, it's still a zombie town," Trev said, puffing and panting as they ran alongside the train. When it slowed down to stop, he hoisted himself into a baggage compartment. Grudgingly he offered Swanny a hand.

"We're getting off at Alice Springs. There's sometimes work to be had there, and maybe we can change some of this money over somewhere."

"What are we gonna do in Alice Springs? I'm not good at nothing." Swanny said. The depression that swept the country after the Plague had killed many homeless kids, and if it wasn't for Trev he would have starved by now.

"Use your imagination mate! We could join some shooters. I hear they're that desperate for meat up there that they'll eat camel."

✳

Shifting the gun belt that held up his fat gut, Chief Inspector Wallis knelt down, careful not to get the bloody mess on his trousers. He didn't get out in the field much these days, and it showed.

"Not zombies for once," he said, picking up the shotgun shell.

"Stupid bastards choose to live outside the wall, you see what happens," the young constable started. Wallis glared at him like he was a dog-turd hiding in a box of doughnuts and he wisely shut up.

"Buchanan was my brother-in-law," he said. "My old lady is beside herself, you little shit! Do me a favour and interrogate the farm-hands, or the pigs or something. I don't care what, just get out."

For what it was worth, the fingerprint guy had been all over the place. He'd found nothing, but since the computers had stopped the police had bugger-all to work with. They had to rely on old methods and equipment, but contingency plans meant nothing when all the records were gone.

"Why did they shoot you mate?" Wallis wondered. There was a square of paper soaking up blood, and he peeled it off the floor with a pair of tweezers.

"Danish money?" he mumbled to himself. "What the hell was he into?"

"Boss, one of the town shooters just got on the radio," the young copper said, timidly poking his head around the doorway. "Says they saw a motorbike circling the town this morning, two fellas. Weird that they didn't come in and fuel up."

"Where'd they go?" Wallis said, shifting his bulk as he got to his feet. There were only a handful of working cars in the district, and no bikes.

"North, towards Pimba," he said, ducking out of the way as the Chief Inspector barrelled through the door. Wallis moved quick for a fat man, and he was angry. Hardly anything got him out from behind the desk these days.

"I pity those blokes when he catches them," the constable said to the fingerprint guy. "They'll be praying for zombies."

❊

Thousands of feral camels died within hours of the first bite. This news should have made most Outback farmers happy, but people still remembered the Plague. Varied reports went over the patchy ham-radio network, speaking of aggressive camel packs attacking live-stock and people. And eating them.

"Zombie camels?" one ham operator in Alice Springs snorted. His ranger friend was noted for telling tall tales. A hundred miles away his friend was dead, dragged from his shattered four-wheel drive by a camel missing half its face. The entire pack devoured his broken body, jostling with each other for a feed.

With blood-spattered jowls and marble white eyes, a vast stinking horde of dromedaries made for Alice Springs, drawn by the bright lights on the horizon and the distant smell of fresh meat. Their great honking howls echoed throughout the night.

❊

"I saw them officer," the mechanic said. "They came in here perhaps three days ago, toting a big bag full of kraut money and a shotgun. The lads and I chased them away, but we lost them after that."

"Great," Wallis said, looking around the filthy workshop. The only car in town lay in pieces before him. "You have a pair of killers gone to ground somewhere in your town. Why didn't you get on the radio? You idiots have put everyone in danger."

"When's the last time we saw the law in this town? No-one cared about this place, not even before the Plague. We look after ourselves here."

"Doing a good job," Wallis said, turning his bulk on the man as he returned to the squad car, which bristled with antennas and rust. He would poke through every abandoned shack and lean-to in this dust-bowl till he found Stephen's killers. The Chief Inspector was armed to the teeth and vengeful; it was not likely they would be brought to trial, or even buried. Law had changed around here.

After a fruitless morning of poking through a town that was post-apocalyptic before the Plague, Wallis saw the train-line shimmering on the horizon. He visited the sidings on the edge of town, and tore the yellowed time-table from the nail that held it up.

"Least the trains still run proper," he pondered, wondering if he had enough fuel to take him to Alice Springs.

✳

"We don't need shooters," the foreman told Trev. "Stupid to shoot them out in the bush, unless you plan on cooking and eating your camel on the spot. Smart way's to round them up, bring 'em into town and to the slaughterhouse."

"I don't have a horse, or a bike. But I've got a gun," Trev said. The outriders laughed.

"Well mate, perhaps some farmer needs help with a rabbit problem. Doubt you'll hit anything with that old thing though."

I could hit you, Trev thought, but bit his tongue. They were in hiding, and desperate for cash. Last thing they needed was trouble with the law, though he ached to lay into the cocky prick.

Swanny had started work yesterday for a local preserver. The days of fridges and canning had gone by the wayside, and he worked on an assembly line, pushing wax seals into glass jars full of fruit and meat.

"That's women's work," Trev had laughed at the time, but Swanwick was the only one with a job. Trev had pounded the pavements 'til he wanted to pound some heads. No luck.

They'd discretely tried to change some of the Danish notes, with limited success. Alice Springs had been left alone during the Invasion, but many sons and husbands had gone off to fight throughout the district. The hostel had accepted one note with great reluctance, providing a week's accommodation. They would not do this again.

"A fortune and nowhere to spend it," Trev moaned, not for the first time that day. He flopped onto the uncomfortable bed, waiting for Swanny to come home so he could hit him for beer money. Literally.

Making sure that the door was closed, Trev went through the bag one more time, in the vain hope that some Australian currency had been in Buchanan's safe. There was nothing but the Danish money and some boring looking papers. With nothing better to do, Trev actually took the time to read them, took a closer look at the maps that they'd snatched from the safe.

What the hell was Buchanan doing? Trev thought, his head spinning. What he held in his hands amounted to high treason, spoke of sabotage and troop movements. *Perhaps I'll get some sort of reward for turning this in. We killed a Danish spy!*

He'd only known Buchanan was a wealthy land-owner near Port Augusta, went there with the pretence of looking for work. *We bungled the heist, but I reckon we've come up with something better than loot!* he exulted. *This will clear my name!*

He was still sitting there on the bed, surrounded by enemy money and plans for sabotage and invasion, when the door opened. It was another person he'd seen in the hostel, another labourer down on his luck.

"Sorry mate, wrong room," the bloke said, doing a double take when he took in the scene. The white and red *kroner* of New Denmark was distinctive, and to be seen with so much of it could only mean one thing.

"Oh Christ!" the man said, slamming the door a moment before Trev blasted away with the ever present shotgun. There were screams of pain, the sounds of running and doors slamming.

"Fuck, fuck, fuck it all!" Trev said, pushing the bed up against the door and jamming more shells into the breech of the gun.

"I'm not a spy!" he shouted through the broken door, letting off another round just to show he meant business. "I'm a fucking thief."

*

Wallis had navigated hundreds of miles of cracked highway, and when the barren landscape gave way to the green outskirts of Alice Springs he breathed a sigh of relief. He was literally driving on the fumes in his tank, the boot full of empty jerry cans. The old car had begun to overheat, and he doubted it would make the return journey.

No wonder this place was spared by the Plague, he thought. *No zombie would ever make it across that wasteland.*

He noticed the smoke from several fires rising above the town, wondered why he couldn't hear the bells of the fire-brigade. There was screaming in the distance, and as he prowled through the streets in the cruiser Wallis saw people darting into doorways as if the devil was on their heels. The engine began to struggle as the tank ran out, and the car stalled in the middle of the road, engine ticking.

Where the hell is the petrol station?

A young lad ran around the corner and didn't see the police car, running into the driver's side door. The Chief Inspector launched a beefy arm out of the window and grabbed him by the collar before he could flee.

"What's going on?" Wallis demanded.

"The camels are coming!" the boy cried. "They're eating everyone. Mister, you've gotta get out of here."

Camels?

✳

"Give me that," Swanny said, pushing the young girl to the ground and taking her bike. His knees knocking against the handle-bars, he poured as much energy as he could into making that pink-tasselled wonder machine go. Something from the depths of hell was hot on his tail, several somethings that had devoured all of the little old ladies at the preservery. He heard the horrible honking cries behind him, heard the sick crunching sounds as the beasts caught the screaming little girl and tore her apart, eating her alive.

"Whatthehellwhatthehellwhatthehell!" he screamed, losing his bladder control and not caring. A great rotting head loomed out of an alleyway, square teeth nipping at him as he sped past. He felt the hot stinking breath of the camel on the back of his neck, whimpering as the teeth barely missed him. The great empty clacking sound of the teeth striking each other made him moan with fear.

"Camels do not EAT people!" Swanny sobbed. He had to find Trev, Trev would know what to do.

He took the side streets when he could, hoping he would be able to find the hostel. They'd only been in Alice for two days. A wrong turn could mean becoming a camel snack. *I've got to get Trev and the money, get the hell out of this place!* Their problems with the law seemed so less important right now.

There was a shot-gun blast, and then another. *Trev!* he thought, steering towards the noise. *He's alive!* There was another shot-gun blast, and Swanny rode into view of the hostel, abandoning the bike in the street. Within seconds, someone else nicked it to flee from the undead camels, but Swanny didn't care. He'd found salvation.

"Take that, you bastards!" Trev yelled from somewhere inside. "I've got plenty more where that came from!"

One of the camels had tried to walk into the front door of the hostel and got stuck. It roared with impatience, and Swanny could hear it bashing at the internal walls with its great heavy head. He wouldn't be going in that way.

Creeping down the back alleyway, Swanny froze as something knocked over a bin. It was a cat, screeching in terror. It tried to bolt for safety, but as it ran across the street one of the abnormally swift camels struck like a snake and swallowed it whole. Then it looked up, pale dead eyes regarding Kevin Swanwick. He felt his bowels release, and ran up the alleyway, undeath hot at his heels.

"Oh sweet Jesus!" he said, leaping through the window. Broken glass and shit covered him, and Swanny lay in a painful pile on the floor. The room stank of cordite, and Trev was loading more shells into the shotgun.

"Where in the *hell* you been?" Trev demanded. "Hang on, did you piss *and* shit yourself?"

"The camels!" Swanny managed, a split second before the zombie camel rammed its dead head through the window, blood-stained teeth snapping at Swanny. Trev emptied the shot-gun into its head, round after round until he was leaning outside the window to finish the job. Finally, the horrible beast was silent and presumably still.

"What in the bright blue fuck was that?" Trev said incredulously. "Never seen a camel do that before."

"Um, Trev."

"Yeah, what."

"What the hell were you shooting at before?"

They moved the bed and opened the doorway. Numerous trappers and shooters had been running down the corridor to deal with the stuck camel; Trev had murdered every last one of them.

"I thought they were coming for me," he explained weakly. "What else was I supposed to do?"

"We need to go Trev, we need to go now," Swanny pleaded. He reached for the duffel bag, swept the bundles of paper and money into it.

"Leave the money!" Trev said. "That shit has done nothing but curse us. I say we burn it." But Swanny held onto it.

Despatching the stuck camel with several well-placed rounds, Trev and Swanny stepped over its twitching body, and stepped into the absolute anarchy that was post-camel Alice Springs. Somewhere in the distance were the sounds of screams; it seemed the movement of the undead herd had passed this spot.

"Not looking for a shooter eh?" Trev said as he walked past the dismembered corpse of the foreman. "'Smart way's to round 'em up and bring 'em into town,'" he mimicked, poking the dead man's head with his boot. "Not too flamin' smart, are you?"

"Trev!" Swanny whispered. "We need to get a car or something. Stop messing about!"

Momentarily stunned by Swanny's rare display of backbone, Trev complied. They both had guns now, though Swanny didn't realise the rifle from the hostel wasn't loaded. It made him feel better at any rate.

There was a noise behind them, and the pair of petty thugs turned, only to see a morbidly obese police officer. Trev swore.

"Behind you," the man said calmly, raising his pistol. The pair turned, firing at the camel that lurched drunkenly towards them. Swanny panicked and threw his useless rifle at the undead beast, which the stranger dropped with a well-placed shot to the eyes.

"You there," the cop said. "Forgot to do your bag up." Swanny looked down, saw the *kroners* sticking out of the open duffel bag. The man had a pistol levelled at Trev, and gestured for Swanny to drop the bag.

"Over my dead body," Trev said, lifting the shotgun. He was so focussed on the fat man that he didn't hear the camel until it pounced on him, all peg teeth and grinding punishment. Swanny squeaked with dismay, and was frozen with fear. Several camels were running towards them, honking and slavering, broad feet kicking up the dust as they charged. The policeman grabbed him by the collar, jerked him into a different direction. Swanny was too terrified to object.

"I've a score to settle with you," the fat man said, "but you and I have bigger problems. I know you can shoot, you shot my brother-in-law." He handed Swanny a revolver, which the young man took with disbelief.

"We need to get fuel, and we need to leave. Help me and I promise not to leave you for the camels."

It was a no-brainer, even for Swanny. They almost made it too.

At long last, the dead man staggered into Alice Springs. How long he'd travelled was beyond his limited understanding, but he'd finally made it as far north as he'd ever been in his previous life. It was glorious, a dream come true, and he took in the vista with a moaning wordless amazement.

Hordes of the undead staggered around in the streets, half-eaten and moving. Even more of a surprise, the great spitting beasts of the desert were there. In a few instances, the camels were quite happy to let the more damaged undead ride around on them.

Shuffling forward, the zombie was greeted with moans of recognition and acceptance from the newly raised dead. Let the fresh ones fight over the other places. The dead would always have this town.

✳

PIGROOT FLAT

The flies should have given fair warning to Hazel. That, or Codger straining at his leash and barking like an idiot. But the dog was asleep, his feet twitching in a dream. Hazel was wool-gathering in the garden, turning pigshit into the red earth and wondering if anything would grow. A dozen flies became a hundred, then the tin-cans began to rattle.

Dropping the shovel, Hazel ran.

Swearing at the useless dog, she knocked him in the ribs with her boot. Codger barked then, barked for all he was worth. Hazel hauled him along by the collar, and the stupid mutt yipped excitedly, doing his best to wriggle out of her grip.

Hazel had done a turn or two as a roustabout, and years spent throwing sheep and feed gave her ropy arms strength. More cans rattled, and she dragged the pig-dog up the ladder, even as he yipped and gagged and choked on his collar.

Early on she'd spent a whole day on the roof, and nightfall saw her sunburnt and thirsty. She had a camp up there now, slept there most nights. A beach umbrella, food and water, a swag and some chairs. The old rifle and the CB, for all either were worth. Codger couldn't be trusted not to fall off the bloody roof, and so he was tied to the TV antenna.

He barked enough to do himself an injury. Hazel sighed, and watched as her visitors ran around the yard, buggering everything up. Dozens of them today, tripping over the ankle-high fencing wire, rattling the tin cans and cowbells she'd attached every few feet.

They were in the garden now, knocking over stakes and squashing the seedlings. The sound of breaking glass came from the green-house, and they even tried the doors on the four-wheel drive, chattering excitedly as they pounded on the windows.

"Ba Ba Ba!" they shouted gleefully. HAZEL'S ECO TOURS, a dusty decal read on the driver's side door. The tires were flat, the engine out and in pieces.

"Stupid bastards," Hazel said, wincing as they clattered around on the porch, ran through the house underneath her. It got that it wasn't even worth fixing up the doors and windows, so she just left everything open now. That way, they'd go through the house with a minimum of damage, and pour out into the backyard when they got bored.

Hazel had set up a playground to draw them out. Toys, bikes, footballs, even a swing-set. She'd visited the Halletts recently, her neighbours from ten clicks up the road. They'd had kids, probably all dead now. Their farm was silent, and she never cared to linger long.

The ladder scraped along the guttering, and Hazel swore. She dropped her half-rolled cigarette, and slid across the hot tiles, grabbing at the top rung. There was resistance at the other end, and she peered over the side. A rotten face stared up at her.

A woman, a few days on the wrong side of dead. She should have been so much rotten meat, but here she was, smiling up at Hazel, hauling on the ladder for all she was worth. The stink was enough to make Hazel gag, and almost every inch of the walking corpse was covered in flies.

"Play?" the dead woman said, rotten slug of a tongue still working in her mouth. In time, she would become like her idiot friends, speaking in an autistic babble, finally communicating with nothing but the click of teeth, the excited wheeze of maggoty lungs. The fresh ones liked to have a chat.

Hazel let go of the ladder, watched as it clattered to the red earth. The dead woman tried to raise it up again, couldn't quite work out the angle. She gave up the attempt to reach the roof and stood underneath Hazel, waving cheerfully. Fetching up another cigarette with shaking hands, Hazel looked down at the corpse, tried to recognize who it was. Probably someone from town, or hiding out on one of the stations. Underneath the shroud of flies, the dead woman wore dusty jeans and a flanno, torn to strips now.

Near as she could tell, the dead woman had been beautiful once. Maybe a tourist, or some fool from the coast, looking to snag a rich farmer. Hazel felt angry at the thought, and then weird, the way she remembered when she saw someone prettier than her. Jealous, wanting to belong to their world.

Now, the pretty girl was just dead meat. Hazel shook her head, vanished the dark thoughts. Everything was different now, and Hazel needed to get used to it.

Codger was going nuts. He stretched out as far as the leash would allow, snarling along the gutter's edge. The TV antennae strained, and bent with a worrying creak.

"Doggy!" the dead woman shrieked with delight, pointing. "Dog doggy. Doggy. Play."

Hazel looked over at her campsite, wondered if it was worth fetching Gilbo's gun. A big .303, it would drop anything worth dropping. As he'd often reminded her after a few beers.

"Play!" the dead woman insisted, reaching upwards as if in benediction. Codger yipped and hauled at his collar till he was bug-eyed, teeth and scrap of tongue dancing along the edge of the gutter.

They were like something out of the old science-fiction movies, like at the picture theatre when Gilbo was courting her. The recently deceased, risen from death and come for the living. But in none of the b-grade horror flicks had the ghouls been like this.

Idiots. Cheerful monsters, who came calling like the Sandlot Kids. When they caught something living, they'd swarm in, babbling and chatting, smearing their rotten fingers all over the poor bugger, slobbering and kissing them.

That was all it took. You'd be dead in an hour, and up and walking by sunset. They didn't need to bite you, not these idiot dead things. They killed you with love, doomed you with a toddler's affection.

Hazel considered their affliction, and decided that she understood them all too well. She had a grudging respect for these lost souls, exasperation rather than anger as they wrecked the place. Turned out it was hard to hate something that loved you back.

The dead woman was caught up in a stream of corpses that poured out of the house. A man who was almost rotted down to bone carried Hazel's toaster. Another an old record. The walking corpses made for the impromptu playground, and the dead woman waved at Hazel.

"Bye!" she called. "Bye doggy!"

Hazel watched the corpses at play, and realised that her distraction worked too well. They clambered over the swingset, and lined up patiently behind the slippery dip. Normally, they'd have lost interest and moved on by now.

There was a pattern to these visits—gangs of the friendly dead visited all these old holdings at least once a month, and back again on their way to town. She'd seen groups heading north to Darwin, others south and maybe all the way down to Alice.

She picked up the rifle. Grimaced. Set it down by the water container. Codger looked up from his paws, whimpered with something that might have been boredom or frustration.

Only a dozen or so of the idiot dead, but she couldn't bring herself to shoot them. They were dangerous, she reasoned, the way that a snake or a dingo could be dangerous. Just part of their nature, and they couldn't help the way they were put together.

They were dead once, but the rules for death had changed.

Even as she watched the joyful corpses, she found her eyes drawn to the dam. A broken tractor lurked by the water, jerry-rigged with a digging bucket. The metal teeth rested on a bank of cracked earth, mud once.

Across the bank, she'd laid out sheets of tin, weighed them down with cinder blocks. Empty beer bottles, anything that would make noise. The beginnings of a concrete slab; a mixer standing idle, cement bags split and gone bad from neglect. Gravel was scattered everywhere. Cursing and crying, she had quit halfway through, tossing the shovel out into the middle of the dam.

Something buried once was buried good enough.

Next to this, the trunk of a long-dead iron gum, bound with chain. Old iron, red from decades in the weather. The links ran down the trunk, ran across the clay-pan until they ended in a single shackle.

The meat chain.

Hazel took her crossword book out of her back pocket, and attacked the squares with a stub of pencil. There was nothing left to do but put her feet up and wait for the pigs.

*

Pigroot Flat belonged to Gilbo's dad, until lung cancer ate him inside out. Young Gilbo didn't have anyone else, and so he spent five years in a boy's home down in Adelaide. On his eighteenth birthday he came back, moved into the old shanty. Now Gilbo was gone too, and Hazel supposed that made it her place now.

Ten acres of scrub, an hour's drive west of Katherine. Gilbo had spent twenty years on this block, trying to turn his old man's leavings into cash. He put up a dormitory for the backpackers who never visited, and bought riding horses that grew fat and lazy in their yard.

"We're too far from town," Hazel said to Gilbo, back when she still had hope of a ring on her finger. "Should look into guided tours. A boat on the Gorge. Take tourists pig shooting."

Gilbo did none of these things. He drank, broke Hazel with his words, then his fists. Introduced her to the meat chain.

*

That old fear tickled through her belly. Hazel bit at her nails as the sun drifted through the scrub, watched as her dead visitors organized a simple ball-game.

She gave up on the crossword. Opening a tin of dog-food for Codger, she heard grunting, the thump of many feet, an excited squeal that echoed through the bush. Codger danced about on the roof, torn between his dinner and the sudden stink of pig.

They came pouring out of the bush, a big hunting pack. Razorbacks with nasty tusks, their fat sows bouncing along behind them. Piglets jumped around, struggling to keep up.

The end of the world meant nothing but good times and fine dining to these residents of the Northern Territory. Hazel watched as the pigs bolted through the playground, knocking the dead over. They squealed and squabbled amongst themselves, stripping the rotten meat from still twitching skeletons. Whatever fear they'd had of people was long gone.

The dead girl had enough sense to climb the slippery dip, but a young boar clambered after her, snapping and slavering. It reached her foot, and tore it loose. Three more pigs joined the first, fighting to get at the freshest corpse.

Hazel wasn't scared of the idiot dead, and the pigs were just a fact of life around here. But that old anxiety still danced around in Hazel, until her gut felt like it was full of bitter coffee. Gilbo taught this feeling to her, even as he showed her how to take it away. There was a process to follow, but now the bloody pigs were ruining things.

Fear. Amplified by the simple fact that she was completely alone. Last woman standing. She trembled all over, moved her dry lips in a silent litany.

Meat chain.

It had to be now. The rules had changed, but it was do this, or lose her mind.

"You bloody well leave her alone," Hazel muttered. She rested the .303 on an old esky, lining up the sights on the next leaping pig.

"Keep away from her."

A thunderous crack, and then the first pig ran in a confused circle, bleeding and screaming. Codger barked fit to burst, as Hazel sent round after round into the pack. Finally they fled, some dragging their rotten meals back into the bush.

She let Codger off the chain, and the pig-dog fought out of her hands, leapt off the roof with no hesitation. He was off, barking and bounding through the scrub like madness on legs.

Gripping the gutter, Hazel lowered herself down, dropping almost a metre to the ground. Wincing, she limped across the yard. The last light of dusk painted the carnage in shades of grey.

The idiot dead never stood a chance. Rotten meat lay strewn across the yard, guts and bones spread wide by the feral pigs. Some of the bodies were still twitching and trying to move. Hazel coughed up a little vomit into her mouth, fought the rest back down. *This is not the time to lose it, love.*

A razorback lay slumped across the slippery dip. Its life-blood ran down the plastic chute, pooling at the bottom. A fat pig, well-fed and fresh, but Hazel wasn't game enough to eat it. Who knew what the zombie-meat did to its insides? She missed bacon and pork chops, but it wasn't worth the risk.

"Piggy?" the forlorn voice came. Still perched at the top of the slippery dip, the dead woman looked down at Hazel with some confusion.

"Piggy's gone," she replied, and crooked a finger. "Come on, love. We can play now if you want."

The dead woman smiled then, lips sliding across a slimy jag of teeth. She slid awkwardly down the slide, clambering across the barrel chest of the dead pig. Hazel moved backwards, beckoned. The dead woman fell to the ground, tried to rise on the shattered bone where her leg ended now.

"It's okay," Hazel said, making sure to stay clear of those reaching hands. Even in the gloom, she could see the rapture in the corpse's face, the joy of friendship, even love. The dead woman rose, crawled forward when walking failed her.

"We can be friends now," Hazel called out, and meant it. "Let's play over here."

She led the dead woman on, past the house. There was a toolshed by the silent dormitory, and Hazel reached into the gloom, found the old school bag just inside the door. Dusty now, wreathed in cobwebs. A familiar weight, and it felt good.

"Keep coming," she said.

Codger came back from his fruitless pursuit of the pigs, trotting through the yard with a human femur in his mouth. When he spotted the dead woman crawling towards his mistress, he dropped the bone, hackles rising. Lips slid away from bared fangs, and a snarl came from deep down in his chest.

"Leave off!" Hazel shouted. When Codger began growling and edging closer, she fetched up a stone and skipped it across the dust. The dog shied away from the bouncing rock. Fetching up the bone, Codger retreated underneath the house pilings, sulking and whining.

"Idiot dog," Hazel said, shuffling backwards. The dead girl crawled closer, beaming, reaching for Hazel's feet almost shyly. This close, the mortal stink almost overcame her. Hazel fought the urge to vomit.

"Play?"

"Over here."

Slow backwards shuffle, ever aware of the disease on those lips, knowing that a single scratch would doom her. She'd fought off this moment as long as she could, held those old feelings at bay.

There were ways to cope with life on Pigroot Flat.

Living woman and dead obscenity inched across the dusty yard, past the four-wheel drive, around the brooding hulk of the tractor. Hazel led the monster towards the dam, beckoning her on.

"You're beautiful. Pretty girl," Hazel said, wondering who she was trying to convince. The dead woman preened at the compliment, the slimy crack of her mouth turned up at the corners.

"Pretty," the cadaver agreed.

"This way," Hazel said with false cheer, beckoning as if to a puppy. She felt her boots crunch into gravel, lead the dead woman across the corrugated iron. Clattering across the iron, the corpse wheezed with excitement, moving faster now.

"Come and play, pretty girl," Hazel said, kneeling in the cracked clay. Behind her, thousands of mosquitos made an airfield on the dam water, dancing on the murky film. On the water's edge, the cracked clay gave way to pig shit and algae. She wouldn't let an animal drink from it, but that was the point of the whole thing, an element of Gilbo's infamous script.

Hazel tensed, held ready. Opening the school bag, she tipped out her tools, checked that everything was there. She'd need to be quick.

When bruise-coloured fingers brushed against her boots, Hazel ran around the iron gum. With reflexes born of farm-life, she snatched up the rusting snake that was the meat chain. Dove upon the dead woman like a calf in need of hog-tying.

She clapped the shackle around the corpse's ankle, just above its remaining foot. Even as it turned and grabbed at her, screaming like a terrified toddler, Hazel dodged the reaching hands. She pushed it face first into the clay, knelt in the small of the corpse's back. Something gave beneath her with a sickening crack. Hazel's whole world seemed like a miasma of rot and flies.

In seconds she had the muzzle on. A wire frame, much like what the greyhounds wore. Next came the oven mitts, strapped onto the corpse's hands with duct tape.

"Yes, that's it," Hazel exulted, looking down on her handiwork. A moment later she staggered over to the dam, and vomited up everything she'd ever eaten.

✳

Gilbo vanished for a week once, took the house-keeping money and the only car that worked. He came back in the middle of the night, and Hazel woke to a furious beating. He was blind drunk, stank of booze and vomit. She begged, pleaded, crawled across the bed. He hauled her in with no effort, dragged her out of bed by an ankle. Boxed her almost into that sweet darkness.

From a dim place in her mind, she noted how he broke her nose, cracked a rib, and snapped several of her teeth. She'd been beaten before, but never this bad. *He's going to kill me.*

"It's time, bitch!" he shouted. Gilbo carried her out of the house, across the yard. Towards the dam, the iron gum stump, the old chain that he refused to speak of. She wriggled and fought, but Gilbo was built like a brick shithouse.

He threw her to the ground, kicked her in the gut for good measure. Winded, she tried to crawl away, tried to call for help. *Stupid.* Even if she had an air-raid siren, the neighbours wouldn't hear. Gilbo knelt on her back, an implacable force. Something fastened around her ankle, a tight pinch.

Next came a muzzle, and she cried out as the steel jammed against her broken face. He placed something around each hand, binding it up tight with tape.

Then Gilbo left her alone, to sob and shake in the dark.

Terror wouldn't let Hazel sleep. She saw the sun rise over the dam as she shivered in her dirty nightie. The house was silent and still, and she strained her ears, heard Gilbo's snoring.

Every movement brought a wave of pain. Hazel worked herself up to a sitting position, tried to tear off the tape. She couldn't do anything with the mittens on, and the muzzle prevented her from tearing at the tape with her teeth.

Heart sinking, she examined the shackle, noted how the rough metal already wore at her skin. The iron was weathered but strong, almost a half-inch thick. Even if she had a hammer and chisel, Hazel doubted she could hack through this. The other end of the chain fed through a bracket, hammered deep into the tree.

Planting both feet against the stump, Hazel strained, pulled the chain as hard as she could. After several minutes, she slumped to the ground, defeated. She wouldn't be leaving until Gilbo unlocked it. Or killed her.

The sun climbed into the sky, and burnt the last of the night chill. Hazel started to roast in the sun, and by the time noon rolled around, she was burnt from tip to toe. Gilbo snored through the day. The sweat poured out of Hazel, and she circled the stump, trying to hide in a sliver of shade.

She licked her lips, wincing as her dried tongue danced across the skin Gilbo had split with his fists. Her whole mouth and throat were as dry as leather, and she ached with thirst.

When he'd had a skinful, Gilbo was known to sleep till dusk. Hazel realized that she might die of thirst before he bothered to see to her.

Crawling across the clay, Hazel inched towards the old dam. Her hands slid around in the greasy pig shit, but she picked herself up, reached towards the foul water.

A tug at her ankle. She looked back to see the chain at full stretch. The water's edge was just beyond her reach. She strained, winced as the shackle rubbed her ankle raw.

Curled around the stump and dozing, Hazel was later woken by the slam of the screen door. She looked up in terror as Gilbo stepped off the porch, a dusty old school bag in one hand.

"Richie, please," she whimpered, daring to use his first name. He crossed the yard like a man with a purpose, and Hazel couldn't remember the last time she'd seen him stand so tall.

He looked at her indifferently, all the anger of last night gone. This dead stare was far more terrifying than the drunken rage, and she trembled, tried to back away from this stranger.

"This is the meat chain," he told her, placing the school bag on the ground. KATHERINE AREA SCHOOL, the faded old legend read. The leather straps were busted, and a canvas flap hung loose. He flipped it open, and Hazel moaned with fear.

Knives. A hacksaw. Hammers and even an old hand-drill.

"My great grand-dad brought this over from Mount Isa," he said, rattling the chain idly. "He had a claim there, ran a thousand head of sheep. Black fellas ran wild over there once, killing stock, spearing folks in their huts."

He tested a big knife against his thumb, found the edge wanting. Even as Hazel moved her lips in a silent plea, Gilbo worked a whetstone over the blade.

"An army of savages, real cowboys and Indians stuff. Their

land, and they fought for it tooth and nail. So, my great grand-dad lost one sheep too many, and saw red. Fixed this here chain into a stump, much like this one. Went out on his horse, sent a mob of blacks running. Killed three or four, dragged an old woman back by the hair."

Tested the edge, drew blood. Smiled, but it was just a quick twitch of the lips, his eyes set in a cold lizard stare.

"Kept her in the chain for a week, shot every black face that came to save her. In the end her mob were just trying to bring food and water, but he shot 'em just the same."

He ran the blade along her leg, little steel kisses that parted her skin, sent a trickle of blood into the red clay. She screamed, and her curses echoed through the lonely scrub.

"Turns out the meat chain was good fun. Character building. This here is a family heirloom. I've worn it too, and now it's your turn."

Gilbo brought her into the family tradition, a long and bloody lesson. He did not kill her that day, or the next. He promised that one day she would die in the meat chain, but only when she begged him for it, and only when he had a kid to pass this dark legacy onto.

Eventually Hazel agreed to these conditions, and she meant it too. Then he let her go. The visible wounds healed in time, and Gilbo never laid a hand on her from that day.

He had another outlet.

Hazel found a new role as Gilbo's apprentice. Lost waifs, hitchhikers and tourists, they all took a turn in the meat chain. Hazel was part lure, part caddy, and she handed over the knives, watched happily as her man carved up the women she'd befriended.

One night, Hazel put sleeping pills in Gilbo's curried prawns, concerned that he was going about things wrong. Quite simply, he didn't love them. Everything Gilbo did to the girls in the meat-chain was hateful, an act of violence, dominance. It was his legacy, and he didn't even understand it.

The true secret of the meat-chain was intimacy, a love that transcended all common sense. She saw glimmers of it, lurking around her man's shoulders as he went to work.

Even as the life rattled out of them, the girls always loved him. Friendship stripped down to a bare honesty, even as their skin parted from flesh and their flesh parted from bone. They shared confidences with their hulking killer, more than even Stockholm's Syndrome could explain.

These girls needed to be treated properly. With respect.

Gilbo woke in the meat chain, and died slowly. Hazel did her best to make him proud. About a week later she put him in the ground with all the others, and took over the family business.

Beautiful backpackers from Europe, leggy blondes with light smiles. They came to stay at her block, lured by the cheap rates. Green-friendly tours, run by a female owner-operator. A safe destination. It was hardly a success, but she got by.

Some came alone or in twos, and these were the tourists she sometimes introduced to the meat chain. Over days she befriended them, learnt their innermost secrets. They grew to love her, as she loved them, even as she ran Gilbo's tools over their bodies.

She wasn't deaf, knew that the tourists giggled at her crooked nose, her gappy smile. Teased her in their Nordic tongues, even as the four-wheel drive bounced their pert bodies around. Time was not kind to Hazel's looks, and no-one kissed her anymore. Still, she gave these girls new kisses, in all the places that the handsome men kissed them.

Hazel's circle of friends grew year by year. In the times that the chain was empty, she'd sit by the dam, reliving these brief friendships. She remembered them fondly, and mourned them with kindness.

Then one day, the world ended. New friends were hard to come by.

∗

"This is the meat chain," Hazel told the dead girl. The corpse smiled up at her, reaching for her with mitten hands. She brushed aside the reaching hands, continued with the script.

"Chain," the dead woman echoed.

Apparently Gilbo's dad introduced the oven-mitts into the ritual; this was about the time that law-men took to scraping dead women's fingernails, to see who they scratched at in their last moments. Hazel figured a mass grave was damning enough, but praised her dead father-in-law today. The resurrected girl could do little to infect her.

Hazel wore a butcher's apron, rubber gloves that reached almost to her elbows. A bandana, soaked in vinegar to keep out the stink, and thick safety goggles from the shed. No sense risking a bit of spit or blood landing in her eyes.

She ran through the history of the chain, told her new friend all about her part in its legacy. She'd always found the initial begging and screaming a little annoying, so it was a pleasant surprise that the dead woman went along so cheerfully. She even echoed the words as best she could, and Hazel had never laughed so much.

But then it all went wrong. The woman happily let her peel off the rotten skin, take off layer after layer of meat. But the pain was missing. There was no communion to this, no intimacy. The dead woman did nothing but gurgle happily, even after Hazel took her slimy tongue out by the roots.

"It doesn't work!" Hazel cried. Wielding knife and saw, she broke the woman down into her individual parts, left with a neat stack of rank meat that continued to writhe. Normally this was a meditative time, a goodbye to a new friend. Hazel was shaken to the core, and hacked away messily. She'd never been lonelier, or more frustrated.

Empty.

Safe or not, it was time to leave Pigroot Flat.

She left the dead woman by the side of the dam. The stack of severed limbs continued to twitch and shiver. When Hazel limped back to the house, an arm rolled onto the ground, kept rolling until it was thrashing around in the dam.

Only then did Codger deem it safe enough to come out of hiding. He was canny enough to know that the pigs would be back, and they'd make short work of all that meat. He stole across the yard, wary of his mistress. In seconds he was back under the verandah, dragging the dead woman's head by a hank of hair. Her jaw still worked, and the remaining eye regarded the half-starved dog with love.

"Doggy," she mouthed, her blue lips curving up into a radiant smile.

✳

Hazel spent a long time by the dam, bidding her friends goodbye. She made her final peace with Gilbo, and left Pigroot Flat, left her history slumbering beneath the earth. Codger trotted behind her but she threw stones and curses, drove him into the scrub. The dog had tasted people flesh now, would probably turn on her if she got too weak.

The township of Katherine was an open-aired graveyard, full of playful corpses. They splashed around in the Gorge, others wheezing rotten laughter as they kicked the footy. One even had a fishing line out, the hook dangling a good foot above the water.

The cars all sat on flats, batteries long dead. Gilbo might have got one working, but Hazel was no bush mechanic. Snatching a bicycle from a dead man's hands, she ignored the invitations to play, dodged their skeletal fingers.

She pointed the bicycle down the cracked highway, and rode.

Every place was the same. The apocalypse had rolled over every farmhouse, every roadhouse, every sheep station and shit-shack. Numb, burnt to leather by the sun, Hazel passed through Tennant Creek, Davenport, Alice Springs. The dead, red heart of Australia.

By now the idiot dead were little more than skeletons in the sun, sinew holding bones together, skin drawn taut. They waved enthusiastically, shuffling after her bicycle.

On the day she saw the crude fort, she was walking like a dead thing herself. The chain on her bicycle had snapped, but she pushed it mindlessly, useless pedals clicking, busted tire dragging. An enclave, set almost a mile from the highway. Behind the barricades, a stand of trees. *Perhaps a waterhole?*

The gate opened. Figures rushed towards her. Hazel dropped the bicycle to the red earth, and shook with silent sobs.

People embraced her. Someone pressed a water bottle against her lips, and she gulped it gratefully, water running down her filthy face.

They led her into their compound, and she gazed around in wonder. Buildings, green gardens, livestock. Kids, playing in the street.

People, dozens of people.

The first she'd seen in years.

They closed the gate behind her, and Hazel clutched the old schoolbag close, the one marked KATHERINE AREA SCHOOL. Dangling from the open canvas flap, a loop of rusty old chain.

"You're among friends now," someone said to her, and she smiled.

✳

THE HOUSE OF NAMELESS

The date had been going well, all things considered. No girl in her right mind ever thought she would sit down to dinner at a minotaur's house, but then again no-one knew that Raoul could cook up a storm.

"I've been saving this for a special occasion," he said, bumping open the kitchen door with his broad hip. He had a freshly baked pavlova resting across the palm of one broad hand, his free hand proffering a bottle of Sauternes that was pinched between his enormous thumb and forefinger.

He stopped short. The girl was sitting rigid in her seat, gripping the edge of the table and trembling. There was a stranger in his house, standing right behind her, resting his hands upon shoulders made bare by her evening dress.

He was a patch of murk and drab, and Raoul found it difficult to look directly at him. His eyes seemed to slide off the intruder's shape, as if he were too greasy to hold light and form.

Raoul growled. His horns were sharp enough to pierce an engine block, but he hesitated. There were measures in place to keep weak minds out of this house, and this intruder had bypassed them all.

The man stank of rot, and was sniffing at the girl's scalp, long and lovingly. The intruder was blurred around the edges, not a definite shape so much as a smudge. He moved in jerky fits and starts until he stood before Raoul.

"I knew you, back in the One-Way-World," the stranger said. "You were Mithras then."

"Get out of my house," Raoul said. "Now."

"I will undo all of your works," the man said, turning sideways and inside out till he was gone.

Raoul hushed his weeping date. He gently licked her forehead with his broad flat tongue, massaging the incident out of her mind. The minotaur sent the blank-faced girl safely home, realising with some embarrassment that he had already forgotten her name.

✳

He checked and refastened every door, even the basement door that led out into the cold vacuum of space. With the girl gone he let the subterfuge drop, and the true nature of his domicile asserted itself.

Gone were the chandeliers, the immaculate mosaic flooring, the tapestries and hangings. His rats-nest of an apartment emerged, complete with flaking stacks of periodicals, weight sets, and mismatched furniture that had started to buckle beneath his weight.

The only true thing to appear in Raoul's spiderweb had been Picasso's *Minotaur Kneeling Over Sleeping Girl*. An original, and the lurid drawing had made his date a little nervous, but ultimately curious. He thought it only fair to give her some hint of what his true intentions were, and it was an ice-breaker if nothing else.

"You looted this," she had said, arching an eyebrow. She touched his arm as she took in the image of the virile bull-man, lurking over the innocent girl, waiting. The date had been going very well, before something with the power to break through his safeguards had appeared *in his house*.

Raoul didn't believe in phones, but he had a battered old note-pad on the counter, propped up against a grimy kettle. It had an elaborate sketch in ballpoint on the cardboard backing, a puppy curled up and sleeping.

If someone phoned him, their words appeared on the topmost page. Raoul found that he preferred to wander around in his squalor and think for half-an-hour or more of what to say, then to write a suitable reply underneath the words of his caller.

This came over on the phone as if he had said the words himself, and the pacing of his speech seemed quite normal. The minotaur liked having the advantage of hours of thought, a chance to reference his various books, or the means to outthink his various lady-friends if one of them happened to call and he was with someone else.

Specifically, he'd invented the device to deal with Lune.

"Hello, it's me," he wrote.

"You'd best be scribbling out an apology," her words appearing in her own neat hand. "I know you just had a visitor."

Long minutes of thought. He knew she was cunning enough to keep eyes on him, jealous enough to wish him harm. Powerful enough to deliver it.

"I had more than a visitor. Someone broke into my house."

"Into your house?" came the writing, cramped together in an excited scrawl. "You've gone to great efforts to keep everyone out. Including me."

"Please, Lune. This man, this intruder, he stank of the old ways. Aren't you concerned?"

"If it's to do with the One-Way-World, I suggest you go see Nameless. I'm done talking."

Her final sentence underlined itself several times, indicating that Lune had terminated their conversation with extreme prejudice.

✳

Raoul visited the house of Nameless. In truth it was the echo of his family home, a sagging mansion full of ghosts and sour days. There was a beach and a caravan park below the cliffs, but these places and the happy sounds that floated up from them were only there to torment Nameless.

"Come in," he told Raoul. The minotaur stepped over the muscle-bound ginger tom that was sometimes one cat, sometimes a dozen resting on every surface, snarling. The cat/s were scared of Raoul now, having attacked him only the once.

They went through the kitchen, past the dining table set with plastic place-mats for a family that would never eat together again. There was room after room full of memories and photographs, and the sunlight drifting through the windows was pale. It was always dusk here, and Nameless would not turn on the lights.

"Up here," Nameless said, and they climbed the stair. There was an old child gate at the bottom, busted now. Up and up, winding, and there were more floors than it looked from outside. They climbed until Raoul snarled impatiently and terrified Nameless into giving him the top floor, the little den of Father.

"I've got this video," Nameless said, and hands shaking he slipped the cartridge out of the paper case. THE FUNNY TAPE! the label read, and he fed it into the guts of a big chunky VCR.

They sat on the dusty couch, the minotaur and the little nothing-man. There was a photo of his family on top of the TV, and everyone but Nameless had their backs turned to the camera.

The tape started, and it showed a young Nameless, back when he had name and life and love. He frolicked on the beach with friends, turning cartwheels to impress the girls.

"Is this how you waste your days?" Raoul asked, knowing the answer. He could taste it in the air, the funk of a house where each day was a hundred years of dusk and loneliness.

"There's more," Nameless mumbled, but stopped the video, cheeks flushing.

"So, given eternity, you would sit here and stew over your misspent youth," Raoul said. "Enough. I would have your thoughts on a matter."

Nameless ejected the tape, reverently sliding it into its case. He rested it on the coffee table, lined it up within its boundary of dust.

"I had a visitor, in my house," Raoul said. "Uninvited."

"In your house?" Nameless pursed his lips, frowned. "That's tricky."

"Stank of the Old Ways, and that from a man who was hardly there. He spoke of the One-Way-World."

"Ah." Nameless drifted into a powerful memory, and Raoul was caught on the edges of this thought, almost drawn into the reverie. The minotaur stood up and with one hand flipped the sofa, knocking Nameless onto his back.

"Why?" the man said, winded. He got up, blubbering and clutching at Raoul's thick furry legs.

"There's enough of the One-Way-World in your head to cause trouble," Raoul said.

"I've been good," Nameless whined.

"You've dragged more than one fool into that mind of yours. Now tell me what you know."

"The man. That blurry, secret man," Nameless whispered. "I thought of him today, when I was making a sandwich," and Raoul knew he was lying, there was never a scrap of food to be found in this house.

"The truth, NOW," Raoul said, and put enough god into it that the knick-knacks on the windowsill bounced around and the window shook. "Or I will turn you out and close this house to you."

"I was reading my high-school yearbooks," Nameless said, terrified into truth. "I was reading the names, and when I saw a photo I thought of the man."

"Show me," and Nameless was hauling a carton out of the nearest shadow. It was brimful of curios and memories, a lifetime of hoarding every encounter, every word. There were lovenotes with the folds worn away, the ink nearly read from the page. Scout badges, speeding fines, broken condoms, the whole box and dice.

Nameless produced the yearbooks, and gave a guilty grin.

"Meant no harm by it. Just looking."

"You were trying to find your name," Raoul said. "Try, it's not in there," and surely Nameless must realise that every mention of it was gone. Excised throughout the whole universe, from his birth certificate onwards.

"Show me the photo," and Nameless was flipping through the pages, past the photos of the formal and the signature page. He stopped at a class shot, rows of kids grinning or scowling at the lens. It was Nameless's class.

Nameless got the faintest of connections to Raoul's intruder, and Raoul carefully captured the very edge of this thought. He had a trail now, and tore the page out of the book.

"Finally, you're useful for something. I'll leave you to it," Raoul said, tapping the video case with his massive sausage fingers. Nameless sat still as Raoul left by the front door, moving only when the wake of the minotaur's far-travel had settled.

Sliding the Funny Tape into the machine, Nameless howled. Raoul had replaced his precious memories with an aerobics programme, and an infomercial for a fruit juicer.

✳

Raoul appeared on the deck of *The Cheerful Misogynist*. The ship was the size of a city, a party boat mounted on wheels and rollers and treads. It was driven by sail, fans, balloons and oars, and rumour had it that a FTL drive could be found deep in its innards.

There was a girl here, Imogen, under his protection.

As could be expected from his entrance, there was a fuss. The sudden appearance of a minotaur can hardly factor into the average fetish, and most of the debauchery stopped wherever he passed.

There wasn't a crew as such, but there were those who liked to think they served the ship, hauling on ropes and scrubbing at the ancient decking when someone yelled at them. The Captain himself appeared, straightening his epaulettes and setting his cap level.

"Milord," he said, offering a lazy salute. "Captain Aurora Luca, if you please."

He wasn't in charge the last time Raoul visited, but the position seemed to be up for grabs whenever the predecessor got bored with it.

"I seek my ward," Raoul said, and for a moment Captain Luca was confused. But the ship itself filled him in and understanding dawned in his eyes.

"Young Imogen," he said, fingering his salt-and-pepper beard. "She's belowdecks, and well cared for."

"I would see her," the minotaur told the man, who shrugged, leading him to a hatch. It was a tight squeeze but the minotaur climbed down the ladder, following the Captain along a cramped passage. When his horns scraped the ceiling beams the ship grudgingly grew to a more reasonable dimension.

"Not welcome, Raoul," Luca said suddenly, now as the voice of the ship. "Do your business and go."

They passed a thousand fantasies, every kind of fetish and whim, hearing the low sobs of those who were meant to cry. Raoul had spent his mandatory season on board *The Cheerful Misogynist* and had no wish to open any of these doors.

Luca led him into an elevator, the clanky old kind with levers and a sliding cage door. After a gut-twisting descent, the door opened onto the Hieronymous Bosch wing, acre upon acre of purgatory. There were other horned beasts here, and he was barely noticed. Luca took them through the yawning mouth of a fat slavering worm.

After a moment of darkness and intense heat, they were climbing a set of stone steps. There was a crude wooden door, and Imogen was behind it.

"Raoul," she said, throwing her arms around the minotaur's waist. She was filthy, her hair matted into thick dreadlocks. "I want to leave this horrible place."

Raoul looked down at Captain Luca, who held up his hands, shrugged.

"She didn't like our games, didn't want to join in," he said. "Her greatest desire was to be left alone, we only gave her what she wanted."

They'd been keeping her in solitary confinement, halfway between a monk's cell and an oubliette. There was a rotten straw pallet with one ragged blanket, and a toilet bucket tipped over in the far corner. They'd nailed a banner to the damp stone wall, higher than she can reach. It read SUIT YOURSELF, YOU STUCK-UP BITCH.

"I'm not happy," Raoul rumbled. "Our agreement was quite clear."

"Keep her safe," Luca said, speaking as the ship. "Keep her hidden from her old lover. That is all."

"Splitter of hairs," Raoul said. "You have wronged me. The girl did not want this."

"You forget, Raoul," said the ship through the man. "Your precious free will does not apply onboard us. We generate our own laws here."

"I'm leaving with the girl. Be glad I take this no further."

"Of course. Still, there is the—simple matter—of our bargain," Luca's lips moved. "You owe us, little cow-god. We want your horns."

Luca blocked the doorway. He was no threat on his own, but Raoul could feel the presence of the ship in him, the weight of centuries of malice. True, he himself still had some power here, but would it be enough?

"You want these?" Raoul said, reaching up and touching the tips of his horns. Luca nodded for yes.

"A deal is a deal," and then the minotaur was upon Luca, goring him and flinging him about like a floppy toy. Imogen was screaming at him, telling him to stop, but he had the rage in him. He cast the broken man to the floor and became all feet and fists, before sense returned, the knowing that the ship would now do its best to destroy them. He heard the stones moving, felt the ship flexing and ready to bear down upon them.

"Get the Captain's hat," he ordered the terrified girl, and the stone wall opened before his horns as if it were paper. They were through and running, even as her prison became fire and wrath and unmaking.

Raoul snatched Imogen under one arm, the better to charge through the walls. The ship was squeezing like a fist, trying to trap them, but Raoul outpaced the changes, ran through desert and castle and future metropolis. Perverts scattered in terror from the roaring bull-man.

Finally they reached the hull, a curving mountain of fitted planks that stretched upwards into a false sky. The hull didn't give for Raoul on the first go, so he set Imogen down on the floor. Taking a few steps back, he charged at the wall, his horns lodging deep. Gouging and twisting he pierced all the way through, till a tiny hole let the daylight inside. Thrusting both hands into the hole, the minotaur stretched out the edges like clay. It was a great wound in the belly of the ship, one that wouldn't mend easily.

"Be ready!" he told Imogen, sliding his bulk through the tear. He was out and hit the ground with bone-breaking speed, rolling to one side as an enormous wheel missed him by inches.

The city-ship was powering along at a terrifying rate, crushing a suburb into rubble. Raoul kept pace and snatched the plummeting Imogen before she could break upon the ground. A hundred hatches opened along the side of *The Cheerful Misogynist* and there was a barrage of cannons, even a trebuchet swinging its great lazy arm. Death rained all around them.

The minotaur veered from the ship's destructive path, legs burning as he cleared white-picket fences and vaulted over cars in drive-ways. When Raoul escaped the shadow of the looming boat he entered far-travel, charting an impossible distance.

✳

"I made a mistake," Raoul said. "It was wrong to leave you with the ship."

They were standing in his squalid living room, both covered in dust and scratches. Raoul was panting like his lungs were about to pop.

"You killed him," Imogen whispered, shaking. "You killed Luca."

"Hush, love." Raoul held her gently, aware that his furry hands were caked with the Captain's blood. "It takes a great deal of effort to kill someone these days. I doubt that he is dead."

He steered her over to the formica dining table, sat her down on a battered art deco chair. She wouldn't look at him, so he busied himself with boiling water on the gas-ring.

"I don't understand you, Raoul," Imogen finally said. "There's rumours about you, about what you are. Yet you choose to live here."

He knew it was a pig-sty. He liked the piles of dirty dishes, the stacks of mouldy books lining the walls. He went to great pains to collect this clutter and arrange it just so.

"It really smells in here," she emphasised, and the minotaur smiled. He put a warm cup of instant coffee on the table, next to Captain Luca's hat.

"We are defined by our ephemera," he said. "Without clutter and junk, we aren't really alive."

"Raoul, this place is a disaster. At least Nameless has an excuse for hoarding rubbish." She played with the hat, and went to put it on her head.

"Don't," Raoul warned. "Do not put that on."

"Why not?"

"Because you will become the Captain of *The Cheerful Misogynist*, and you will bring that murderous boat into my house."

Raoul found an empty shoe-box somewhere under all the junk, and jammed the hat into it. He wrapped it up with an entire roll of sticky tape and tied an extension cord around the whole mess. It went deep into his pocket.

"Why did you come for me? I thought you'd arranged to hide me on the boat for exactly one century. What's going on, Raoul?"

"I need you, Imogen. Not for that," he snorted as she rolled her eyes. "I need your help with something."

He pulled the rumpled year-book page out of his pocket, flattened it out in front of her. He pointed at the class photo.

"One of these people invaded my home. Found where it was for starters, and got past everything I've thought of to keep people out.

No doubting in my mind, he knows the old ways."

"Hmm." Imogen stared at the photo. With free will restored she'd already changed her hair from ratty to natty, and her outfit flickered between a slinky dress and a power-suit.

"You have to try harder," Raoul said, and gently licking her forehead he passed over the thread of thought that he took from Nameless. "You were one of the last ones to leave the One-Way-World. Can you feel anything in this photo?"

"Quick, gimme a pen," she said, finally settling for khaki pants, Docs and a Rolling Stones t-shirt. She drew a biro outline around one of the boys.

"Oh. It's just Nameless," she said.

"As always, he thinks of nothing but himself, his past. What a waste of time."

✳

There was a letter in the mail-box, marked RAOUL MITHRAS. The envelope was marked "card only", and Raoul sniffed it cautiously. Deciding it was safe he slit it open with a thumbnail.

"SHH, IT'S A SPEAKEASY!" the card cried out loud, a cut-out in the shape of a wine barrel. A muted jazz riot could be heard blasting out of the card when he opened it. Imogen could see the reflections of a turning mirror ball on the minotaur's face.

"'You and a friend are invited to Madam Lune's top secret party,'" Raoul read. "'Don't tell the law.'"

"Fun!" Imogen said.

"I don't know. Lune and I are having—problems."

"What have you done now?" Imogen said, exasperated. Raoul scowled but didn't answer.

"I leave you alone for five minutes. Sheesh. Well, I'm going. I've been stuck on that boat for ages."

"This is a bad idea," Raoul rumbled, but he stepped into a zoot suit, with a trilby that sat nicely in between his horns. Imogen wolf-whistled.

"You look snappy."

She dreamt up a flapper outfit, with her make-up caked on and a bob hair-cut to match her laddish physique. She had a cigarette holder and a fur stole.

"Well aren't we the cat's pyjamas?" she purred, and they leapt into the card.

Lune was famous for her parties. The last one she threw was the Egyptian Extravaganza, and it went for two hundred years. *The Cheerful Misogynist* turned up and forced its passengers to build her a scale model of the Great Pyramid. By hand.

This one was an amazing replica of a speakeasy, if the entire city of prohibition-era Chicago had been a boozy party held openly. It was an art deco nightmare, and Raoul shook his head at Lune's twisted take on history. There was an army of federal agents splitting barrels of moonshine over the gutters, but only so that the guests could dip their cups into a ready supply of booze.

"Let's boogie," Raoul said, over the music of the nearest big band. They did the Lindy Hop, the Bunny Hug, the Charleston. For a man-bull hybrid, Raoul was light on his feet and Imogen floated around him like a butterfly.

"Raoul! Darling!" and Lune was there, draped all over the surprised minotaur. Even though she was Aphrodite and Gaia and everything else femme, Lune managed to look cheap. She had too many feather boas and a carafe of gin clenched in one hand, with one of her stockings unstuck and sagging around her ankle. She bumped Imogen aside, covering Raoul's snout with sloppy kisses.

"Lune, it's good to see you," he lied, gently peeling her off. "You remember my ward, Imogen?"

"Not really," she said, turning from Imogen's death-stare. "So, who was your visitor?"

"No-one. A friend," Raoul started, but Lune laughed, a short sharp bark. There was something of her Durga aspect in the sound and he knew he needed to tread carefully. For all their sakes.

"Bullshit from the bullman. Here I thought you were a gentleman. No, I've had to invent a *chevalier*, all on my ownsome."

Lune stuck two fingers in her mouth and let rip with a world-shaking whistle, so loud that her costumed guests clutched their heads in pain. A man came trotting to her side, and for a moment Raoul tensed up, nostrils flaring. He could swear that the man had a blurry face, until he realised that the man has no face at all. In fact it was a mannequin given motion, with a judge's wig sliding around on its head. She'd dressed it in robes befitting the judiciary, and Raoul understood the irony. The only guest likely enough to obey the prohibition should symbolise the "law".

"This is King James," Lune said. "Say hello."

"Open your hearts to us," the dummy said, in a rumbling baritone. Where its mouth should be, the moulded lips tried to move. "We have wronged no one; we have corrupted no one, we have cheated no one."

"Paul's Second Letter to the Corinthians," Lune said, a drunk's grin plastered across her face. "I made him and he always knows what to say."

"It's madness is what it is," Imogen said. "Don't tell me you fed a bloody Bible into that thing."

"Let us walk honestly," King James said, "as in the day—not in rioting and drunkenness, not in chambering and wantonness, not in strife or envying."

"Well, he's got your measure," Raoul said. "Maybe you should have fed it some Henry Miller or something."

Everything shifted, and Raoul was knocked onto his side. A couple of the faux buildings toppled, and screaming and terror from those who shouldn't fear anything.

It was the blurry man. He'd busted into Lune's party, taking gate-crashing to a new level. He was walking towards Raoul, then running, and with every step great cracks opened in Lune's pocket-world. People were falling into the holes and Raoul knew that they would fall forever.

"Foul little cow," the blur yelled, and they met with a crash, grappling and rolling through the wreckage. Raoul was strong even back in the One-Way-World, but this stranger matched him. A blurry hand gripped one horn, shaking his head back and forth till he feared his mighty neck would snap.

Then the intruder gasped and froze up with pain, so Raoul picked him up, threw him as far as he could. It felt like he was hurling a mountain. The blurry man landed just shy of a nothing-hole, curled up and screaming. A bright silver arrow pierced his side.

Lune wore her Diana aspect and stood as tall as a tree, her bow held steady. She was pulling back on the second arrow when the man made a run for it.

"Where's your bloody invite?" she laughed, but her joviality was short-lived when the man slipped through the only door and took it with him.

*

"We've got to get out of here," Lune said, and Imogen mimicked her silently. Like everyone else they were crowded to the very edge of the pocket-world; everything in the middle being eaten up by the spreading doughnut-hole of nothing. Every minute or so another building collapsed, and the roads and sidewalks were being drawn in like strands of spaghetti.

"Well, this is some party," Raoul said, and got grief from all directions. "What?"

Lune was shifting in between Diana and Durga aspects, which had the minotaur quite nervous. She even had a bit of Bast going on, and her cat tail flicked angrily underneath her chiffon dress.

"All I'm saying is that it's always a bad idea to suspend free will." Raoul raised his hands, tempting fate.

"It was for authenticity," Lune sulked. "I didn't want people changing into robots and dragons when they got bored."

She was the only one who could change in any way, but all she could do was flick through her aspects, impotent and furious. Everyone else was stuck in their period clothing, and there was no reaching outside.

Lune padded over to the edge of the abyss, to where the blurry man fell. There was a spot of blood there, and kneeling she dabbed at it with Bast's cat tongue.

"I know this one," she said. "Yon gate-crasher has the taint of YHWH upon him."

"Yahweh," Raoul said. He'd brought her up to speed with the events of late. "It makes sense I guess. He had the most to lose from the closing of the One-Way-World."

"Yes." Lune nodded sagely. "He was most bitter, where everyone else was eager."

The pocket-world gave a great shudder. There wasn't much time left before the bottom fell out completely.

"Raoul, the hat," Imogen said. "What about Luca's hat?"

He dug the box out of his pocket, squashed flat and wrapped tightly. It fluttered around in his hands, and he unwrapped in nervously.

The hat made a leap for his head, and he snatched it out of the air. It twitched and shook with frustration, and Raoul was tempted to lob the thing into the nearest pit.

"It's a really, really bad idea to wear this hat," he said. "But if anything can break into this place, it's *The Cheerful Misogynist*."

"Don't," Imogen said. "I'll do it. It'll hurt you, Raoul." She made to take the peaked cap but he lifted his hands up so high that she couldn't reach.

"No bloody way, José," he said, taking off his trilby. "You are not going back on that ship and that's final. I'll become the Captain."

"I believe I have a better suggestion, much as it pains me to dream it up," Lune said. "What about King James?"

They all looked at the mannequin, puttering around in the rubble and soliloquising about meekness and inheriting the earth. Raoul jammed the hat onto James' head.

"Remember Sodom and Gomorrah," King James rumbled, and a moment later the prow of *The Cheerful Misogynist* breached the pocket-world.

✳

"What crime is Nameless being punished for?" Imogen asked. Raoul brought her in close, wary of the passengers and crew. *The Cheerful Misogynist* was tolerating them as a necessary evil, but only for now.

"We're not exactly sure," the bull-god said. "Nameless hasn't done it yet, and all we know is it's going to be big. Made sense to punish him straight away."

"But you made him a no-one. That's a bit harsh." Imogen went as if to say more but sat down on the deck, spinning a badminton racquet in her hands. She'd shifted into a goth get-up, a nightmare of black and lace.

Aurora Luca was onboard and very much alive, a mess of stitches, bruises and cuts. There was a loop of intestine hanging loose from a wound, and he picked and worried at it. Luca shied away from Raoul, only to continue moaning about "being replaced by a bloody bible-bashing robot."

Captain King James had been thoroughly infested by the ship. The captain's hat had become a tricorne, and he paced the deck in finery that would make Napoleon jealous. He still had no features, but now sported a moulded plastic moustache.

"Render unto Caesar," he said again, pointing at Raoul's horns. The ship just wouldn't give up, even if its only mouthpiece could do nothing but quote the Bible.

"No deal," Raoul said. "You cheated me."

"But one of the soldiers pierced His side with a spear," the ship said through the new Captain, and Raoul remembered the damage he saw on boarding. His previous escape had left a puckering wound in the side of *The Cheerful Misogynist* that would take years to close.

They'd convinced the boat to take them to the house of Nameless. There was no love lost between Yahweh and this, the most sinful of boats, and it had some score to settle that not even Captain King James would speak of.

The ship grew a trio of great zeppelins, each a rubber moon fastened to the deck by cables thicker than a man. The landscape passed in a blur but the wait was agonising, Raoul deciding that the rumours of the ship possessing an FTL-drive were just that. Still, it was quicker than far-travel.

"Mighty son of Minos, what brings you to this pervert's boat?" Lune purred from beside him. She'd sidled up to the prow where he gripped the railing, and gently entwined his arm. Raoul blinked and then she was holding air, he a few steps away. The best his magick could do while onboard.

"Don't, Lune. We've spoken on this."

"I don't know why I'm surprised. You've broken every heart but hers," Lune said, pointing at Imogen who was now playing quoits with a leather-bound gimp.

"I'm not for mazes or any who build them," Raoul said. "Be my friend if you will, but you'll not bind me."

For a long minute they looked at the yawning distance ahead of them. *The Cheerful Misogynist* was about to blast through lands which were a mad blend of downtown Chicago, the Katherine Gorge and parts of an arctic tundra.

"How do you posit that YHWH and Nameless are in cahoots?" Lune said.

"Only Nameless kept the Old Ways in his head, hoarded every scrap of the One-Way-World he ever had. Yahweh could use that poor fool as a gateway, a focus."

"We expected war from the Lord of Hosts," Lune said. "I helped to guard the waypoints when we closed the One-Way-World, but while we marked his mob of hang-tailed bullies none of us saw him enter."

"So it's to be Yahweh, again," Raoul said. "We crossed paths long ago, back when he took the Romans from me. From Mithras," he corrected.

"I thought *he* was meant to be the jealous god," Lune laughed.

"If I were Yahweh, I'd be heading to the house of Nameless. He thinks us trapped in the pocket-world, which gives him time to act."

"Yahweh won't be able to bring it all forth," Lune said, but Raoul could smell her uncertainty, the bitter beginnings of a strong fear. "Without a name, he's nothing to bind it to."

*

They saw the house of Nameless, slumped across the cliffs like the broken man who lived there. Some time back they caught the far-travel wake of Yahweh, and through a sticky field-glass that King James offered Raoul he could spot the broken god entering the front door.

"Curse your sluggard of a boat!" Raoul said, snapping the glass closed. "Ram it! Bring the whole place down!"

But there was enough vinegar left in the old god to keep the ship at bay. Try as it might, *The Cheerful Misogynist* was grounded, straining against Yahweh's invisible hand.

Raoul and the others were out, rappelling down ropes or gliding on dreamt-up wings. There were enough holes in Yahweh's fence that they could slip through on foot.

Imogen was back to khaki's and a t-shirt, and for some reason had the remote control for Raoul's entertainment centre in her hand. Lune was passive, reining her aspects in till she needed one of them. Captain King James hobbled along, a plastic fop with nothing but a bunch of scripture in his head.

They were through the open front door, and the cat/s bombarded them, a hundred toms from the size of a kitten to tiger size. They snarled and hissed and scratched until Lune brought forth Bast in all her awful glory. The cat/s disappeared into whatever shadows they could, slipping from the anger of their lady.

"Puss is an Egyptian word," Lune/Bast said. "They've never been allowed to forget me."

It would take hours to search the house, but Yahweh left a sour funk that Raoul could easily follow, a smell that spoke to his delicate nostrils of loss and lust, of spilled seed and dust.

"The stairs of course," and they were up and running, Raoul running his horns along the banister when the house itself sought to delay them. Then they were up in the den, and Raoul saw Nameless kneeling on the ground, his box of mementos tipped over and spread on the floor around him.

"Be wary, Nameless," Raoul said. "Your old master walks in your halls."

Nameless looked up at the minotaur, and Raoul saw the ripple, the signs of a limitless being that has hidden in flesh for too long.

"Mute him!" he instructed Imogen, who thumbed the appropriate button on the remote control, but she was too slow. Yahweh spoke through the mouth of Nameless, and returned his name to him.

The One-Way-World began to slowly erupt from his mouth, an obscene bubble of galaxies and sparkling nebula. Every muscle straining against that impossible weight, Raoul lifted Nameless, a floppy doll with eyes rolling, oblivious to the intrusion.

"Call your boat," he told King James. "Do it!"

He could see the plastic mouth moving, but the words coming out were like treacle, mere sounds against a greater darkness. Raoul was being drawn into the maelstrom, the One-Way-World that was growing by inches.

He dimly noted that Lune brought out the feared Durga aspect, and the trendy flapper outfit peeled away to reveal a three-eyed ten-armed killer, bristling with weapons. She was hacking away at the walls and one hand was contorted into a little-known mudrā, negating the very house beneath them. She wanted to put a blade through Yahweh's throat but Raoul kept her at horn's length, circling him protectively with his enormous arms. Injuring Yahweh at this point could mean the undoing of all things. No second chances, not even a One-Way-World to fester in. Nothing but oblivion.

"The boat," he cried through the treacle darkness, and when he saw Imogen it all made sense. Imogen had the remote held level, and was thumbing a button over and over. Raoul guessed it to be 'pause' or 'slow-tracking' or similar. Either way, Raoul hadn't replaced the batteries for a thousand years, and they were only held in with duct-tape anyways. This wouldn't work for long.

Lune/Durga cancelled a wall of Nameless's house into shivers of nothing, and slipping into her Diana skin she launched arrows at something in the distance. Each shot was an eternity as she nocked the arrow and drew it to her cheek, the same cheek that Raoul had kissed and nuzzled and made false promises to. She blinked as she was aiming, and set her tongue just so. Release, and the arrow slowly glided forward.

She's cutting a path for the boat, he realised, and even as the remote control finally failed and Lune/Diana was firing dozens of arrows per second, Yahweh's fence shattered. Captain King James touched the tip of his tricorne with a plastic hand, and a moment later the enormity of the boat pulled alongside the shattered house.

They were level with the tear in the hull, the evidence of Raoul's escape that should be down near the ground. Raoul guessed what the boat was planning, and with no other choice he pitched Yahweh and Nameless through the hole. They fell into the guts of *The Cheerful Misogynist*, along with the growing seed that was the One-Way-World.

*

"Well, it's a fetish boat, and the One-Way-World just happens to be Yahweh's fetish," Raoul said. "It makes sense to trap him there."

They were following the secret paths to Raoul's house via far-travel, Imogen clutched to his broad woolly chest as his legs ate up the miles.

"He'll figure it out," Imogen said.

"Yahweh thinks he won, and who are we to tell him any different. Let him run his little play-world, I know *I* won't bother him."

Imogen stared at him again, at the stub where his left horn was. It would take perhaps a hundred years to grow back, and he'd been halved in more ways than he cared to admit.

"A fair deal," Raoul said. "The ship hid you for fifty years, so they get one horn."

They stood at his front door now, and as Raoul reached for the key Imogen snatched it out of his hand, with a speed that was suspiciously reminiscent of Lune. She tucked the key into a fanny-pack that she had suddenly decided was cool.

"I want you to help Nameless," she said, gamely blocking the minotaur from his house. "You've punished him enough. It's wrong to leave him stuck in that boat with Yahweh, the pair of them dreaming over a seed of a world. Or a universe, or whatever."

"It's what they both want," Raoul sighed. "Neither of them want to be here, surely we owe them this small kindness." Imogen was defiant, but even she could see reason and fished out the chunky brass key, the one that could open the Great Library at Alexandria as well as a Starbucks in Melbourne.

He unlocked the door and jerked it open, but instead of his filthy apartment he could see a great frothing sea, and perched on a murderous wave was *The Cheerful Misogynist*. He could make out Lune's dummy on the prow, holding up a yellow curve that was his horn.

Raoul slammed the door shut.

"I wanted to move anyway," he said.

GOODNIGHTS TO HEAVEN

It was spotting the man on the roof that made her change direction, and probably saved their lives. He was obviously a lookout, some poor frozen bugger lurking in the mess of old chimneys and tiles, anorak up around his ears. There was no other reason for a breathing body to be sitting up there in the cold.

"Back this way, Toby," Mary whispered, pulling the little boy back around the corner, holding him close. Her heart was racing. *Were we seen?*

"I'm tired, Mummy," the boy whined softly.

She led him away from that reasonable looking street, a row of terrace houses with most of the windows intact. She pictured the untouched larders, clean beds, maybe left over toys and books for her son. And then she remembered that man on the rooftop, and knew that where one man watched, others waited, and that soon enough this place too would be stripped bare.

They trudged back into streets long since picked over, endless blocks of waste, the houses all cracked open like eggs and open to the elements, doors flapping or off their hinges, windows broken by angry starving kids. And always, always the stacks of bodies, thick on the ground here and putrid, but at least they weren't up and walking about.

The sun was starting to sink through the rooftops, a thin watery orb sliding down that freezing clear sky. With an eye to the remaining daylight, Mary found a semi-detached house, less damaged than its neighbours. Stepping gingerly over an eviscerated corpse, spread out and rotting on the doorstep, Mary took the boy inside, looking at the thick layers of dirt coating the floors, noting how every corner and nook had trapped the autumn leaves, blown in through the destroyed windows.

"See that," she whispered to the boy, pointing at the grimy floors. "No tracks, nothing for a long time. We can stay here."

"Mummy, I'm hungry," Toby grizzled, looking up at her. His eyes were sunken, his cheek bones far too pronounced. She'd dressed him in several layers of clothes and he still looked like a ghost on legs.

The last of their food had been taken from them at knife-point, by a sad-eyed man who tried to apologise for robbing them, even as he was doing it. He'd left them a can of dog-food, which they'd bolted down as soon as he left, Mary gagging on the gelatin slime. Between them they ate every mouthful, scraping the sides of the tin clean.

That had been three days ago.

They looked through the cupboards and shelves, even checking the mess of drawers that had been pulled out and dumped onto the lino floor. The place had been picked over, and good. Feeling around underneath the kitchen sink, she cried out triumphantly. A single can had fallen behind the drain pipes, overlooked by the human locusts who'd last visited.

"Halved Pears in Syrup!" the faded label read. Hands shaking, Mary worked her can-opener, mouth running when she saw the fat slices of fruit, bobbing in thick liquid. Even though her stomach growled, Mary made sure that Toby ate every single mouthful, saving only a little of the juice for herself.

"My tummy hurts," Toby said, a few minutes after wolfing down the pears. He danced on the spot, clutching at his stomach, which gave an ominous rumbling sound. The toilet stank like a morgue, with a rotting body still clutching the bowl, so Mary helped her son squat over a large saucepan, the boy sobbing as his meal ran right through him.

"My poor darling, my sweet boy," Mary said, wiping his brow. They had a little clean water left, and she let him drink it all. "I know, my heart, I know."

They found a thick quilt in the linen cupboard, and slept in the top of the garage, a converted stable complete with the old hayloft. With the ladder pulled up they were safe enough, if a walking dead thing should sniff them out.

"I can see the stars," Toby whispered, pointing out through the dusty louvre windows. "I'm gonna do my goodnights to Heaven."

Mary clutched her boy close, tucking the quilt in around them. The boards beneath them were hard and cold, and the backpack made for a poor pillow. Her limbs ached with exhaustion.

"Goodnight Grandpa, and Daddy, and Sally, and Moggy. I love you lots and lots." He ended the ritual with a blown kiss, the way he'd always done. Cradled in his mother's bony arms, the boy was asleep in seconds. Stifling her sobs, Mary cried and cried.

✳

"It's a special day today," Mary told Toby, pointing to her diary. She always recorded temperature, locations visited, numbers of undead seen, her general condition and Toby's. Bevan had told her she was an obsessive diariser, "a mad Samuel Pepys, except you've got nothing interesting to write about."

In the early days of this feral new world, he sure changed his tune as to the usefulness of a diary, and then he was bitten and had to be put down (this event marked in a somewhat shaky hand as having happened on the 5th of February, 2014), marking the end of married life and all of its comfortable nitpickings.

"It's Christmas day," she said. "You might have been too little to remember it, but we used to put up a big tree with lights on it, with presents underneath and everyone would come over for a big roast lunch."

Toby chewed his lip for a long moment. He always looked thoughtful whenever Mary spoke about the world that once was, as if was telling tall tales, making things up to keep him cheerful.

"I do so remember Christmas," Toby said. "We ate a tin of pudding last year. Daddy put a fire on and he gave me my colouring book."

"That's right. But I've got something better for you this year."

They left the semi-detached, Mary making a careful note of its position in her diary, wrote "A SAFE PLACE?". The two walked through the streets, pausing only once to hide from a small pack of zombies, leathery corpses weaving all over the street like drunks.

Roughly twelve corpses, when last month they'd run from a mob in this neighbourhood that was three hundred strong. *Suits me fine,* Mary thought. *Move on, you smelly buggers.*

They waited in an abandoned Kombi van for the mob to pass, and Mary tipped a sprinkling of vinegar onto herself and Toby. It would mask their scent, confuse the keen senses of the undead. If they kept out of sight, they would be fine.

We creep through this strange new world like a pair of mice, Mary thought. Licking her cracked lips, she eyed off the vinegar, perhaps two fingers worth left in the bottle, but wrote it off as a bad idea. *It will only make us thirsty, and we need every drop of this stuff, need it to move around safely.*

When the last faint moan had faded into the distance, they slid out of the van, walked quickly. Once, Mary heard arguing, a man and a woman, and lingered on the corner of main street, wondering if it was worth the risk. It would take them straight to where they were going. A moment later and there was a gunshot, the sharp crack like a fat hand swatting the life out of something.

There was no scream, and the angry words had stopped. Mary scooped Toby up into her arms and ran back the way she'd come, changing streets, slipping down quiet alleyways, doubling back on herself until she was thoroughly lost. The young boy trembled in her arms, and she felt the warm trickle of his urine as it soaked through the seat of his pants.

"It's okay mate, we won't see any of the bad people," she said, stroking his hair. "We're okay now."

The street directory gave her an alternate route, through the old industrial area. They'd passed through about nine months ago (9th November, 2013 to be precise, "STUFF ALL HERE" Bevan had added to her brief jottings), and the place was of no interest to anyone alive—all the fuel was gone, as well as anything useful.

A handful of the rotting walkers spotted them in the old cement plant, and gave limping chase through the tank farms and plant rooms. Mary dabbed on the last of the vinegar, making sure to rub the last few drops into Toby's face, behind his ears, all over his hands. Befuddled, the slavering monsters shuffled past their hiding spot, close enough that Mary could see the fat bloat of rot pushing at leathery skin from the inside, eyes frosted like a fish hooked and bled out.

Look at them. They're having trouble walking, Mary thought. *Their joints are all fused together or something.* A fat chunk of maggot-ridden flesh slid off a zombie's back, dropping onto the floor at their feet. Gagging quietly, Mary fought the churning rebellion in her empty stomach.

The stink of the undead things washed over them, the decomposed corpse smell that no-one should ever have to breathe in, and that time did not improve. She held Toby close, covering his eyes and ears, barely daring to breathe. Her boy shook, but he was smart for his age, knew how to hide from the undead.

Slipping through a chain-link fence the woman and boy were across a vacant block, sneaking through the car-choked ruins of the old highway, stopping still when the gusting wind rocked a dead car on its springs. There were infected bodies in some cars, too stupid to get themselves out, quiet enough to snatch you should you pass too close.

"There's the city," Mary said, pointing at the mess of skyscrapers, the glass edifices peppered with broken windows, some of the buildings burnt out in their entirety. "I've got a nice surprise for you Toby, but you have to keep close and be very quiet. It's dangerous here."

"I know, Mum," Toby sighed. "I'm not stupid."

"Look at me," Mary said, kneeling down so that her face was level with the boy's. "I don't mean to nag at you. I just don't want to see you get hurt, okay?"

"'kay," Toby mumbled.

"Just keep your eyes open and tell me if you see anything," she said. "It might be a bit smelly in there, so try to breathe through your mouth."

Smelly was the understatement of the year. The streets were carpeted with bodies, and little bones crunched with every step. In some places the footpaths was slick with gore, and it was all Mary could do not to slip over. She tried her best not to think about the diseases they were wallowing through, promised them both a bath the moment she could boil up enough water.

Where are all the zombies? she thought. The last time they'd looked at the place through Bevan's binoculars, it was a hive of dead things, an enormous tomb. Millions of dead things, hungry for human flesh, and no point dropping in to Tesco's if you didn't want to be nibbled on.

But now, there were only a handful of zombies walking the street, and they were in bad shape. A body that was little more than sinew and bone was standing in a doorway, swaying gently, and another was in an alleyway, knocking the bins over, moaning in confusion.

"Look, they're sick Mummy," Toby said. What was once a nun dragged herself down the front steps of a shop, nothing left to her but the top half and a little tail of spine. Its descent was laborious, and when it reached the bottom it lay down with a sigh, eyeing off mother and son with malevolence. But apart from one shuddering attempt to rise, it did not move.

"That bloody nun should be chasing us to the ends of the earth," Mary said. "Maybe it's kicked the habit."

Toby looked at her with confusion.

"Don't worry, it wasn't that funny. Come on."

Some minutes later they stood hand-in-hand before a huge shopping complex, the car-parks completely coated with rotting flesh. Ignoring the smell and the flies, Mary led Toby towards an enormous store, with an enormous giraffe mascot blazoned on the side of the building.

The glass sign had been smashed, but there was enough left to spell out TOYS in ten foot high letters. When Toby saw this, a gap-toothed smile shot out across his filthy face, and he darted forward, dragging his mother by the hand, shouting at her to hurry up.

"Merry Christmas kid," she laughed.

✳

25 December, 2014:

The zombies are dying out, pun intended. Looks like we're the first ones game to come back here. A horrid smell everywhere, someone needs to fire the maid! Found two cans beans, one box ramen noodles, one can of Glen 20 to disinfect EVERYTHING.

Toby had a V. good day, all the bikes had been pinched months ago but no-one wanted the other stuff. Found a box of batteries and he had the time of his life—I've never seen so many robots and dinosaurs walking around.

Turns out that happiness still is a kid in a toy store.

FOR WANT OF A JESUSMAN

Lanyard Everett knew a sheila once, who didn't want a crooked man but liked the idea of being kept by one. When he talked of being prentice to a jesusman, she tried to stab him and he had to hurt her some. He left her there in a bubble of blood and teeth, and followed a man named Bauer into a new life.

"There'll be hatred for you and yours," Bauer tried to warn him, but Lanyard laughed. He'd never known anything else, didn't have anyone anyway. The old jesusman had smelled him out, pulled him from his crooked ways. First thing he made him do was burn a bible.

"This is just to let you know that the old rules are gone. The jesus doesn't have a book for Now, and you'd be mad to want to write it."

They sat there in silence, the old man poking the burning paper with a stick. Lanyard couldn't remember ever having read it, and the tiny print made his eyes swim in their sockets. He was glad to see the pages curl and blacken.

"No books anymore. You ever need guidance, you make his mark," Bauer said. "But don't let anyone see you making it. Certain folks will kill you over it."

Lanyard killed Bauer himself, in what some would call a crisis of faith. He killed the next jesusman that came for him, and then they left him alone. One year with Bauer and he learnt enough to hate their kind, just like everyone else did.

✳

"If he carries that mark, then he serves the jesus," said one of Gareth's new men. Lanyard pretended he didn't understand the river patois, which sometimes served him well. Comments like that were meant to end in blood.

"Lanyard?" Gareth laughed. He was the bossman, and it was never "Gary" unless you wanted drama and hurt. "No, he's not. My oath, he's as far from one of those fools as a man can get."

He ignored them, worked on rolling another cigarette and trying not to drop his tobacco each time the barge pitched. The gun often got comments, but he'd be a fool to be rid of it. It was Bauer's shotgun, the wooden stock carved with jesus marks and pictures, the barrel etched with words no-one knew how to read. It brought a lot of trouble, but a gun was a gun. They were rare enough in the Now.

"Get them ropes ready, we're here," Gareth said, cutting the motor. The men threw the ropes to the dock and some taursi fellas tied them alongside the crude pier. Taursi were taller than a man, bristling with sharp spines on their head and back. Lanyard knew the river folk called them spiny or worse. A better word he might have used was echidna but he'd only heard it in dreams so he kept that word tight.

They unloaded the gear. They were running grog to the taursi, as there was more profit in it than medicine or food. Nevermind the misery they were causing and the fact that a patrol would shoot them on sight for breaking town-law. There was trade and profit to be had and damn the indigenes.

"Where's your bossman?" Gareth asked one of the deckhands. He spoke loud, as if the taursi were deaf or simple. A taursi could hear a bird's shadow and tell you its name but men were men and they laughed and told jokes.

The deckhand gestured, his coat of quills expanding. This taursi was getting huffy. Lanyard was always wary around them, they ate sand and had workings inside them hot enough to make sharp glass. Gareth's men followed, all but the man with a working gat who was made to watch the barge.

"You see anyone on that river, they get the bullet," he told the man, a trusty and not one of the new recruits who'd as likely nick the gun and the boat. "None meant to be here but us."

Humping and lugging the rattling crates of moonshine, they followed the taursi back to their settlement. It was a rude place, all shanties and humpies and campfires. This mob had some of the yellow-furred native dogs, half-starved and whining. For all their bravado on the boat, none of the grog-runners said a word, or met any of the sullen looks cast at them by the locals. Though these were half-civilised addicts, a taursi could launch battle-glass through a man's heart at twenty steps.

At last they were at the trade-stone. The bossman of this settlement was an old buck named Pauryah, his spines turning white and his eyes near eaten by cataracts. Near as Lanyard could guess he intended to drink himself to death and take his mob with him.

"We brung it," Gareth said, placing an unlabelled flagon on the stone. "What you got for us today?"

"Nothing for you," Pauryah spat. "You would destroy our people, I give you nothing."

Gareth smiled, put another bottle on the trade-stone, then another. Pauryah relented, reached into the pouch that was part of his skin. He unwrapped something wrapped in a thick leaf, gave a heavy sigh that made his quills rustle and click together.

"Very old," he said, placing the delicate glass sculpture on the stone. It was a master work even by taursi standards, a beautiful abstract catching the sun how it was meant to. It would hold the sun long after dusk, twinkling in the dark like a little star.

"A good start," Gareth said. "What else for the trade?"

"No else!" Pauryah said. "This is our history. Worth more than you or any man."

Gareth said nothing. When he made as to take the booze from the trade-stone, Pauryah put up his hands. More glass was brought out and they both kissed the stone, striking a deal.

Lanyard was ready, knew that this was the time things could sour. The taursi had no love for the grog-runners, and sometimes their crushed spirits flared into violence. It would happen quickly, they would fill the air with glass and death before the men could raise their guns.

Gareth was getting greedy and stupid. The taursi may sell their treasures today for his poison, but they would regret their loss, doubly so through a hangover. The next visit to this settlement would end in tears.

Lanyard Everett did nothing to stop this, never did. Even if he were a great and noble man, that type went hungry these days. Gareth's coin brought his guns and his silence.

Lanyard had not meant to fall into this line of work, but Gareth was right. He was as far from a jesusman as you could get.

*

Lanyard had a little rat's nest of a room, it was in a Before-Time building and it cost him nothing. Few people were mad enough to squat in one, and when the twisted structure sprang out of the ground, all melted and crooked looking, Lanyard leapt at the chance to move out of Gareth's place. He did not wish to have all his eggs in that particular basket.

Near as he knew there were three or four others living in the building. What furniture was left in it was twisted and wrong, but this place was big enough that the squatters hardly saw each other.

There were other places like this. He'd seen skyscrapers jutting sideways from cliffs, cities underwater, half-melted houses out in the middle of nowhere. It was just rubbish from the Before-Times and these dead places did nothing but confuse and upset folks living in the Now.

There was still water in the pipes, though Lanyard wasn't that foolish. A lad could bring you a cask of boiled river water for a crown, but Lanyard always boiled it again. He'd worked on the delta long enough to know how filthy the water got.

"I got a job for you, Mister Everett," Gareth said. He wasn't scared by his new Before-Time place, seemed to respect Lanyard more for having moved out.

"A grog run?" he asked, and the portly criminal shook his head. He took in the cramped little room, the walls at odd angles. Lanyard had made a bed of sorts, a jumble of rags and boards. He'd tacked mosquito netting over the doorway; the window was fused and didn't open. The glass was all warped, and looked like a sheet of toffee.

"You get any ghosts in here?" he asked Lanyard. "My friend tells me these places are a home for ghosts."

"No ghosts. Just Before-Time dreams," Lanyard said. "The job?"

"Ah. We need to go overland and inland and maybe further. Man wants us to kill another man. You in?"

Lanyard nodded.

✳

"That's far enough," Lanyard told the boy.

He held the shotgun to the lad's head. The boy looked from the gun, the wooden stock completely covered in mad etchings, to the whip-thin man glaring at him from under a battered slouch hat.

The boy dropped the sharp little rabbit knife, never taking his eyes from his, tender little mouth a black O of fear. He looked like he was about to cry.

"That your pa?" Lanyard asked the boy, who nodded yes. The body was folded up in the dirt, a great hole in his belly and a kinder one between his eyes. "I had to kill your pa, but I won't harm you if you don't do nothing stupid."

The boy must have been all of ten years. He didn't have a friend in the world now but he had the balls to stand up to his daddy's killer.

Lanyard felt an ache then, deep in his bones. He'd been feeling it for months now, on and off, but never this strong. His teeth felt sore, and his skin itched like crazy. Someone was watching him, had seen him murder another man out here, deep in the bush and as far from town-law as you could get.

"Damn you Bauer," he said. He knew the signs now for what they meant, wish he'd never met the old man. A man just didn't need to know some things. He could feel the witch, somewhere close. And the witch would feel him, and know him for a witch-sniffing jesusman.

The boy looked a little less scared now, thinking Lanyard was the worst of his problems. Lanyard picked up the boy's knife and threw it as far as he could. He broke the shotgun, primed another round into the breech.

The boy was staring at his gun, covered in the forbidden jesus marks. It told the story of a man what let himself get pinned to a tree, led everyone to a land of flies and dust. Not to paradise, not to heaven. Here. The boy's pa might have told him stories of the jesus late at night, to give him delicious shivers around the campfire.

At last, the distant sound of the skiff. Gareth must have had trouble getting the ancient motor started. "Five minutes after you hear shots", he'd told his bossman. Damn noisy thing would have scared the dead man to ground, who must have known that someone would be gunning for him. He'd stalked the mark on foot before shooting him dead.

Lanyard started to get the shakes then. A very bad sign. He started, seeing a white shape through the trees, and knocked the boy to the ground with his free hand. Almost let off a round of buckshot before cursing himself. It was a termite mound, half-hidden by trees and spinifex, bleached by the sun.

He was right to be scared. He could feel a great dark presence, something lurking unseen in the scrub. If he was right, it would sniff him out and come for him. They hated his kind, and with good reason.

He could see the familiar shape of the skiff through the trees, felt the beginnings of hope. Gareth pulled up in the rusty old wind-cart, the machine coughing and belching blue smoke. The sails were limp, the air sticky and still, and if the motor gave out they'd be walking.

He raised an eyebrow at Lanyard and nodded meaningfully at the boy, as if to say *why don't you kill him?* but Lanyard ignored him. If he was right, and there was something out here, it could feed on the boy, and they'd have time to run.

Lanyard had the presence of mind to hack off the dead man's pinky finger with his Bowie knife. Proof for payment. He climbed into the passenger seat of the skiff, the tube frame rocking under his weight.

"Don't leave me here," the boy yelled out over the spluttering engine, but Lanyard shook his head and told Gareth to go. With a roar of the dying motor and a cloud of dust and stones, they left the lad in the middle of nowhere.

It was a long minute before the ache in his bones left him, and even then he watched their backtrail till sunset. He'd never been a real jesusman, but try telling that to a hungry witch.

*

"I guess it doesn't matter about the boy," Gareth said. "Should have killed him out of kindness. Mark my words, an orphan is just a bum in training." Lanyard said nothing, just stared into the depths of his beer. His soul was already filthy with shame, but this was a new low.

They were drinking in a shanty that straddled a crossroads. The whole place was on stilts, more for the gimmick than for avoiding the overland heat. Still, it helped a little.

There were taursi at the next table, nasty drunk and quills flared. Gareth hated the natives, hated their weakness and exploited it. Lanyard did not like what Gareth did but he'd advanced him some coin and never cheated him that he knew of.

"You're my best gun, Lanyard. You never lose it when they're throwing glass and shit at you. Men die and I always got to press new recruits, but you . . . " Gareth was rolling, sweaty drunk, the way he got when a job went well. Lanyard drank very little, knowing that part of his job was to guard this man. Focusing on work kept a man from thinking too much.

"You worth ten of them river bitches," he said, glassy eyed sincerity. "I love you Lanyard, I do."

"You don't love anyone," one of the taursi said. He was standing over them both, sharp spines puffing out aggressively. Lanyard already had the shotgun and a pistol out, covering the room. He could see the tip of a battle-glass, the sharp point pushing through the webbing of its hand.

He could see the tell-tale dull glow of the spines drawing the heat away from its body, knew the native was brewing up a batch of hurt. A taursi could cut up a man slow on the trigger.

"This one here, he only loves money. If things went wrong, he would leave you to die." Lanyard agreed silently but kept pressure on the triggers. He was running low on ammo but no-one needed to know that.

"If you know who I am, you know you court strife," Gareth laughed. "You touch me, a crew will wipe your people out."

"You groggers already wiped my people out," the taursi said. He backed down, quills lowered. Nodding once at Lanyard, the enormous creature returned to its seat and its drink.

He stood guard at the door when Gareth went to relieve himself. That was when the taursi made a quiet offer to Lanyard, and he wasn't surprised. They'd only been testing him.

"We've heard whispers of what you are."

"I'm no-one." Always, the tired denial, eyes wary for a fist or worse.

"A dark day when we need to search out your kind," the drunkest spiney said. "This was our land, till your dying man brung you lot here."

"That's not my problem. Be quick, Gareth returns."

"We were sent for want of a jesusman. We have a witching fella what needs seeing to."

They slipped some taursi glass into his hands, which he didn't even look at. He left Gareth snoring that night, knowing the fat gangster would only pretend to be mad if and when he returned for more work.

They made good time through the scrub and then cut across the salt-flats, the taursi bounding along a path that Lanyard had trouble seeing in the dark. They slowed down for the man, he didn't have the long sweeping dog-legs that they did.

Every few miles they passed a great mound of glass, tall like a termites' nest. They were like beacons, great spires that lit the plains. There was no sense to these sculptures, he guessed they were for navigating but the natives wouldn't talk about them. He was glad to pass them by, he gauged them to be the size of your average taursi and didn't want to know much more.

Just before dawn they reached the camp. He could see the dim glow of much taursi glass, knew that this tribe hadn't sold its heritage. He'd heard of wild taursi, pushed from the good land but still living the old ways. Perhaps was only these young ones what snuck grog beneath their elder's snouts.

Lanyard didn't speak taurse, but he knew some of their signs. He'd never seen a tribe like this before, a dozen different clan standards dotted the fire-ground. Their best clan glass glittered in the morning light, tied with long ropes of sinew along a cross-stave. He knew the patterns of knots meant something, like a calendar or something to do with numbers, but then again no-one cared about the natives save for what they could steal from them. A clan standard went for a small fortune in the towns, for streetlights and such.

"We're a mob of leftover tribes, bits and pieces," one of his guides said. "Them grog-men and the slavers have ruined the rest." Lanyard had been both things and deemed it wise to say nothing.

They called for their elders in their sharp honking tongue, and they came out, suspicious and hateful of the man-folk the young taursi had brought to them.

"There's a witching fella roaming our lands," one of them said in halting man-talk. "We've sent our kin to drive him away, but none of them come back."

"I'll give you advice," Lanyard said. "Move on. You got witch trouble, you leave or it will kill you."

"No moving on," the elder snarled. "You man-folk take all the good land. We got nowhere left but here."

Lanyard gathered his thoughts, rolled a cigarette. He was running low on tobacco, but offered the pouch to the taursi. He was just being polite and knew they would decline, smokes making most taursi ill. They looked ridiculous when they tried, with a lit durry hanging out of that droopy snout.

"I can track the witch and find its home, so you can mark it and avoid it. No more than that, not for all your glass. Move on and live."

"Why you come then?" the old one said. "You knew we got a witch. Most man-folk say, "they just stupid taursi, let them die". Why you really here?"

He could have talked about a young lad he'd left to die in his place. Shame was a currency the taursi definitely understood, but Lanyard didn't speak. He just put down the glass what they'd paid him with already and walked away. He heard them cursing him in their tongue but he didn't turn around. When he was out of their sight, he checked his pockets. He had enough ammo left to do what needed doing.

※

He lay flat on a broad rock and looked like a denim gecko, an overhang shading him from the murderous sun that was already baking the salt-flats below. He'd felt enough signs to guess he was close.

There'd been the distant buzzing, like a mosquito was trapped in his ear. His teeth began to ache, just a little.

"Come out, you pale piece of shit," he muttered, checking his gear again. The shotgun was ready, both barrels. He had a revolver and a newer gun that loaded from a clip, but these might not be much good. Still, a rain of bullets should give anything a moment of doubt.

He reefed out a pair of field-glasses from his battered satchel. They'd come through the shift from Before-Time with almost no damage, just a scratch on the left lens. Cost him a fortune, but worth every coin.

He thumbed the focus dial, and Lanyard could see a pair of taursi, hunting some small creature far below. They brought it down with battle-glass, and while they were busy skinning it the witch showed itself.

There was nothing Lanyard could do from this distance. He could only watch as a white shape loped across the ground with great mile-eating strides, unnaturally quick. The low buzz in Lanyard's ear jumped to a painful screech, and then there was just the horrible vision of a great shifting shape eating the taursi alive.

A witch knew the right words, the ones to persuade the living to keep perfectly still while it ripped at their flesh. They would feel everything.

Lanyard Everett was no fool. He did not slither down from his hiding place, go charging across the open ground with guns a blazing.

It took hours, but the witch ate the pair spines and all, finally cracking the last bone open to get to the marrow. The pain in Lanyard's teeth had been greatest by this spot, so he knew the witch had a lair in these hills. It wouldn't be the true nest, just the crossing point. The witch would pass by, with a full belly and dull wits, and Lanyard would do his best to kill it.

He could see the witch clearly now, weaving as if drunk. It had the form of a great obese man, and then the pasty white flesh ran like wax until the witch was a dog whose belly dragged upon the ground, then it became a great fleshy cloud out of a nightmare that had trouble moving. It settled for wearing a man's skin, and came lurching up the path. The pain grew, a dull ache in his bones as the witch approached.

The witch would only be thinking of sleep now, and so it didn't see Lanyard waiting on the rocks above. The sun flashed on the barrel of the gun, etched with little signs of the crossing-man, words from another world.

Close now, and he leaned over the edge, tracking the witch. His fingers caressed the double-trigger, but there was a noise on the rock next to him. He swung the gun up but suddenly his skull was a firepit and noise filled his universe like a thousand screams as a second witch sang him into oblivion.

✳

"Wake up jesusman," one of the witches said. He knew without looking that they would have him in one of their nests, those gray spaces halfway between Before and Now. If he were awake they'd never have got him through the door, they needed him asleep for that.

"Yes wake up jesusman, we know what you are" the other said. They spoke in a mixture of words and mind-raping thoughts that sounded like radio static and made his head throb. He was tied up, against something hard.

"You know nothing," Lanyard said. They had him naked in the gray place and bound to something, and he could see both whens as if through filthy glass.

One witch ran a sharp stub of yellow fingernail across Lanyard's chest, tracing the outline of his jesus tattoo. It would have been elaborate, but he'd abandoned it years ago, half-finished.

"Such beautiful ink, a shame to be left undone," the witch sighed.

"We can't find many of your kind in the Now," said the other witch. It took the form of Gareth from his mind, wore it to make a point. "It is delicious to eat a misguided fool."

"Most jesusmen found a way back to Before," the witch touching him laughed. He dug his nails in hard, lifting skin. "They're not welcome in the Now, are they Lanyard?"

"Neither are you," Lanyard said. His arms were really beginning to ache, and then he realised. They'd crucified him.

"We've half a jesusman and eternity to play with it," not-Gareth said. "What shall we do?"

"The tattoo," the first witch said, maggoty flesh melting and reforming into the skin of Lanyard himself, not a mirror image but something crooked and wrong. "If it wants to wear a picture of the crossing-man, it needs finishing."

"Fool! Shut your mouth."

Terrified, Lanyard looked through the dirty glass separating Before and Now, wondering what they were going to do to him. Knowing that he would die here, and hard.

✳

An age they kept him there, stuck between the wheres and the whens. Not-Lanyard and Not-Gareth were well-fed and did not need to hunt. From what Lanyard knew, they didn't need to eat often, not till their world-hopping and phantasms drained them.

They visited every kind of torture on him, short of eating his flesh. He was violated, hunted in mazes conjured from nothing, made to confess his darkest secrets while screaming in pain.

They broke him down to nothing, he who wasn't much of a man to begin with. Then, just to build up his hopes, they let him go. He took ten steps through the salt-flats, breathed in the clean fresh air of the Now, then they snatched him up, dragged him screaming back through the ether, back to their nest and the cross. This time they used spikes, not rope.

He flexed his fingers, whips of agony dancing around the spike through his palm. Touching the ragged wound, his fingertip was soaked in his own blood, and on his palm he made a mark he'd never meant to, a simple cross.

"Help me," crucified Lanyard said, and was suddenly somewhere else. He was sitting by a cookfire in the middle of scrub, ten years younger and dressed in the patched manner of a crooked man. Bauer the old jesusman was sitting there, wearing the slouch-hat and poking at the little critter he'd killed for their supper.

"Never could understand you, Mister Everett," the dead man said. "You coveted my stuff so much you bust my head open with that rock," and crooked Lanyard saw the jagged stone in his own hands, seconds before being covered with brain and bits of skull. "If you'd asked, I'd have given you everything I owned."

"Where am I?" Lanyard asked, dropping the stone.

"Oh, you're still in that gray place, two witches tormenting you. You're just paying an old man a visit. You made the mark of something you don't believe in, but make the mark you did."

"The jesus?"

"Enough with the semantics. You have perhaps a few moments before your hosts discover you're not in your head." He hoisted up the shotgun, threw it to Lanyard who caught it. The weapon felt real, cold and mean. "You need to bring this to the gray place."

"Send me back. I'll deal with them."

"The gun's not real, just a shadow of a dream," Bauer said. "You need a mark to get it to you."

"I already made the mark," he said, confused.

"Not enough. You need to somehow make this," Bauer said, poking the fire a little more. With his free hand he popped open his shirt studs, revealing the jesus tatt on his leathery chest. The ink was of a bleeding man bound tight, hands clenched into fists but for his pointer fingers, one to left, the other the right. BEFORE and NOW were writ under each hand.

"You need a true image of the lord of the crossing, and only that will open a way for you."

"Why are you helping me? I killed you."

"You went gunning for a witch, not for coin or even to save yourself. You're following the rules and that makes you a jesusman. Like it or not."

Then the scrub was gone and Lanyard was back in the witches' nest. They knew he'd been somewhere else, and they brought the hurting to him worse than ever.

✳

They broke him over and over, till even those base creatures grew tired of such games. They meant to eat him, a failed jesusman, munch his marrow in that nowhere land. Lanyard had lost all novelty for them, and they grew hungry.

"Enough of this," Lanyard wheezed, before they could maul him where he lay bound. He was starting to die the slow death, every breath an agony as his weight pulled against the slivers of iron driven through his palms. "You mean to eat me, then do it, but at least give me a belt of grog. The good stuff, so good you'll even taste it as you gorge on my gizzards."

They laughed at this, and Not-Lanyard gave a solemn bow. "A final request it is then," he said. They set to searching the Before-Time for a grog-shop, and he knew they'd be some long moments breaking through the dirty glass of this between place. He saw them pilfering often from the various whens, like bower-birds.

His right arm taut and trembling, he made a clumsy fist, pushed forward. The spike slid through his ragged palm, grating against the little bones and making him moan in pain.

When he'd been bound only with a loop of hemp, he'd been picking at a long sliver of wood on the wooden cross-beam, slowly working it loose. He snapped it free now, saw that it had a long jagged end. Perfect.

The witches were concentrating on their thieving, had torn a narrow hole into the Before-Time. Not-Gareth was pushing a waxy tentacle into a shop, reaching for a bottle of scotch. He'd need to be quick.

Lanyard stabbed his stomach with the sharp splinter, biting down on his lip so he wouldn't cry out. He tried again, breaking the skin. With agonizing slowness he made a shallow cut, tracing the broken outline of his tattoo. It bled like a bastard, and he found it hard to guide the cut where it had to go. He completed the outline on his torso, crude but a true enough mark.

Bauer had spoken of the crossing-man, the jesus who'd dragged his mindless followers through this gray nothing place and was still in between somewhere. Lanyard finally understood, himself stretched out between the Before and the Now, and reached into the Now with his free hand.

All his kit, left out in the sun. Clothes, torn to shreds.

The gun!

Not-Gareth turned from its thieving to see that he'd freed an arm, and came running, the grog forgotten. The last thing it saw was the double-O of the shotgun, and then Lanyard drove eternity out of the witch with one thunderous round. Not-Lanyard lunged for him with lightning speed, and Lanyard fired the second barrel. His shattered hand was aching, and his aim wasn't true. He only wounded it, and the witch crawled from him, shrieking and cursing him and trying to open a door to somewhere else.

"Come and eat me!" Lanyard cried, struggling with his left hand. He pulled it free from the spike, and then fell sideways like a sack of stones, feet still tied to the main shaft of the cross and his legs twisted together painfully. They'd wanted his feet intact for hunting him, did not drive a spike through them for authenticity.

He tore the rope free with his fumbling bleeding hands, even as the witch used the last of its strength to tear a hole through the dirty glass. It crawled for freedom, gibbering and changing shape and looking at Lanyard with terror in its eyes. He limped across the nest, put his naked foot across something that might have been the witch's neck.

"Put you down, like the dog you are," Lanyard said, hefting the empty gun by its hot barrels. He hammered the life out of the witch, and then some.

✳

He left that place through the hole the witch had torn. He was terrified that the passage would drive most of the knowing out of his head, but it seemed he really was a jesusman, a true guard of the crossing. He remembered it all, and stood naked in the Now. Bauer had once spoken against breaking through to the Before-Time, that it wasn't a golden world but an ending one, that witches were jesusmen who went back once too often. Lanyard only wanted his kit, a room in a squat. Perhaps a sheila and a bottle if he had coin enough.

Staggering through the bush he found the spot where they'd jumped him, all his kit still lying there. He'd thought to see his handguns all rusted and jammed, but they were as fresh as the day he'd dropped them. He snatched up his satchel, found the last hunk of bread how he'd left it, and knew he hadn't been gone more than a few hours.

His clothes were useless rags and the only thing left to him was Bauer's old slouch hat, snagged on a thorn bush. He laughed and cried and laughed again, and wore that hat for all the good it could do him.

A taursi found him half-dead and wandering naked over the salt-flats. He was laughing and covered in the yellow life-blood of a witch, which stank of corruption and stale piss. The young buck swept the man into his arms, cradling him as he bounced along the hunting trails and made for the camp. Lanyard knew no more.

He woke to see the taursi elders fussing over him. He was strapped in hemp bandages, aching all over. He hurt too much to be anything but alive.

"Two days now you slept," the greyest native said. "Killed our witching fella, jesusman."

Lanyard Everett wore that most hated word, and said nothing.

HUNTING RUFUS

The ute bounced and jolted down Yurla Crossing's main street. Loud country music belted out of the stereo, and the driver sang along badly. The rusty Falcon was an antique, somehow holding together despite the corrugated dirt roads for miles around.

Pulling up in front of Government House in a sliding mess of gravel and dust, the driver killed the improvised hydrogen converter and jumped out.

"Bob! Hey Bob! Come out here!" the lean man hollered, all bones and faded denim. He had the wrinkled skin of someone too stupid to wear sunblock. The remains of a rolled cigarette stuck to his thin bottom lip.

"Damn roo shooter." Bob Filcher said, walking out of his air-conditioned office. "What've you got now, Terry? Another rabbit or something?"

"Nup!" Terry grinned stupidly, ushering the official around the back. "Just you have a look at that."

"Shit, Terry." Bob whistled appreciatively. "You've bagged yourself a bloody monster."

The two men stared at the pickup's tray, and at the mass of dead meat that filled it. At three metres tall, it was easily the biggest kangaroo Bob had ever seen. It hung almost a metre out of the back, and its tail had rubbed raw against the road.

"That's gotta be worth twice the normal amount, right? Coz it's such a big mongrel?" Terry asked, carefully eyeing Bob Filcher's face. Though Bob had been here two years, he was still considered the new Remote Administrator, but he wasn't a pushover like the last fella. Commonsense never stopped Terry, though.

"No . . . no, Terry. It's one set bounty during the cull."

"You've got to be kidding! I nearly slipped a disc lifting that thing! I should claim for compo or something."

"You can't get worker's compensation. You work for yourself, dickhead." Bob swore, finally lifting his eyes from the giant carcass. "Bring it round the back."

"Sarah, Joe, run over to the pub and ask Brenda for some ice," Bob told his staff through the flyscreen. "Lots and lots of ice."

✳

"What the hell is that?" Sergeant Trickham yelled. His little police station was part of Filcher's building, and consisted of his office, a filing room, and the cells. Like Bob, Ken Trickham loved Yurla Crossing, and firmly believed he would live his whole life there.

Entering through the rarely used cell-block, Ken had nearly choked on his knock-off beer. There in a cell, partly covered in ice, was a kangaroo corpse that reached from one end to the other.

"Bob, where the hell did this come from?" he yelled through the partition. "This one of Terry's?"

"Yep," Filcher said, a smirking Terry in tow. The three men stood outside the bars, looking at the massive carcass. The only sounds were a fly buzzing somewhere, and Ken working wetly on his beer.

"So do you believe me now, Sergeant?" Terry asked. "Said I was seein' things, you did."

"Alright Terry, I can see the bloody thing." Ken snarled. "Where'd you bag it?"

"Josephine's Gorge." Terry said proudly. "There were more of 'em, but they got away."

"Make yourself useful Terrence, and hold this for me," Bob said, pulling out a tape measure. They measured the bleeding hulk from top to toe.

"3.16 metres tall." he said, retracting the tape. "I hate to say it Terry, but you were right."

"Told you, told you I'd seen giant roos." the rooshooter gloated. "I've seen them moving at dusk. The damn things can outrun cars off-road. They don't behave like normal roos."

"What do you mean?" Bob asked. Terry was well known for telling ridiculous stories. He wasn't sure if the shooter was having him on or not.

"I've seen the big ones, the monsters like this one, *chasing* the normal kangaroos. When the group caught one, they ripped it to bits. Scariest thing I ever saw."

"Oh come on," Ken groaned, rolling his eyes. "This roo is a freak. Some kangaroos are, what, two metres and more? It's just a lot of kangaroo."

"Yes, some roos are about two metres high. They're your alpha males." Terry said.

"So what's your point?"

"That thing there, it's a female. And it was one of the small ones too."

"*Bullshit,*" Ken said, but gulped the rest of his beer nervously. "You just saw this one fighting another roo. Happens all the time."

"I know what I saw, Sergeant. The big roos were hunting other animals. They moved just like dogs in a pack."

*

Bob Filcher made some calls, and transmitted images of the animal to Tandanya University. Within a minute the phone was ringing. When Bob calmed the girl on the other end, he asked her if she would come and have a look at the roo.

"A zoologist, a Miss Yarrow. She'll be up on the next mail-plane," Bob told Ken.

Two days later, the plane reached the tiny air-strip. The three men greeted her as she lugged a heavy bag down the ladder, and breathlessly shook their hands.

"Kimberly Yarrow, gentleman. Thanks for asking me up." the young academic smiled eagerly.

"Thanks for coming. The roo's still kinda fresh." Bob said.

"We keep putting ice on it." Terry said, grinning goofily. "I shot it, Ms Yarrow. I was the one who found it."

They returned to the cellblock, and Kimberly made a bee-line for the kangaroo. Kneeling in the muck and half-melted slush, she swept the ice away from its body.

"My god," she whispered. "I've never seen anything like this."

The zoologist performed various experiments on it, taking more photos. Breaking its sternum with a hammer and chisel, she sawed open its ribcage. Prodding the exposed organs and taking notes, Kimberly finally looked up. The three men had not moved, not even to get more beer.

"Gentlemen, this is not a kangaroo."

"What do you mean?" Bob said, puzzled. "It's not a bloody wombat."

"It's very close in some respects, but there are many differences." she continued. "Terry, it looks like you've found a new species of animal."

"I did?"

"Look here," she continued, lifting up the animal's lip, exposing a series of sharp fangs.

"There are still flat molars at the back for crushing vegetation, but these canine teeth shouldn't be here," Kimberly explained.

"Look at the claws too," the biologist continued. "The ones on her "fingers" are about fifteen centimetres long, and on her "toes", almost thirty centimetres. These are still much bigger than what a kangaroo of the same size would have."

"So what are you saying, Miss Yarrow?" Ken asked uneasily.

"This animal is either omnivorous or carnivorous. It eats meat, Terry." she finished as the rooshooter opened his mouth.

*

Determined to learn more, Kimberly Yarrow made arrangements to stay in Yurla Crossing. Eager to capture a live specimen, or at least get some photos, she commissioned Terry and his aging vehicle. They had searched all around Josephine's Gorge, but with no success.

Excited by the find, Tandanya University had asked Kimberly to secure more evidence of the beast she'd dubbed "Magnaroo". A small team of scientists were to join her later in the week, but the biologist did not want to wait that long.

The pair wasted long, frustrating days. Terry spotted what must be a Magnaroo print near Josephine's Gorge, but lost the trail after an hour's drive. When darkness fell, they continued searching with spotlights.

"I seen their alpha male once, Miss Yarrow." Terry grinned, face aglow in the dashlights. "Big red feller, more than four metres tall. Called him Rufus, I did."

"Rufus, sure." Kimberly said absently. She had heard all his tall stories in the last two days.

Scanning the landscape with Terry's nightvision binoculars, Kimberly called out directions whenever she spotted the loping bound of a roo. Apart from scaring kangaroos of the normal variety, the nights proved just as fruitless.

On their fourth day, the long-range radio suddenly squealed, screeching till the auto-tuner found the signal. It was Ken Trickham. He sounded excited.

"Terry, get your arse up to Banross Station! Tell Ms Yarrow that I found her damn roos!"

Bouncing and sliding over the back roads, Terry made it to Banross in under an hour. Ken's four-wheel drive was in the middle of the road, and the copper flagged them to a halt.

"Something's munched on the Banross cattle. Wasn't dingoes neither." he said. "Follow me, and be careful for God's sake!"

They followed Ken across a bumpy paddock, mostly dust from the drought. When they drove around a scattered pile of hay, Terry slammed on the brakes. The shooter swore, and Kimberly gagged, almost vomiting.

Dozens of cows had literally been ripped to shreds—eviscerated and left to die. Intestines and organs had been pulled out, and the mess spread for metres around each body. Already rotting in the Outback sun; the stench was horrific.

Terry piled out of the car, eyes wide and rifle in hand. Kimberly scrambled after him, but fell to her knees, retching loudly.

A group of eagles hopped around on the carcasses, tearing at the flesh. Terry let off a shot that sent them flapping into the sky, screeching in disgust. Bellowing in pain, one of the cows had actually survived, wide-eyed and surrounded by its own entrails. Ken put a mercy round through its brain.

"This was definitely a Magnaroo pack." a white-faced Kimberly said as she rejoined them. "Look at the ground."

Big bloody footprints circled the killing ground, and led to the west. Terry knelt by the spoor, frowning.

"At least eight of them. And these ones make my roo look little."

"This is incredible." the scientist breathed as she investigated the carnage. Taking several photos, she made sure to include the bloody paw-prints.

"These will tell us how they attack, and how they work together. They might help me to figure out the most fascinating part of what happened here."

"What the hell do you mean?" Ken growled, gesturing at the carcasses. "It's not fascinating, it's a bloody mess. Look at what they did! They're a menace!"

"They're built for meat eating and speed, but they don't know what they're doing yet. They're learning how to hunt."

"Seems to me they know what they're doing." Terry commented dryly.

"No, no. That's not true. Have a look here. They've rounded up their prey, and played with it. There's quite a bit of meat left on the carcasses, and predators usually kill just enough to meet the requirements of the pack."

"I'll radio for more shooters." Ken said. "I don't like our chances against that mob."

"No!" Kimberly shouted. "You can't just kill them off! This is the most amazing find in modern history, and you'd simply wipe the species out?"

"I don't think Ted Banross is gonna see it that way." the policeman retorted, gesturing at the dead herd. Clouds of black flies crawled all over the bloody mess.

"They're predators! They kill things! It's the way of nature." Kimberly yelled. "The only shooting will be from my camera."

"What if one of those things attacks *us*, Miss Yarrow?" Terry asked, worry wrinkling his leathery face. "We'd have to drop it then."

"I brought a tranquilliser gun." Kimberly assured. "If we can capture a breeding pair of Magnaroo, we will enter the history books!"

"Maybe for the wrong reasons," Ken Trickham grunted as he headed back to the four wheel drive. They began their cross country crawl, on the bloody trail of the pack.

Drawing up level with the treetops, several giant creatures watched the two vehicles pass, ears twitching. When the noisy vehicles had vanished from sight, they slowly followed them through the scrub.

*

"I hear you loud and clear, Ken. Over." Bob Filcher replied, releasing the button on the handset. Remembering the animal back in the cell, he frowned.

Science and Miss Yarrow be damned, he finally thought. *If those things bred anything like kangaroos did, the Outback would be overrun in no time.*

He read the email again. There's been an unspecified accident at the Woomera Test Facility, *last week*. Typically, the powers-that-be had only just informed the surrounding RA's of the "incident'. The only news was that the Prohibited Area quarantine was being "lethally enforced', and to expect additional Defence Force movements in the area.

Did they do it? he thought. *Did they breed these things? What the hell are they?*

As mental images of the monsters hopping into Yurla Crossing ran through his mind, Bob contacted Tredrea Station. They had a chopper and several good shooters, and helped with the cull in quiet times. Though at first they didn't believe him, they promised they would look for whatever had attacked the Banross cattle.

Sitting by the radio and worrying, Bob finally got up and using his spare key, unlocked Ken's gun-rack. He shuddered, remembering the Magnaroo's fangs.

*

"Geez these things can move!" Terry swore, looking at the sinking sun. "We'd better catch up before it gets dark, or we'll lose them."

The Falcon bouncing around in the scrub, Kimberly was thoroughly sick of being jolted around. Terry's keen eye could still make out the tracks, though every now and then he had to stop and search for the trail on foot.

"C'mon Terry!" Ken Trickham bellowed from the white four-wheel drive, after what seemed the fiftieth stop. "Don't tell me you're lost!"

"I'm not bloody lost, you bloody pig bastard." Terry muttered, giving the policeman a dirty look. Getting in the Falcon, he jammed it into drive and flattened it, leaving Sgt Trickham in a cloud of red dust.

"Stupid copper, wouldn't be able to find his own stupid nose in the dark." the rooshooter grumbled, manoeuvring the ute around a fallen tree. A large dark shape bounded through the scrub, and Terry hollered in triumph.

"We found 'em!" he began, when a large shape threw itself into the side of the Falcon. Kimberly began screaming like crazy, and even Terry shrieked like a little girl. In the dim orange light, they could see the Magnaroo, grabbing onto Kimberly's window sill with its front claws. Trying to ram its massive head through the window, it snapped at Kimberly with its fanged maw.

"Get down!" Terry screamed, and madly grabbing for his gun, let off a wild shot out of his passenger window. Shrieking horribly, the giant roo let go of the door. Ears still ringing from the gun-fire, Kimberly cowered down on the floor, shaking and moaning.

"Wind up the bloody windows!" Terry yelled.

"*Don't stop driving!*" Ken's voice crackled through the radio. "*They're all around us!*"

Bounding through the trees, the Magnaroo pack came for them. Towering over the vehicles, they rammed into the sides as Terry passed, pounding on the roof and hissing sinisterly.

"So . . . big!" Kimberly said, somehow keeping the presence of mind to take photos. Some of the Magnaroo were nearly three and a half metres tall, and they easily outpaced the machines. She counted eight of them, flitting in and out of the scrub.

"We're being rounded up." she whispered, then shrieked as Terry slammed on the brakes. The cloud of dust cleared, and in front of them stood the biggest, meanest Magnaroo of them all. Large fangs extended past his top lip, and he was well over four metres tall, dark red fur just visible in the fading daylight.

"Rufus." Terry whispered, and then the monster pounced. Landing on the bonnet of the Falcon, he crushed the exposed hydrogen converter with his giant feet. Bellowing deep within his chest, he tore at the roof, sharp claws scoring the steel.

Madly reversing, Terry narrowly missed Ken's four-wheel drive, which was covered in the giant beasts. Rufus continued to pound and tear at the roof, sharp claws finally puncturing the steel. Blood trickled into the cabin as the alpha male cut himself on the sharp edge, and Kimberly fumbled for the tranquilliser gun.

"Drop that useless piece of shit!" Terry roared, pulling a loaded pistol from the centre console. As Rufus wrenched at the roof, he emptied the clip through the roof. Shrieking, the massive creature fell to one side, and the lanky man cackled in triumph.

"That's why you should always keep a gun loaded." Terry chuckled, then cursed as the engine suddenly coughed and died. The antique Falcon, rolling on Australian roads since 1998, rolled no more.

"Damn hydrogen converter! I knew I should never have . . . " Terry began, and gasped as the driver's side window smashed. Kimberly shrieked, and could only watch in horror as massive paws reached into the cab and wrenched the screaming man out. His screams turned into agonised squeals, and then there were nothing but horrible crunching and snuffling sounds. The Magnaroo were feeding.

Cowering on the floor, Kimberly shook in terror. Lying in a pool of her own urine, she tried to keep absolutely quiet. Absolutely still.

"Terry! Terry! Come in!" the radio crackled. It was Bob Filcher, back at Yurla Crossing. Frantically, the biologist grabbed the handset. Hands shaking, she thumbed the button.

"It's Kimberly Yarrow, Mister Filcher." she whispered. "They got him! The roos got Terry. I think they've got Ken as well."

"Shit!" Bob swore loudly. *"Where are you? Are you okay?"* The feeding sounds stopped, and there was a sharp hiss. Kimberly could only watch in horror as a giant head peered through the broken window, and she pounded at the radio controls till she found the off switch.

Please god, please, she silently prayed. Leaning through the window, the Magnaroo stretched its long arm across the cab. Breathing with frustration, it couldn't quite reach her.

Sobbing hysterically, she primed the tranquilliser gun. As the beast managed to get its claws snagged in her hair, she fired the dart between the Magnaroo's eyes.

Squealing, the roo snatched back its paw, ripping out some of her hair. Scrabbling at the dart, its eyes rolled backwards and it collapsed into a drugged snooze.

She had five darts left in the clip, and pulling the bolt back, primed the air-gun for the next shot. She had no idea how many Magnaroo surrounded her, and if that would be enough. Quietly reaching across the cabin, she wrapped her hands around Terry's rifle. The cabin rocked slightly.

With a god awful screech, the bloody paws of Rufus smashed through the windscreen. Screaming and crying, Kimberly dropped the rifle as she cowered from the giant. Rooting around in the cab, the injured Rufus finally dug its sharp claws into her side. He pulled the wriggling woman out of the ruined vehicle.

Lip curling back as it growled, the giant red beast towered above the Falcon. Drool fell from its fangs, and it lifted Kimberly up to its mouth.

Managing to land a dart in his chest with the air-gun, the gun dropped from her trembling fingers. Snarling and hissing, Rufus staggered around, shaking his head. The tranquilliser wasn't working!

"No!" she shrieked, beating at the strong arms. Tears pouring down her face, a thousand thoughts racing through her mind in those last awful moments. A week ago, she had been tinkering around in the Uni lab, and now she was about to die horribly in the middle of the Outback.

The towering marsupial squeezed his claws, and they dug into Kimberly's side painfully. The blood rushed to her head, and there was a throbbing sound in her ears. Sniffing at her face, he gently began to worry at her with his teeth, alternately licking and biting at her. His breath stinking of rotten flesh, Kimberly gagged. Rufus was playing with her, like a cat with a mouse.

It took a second for Kimberly to realised that the drumming sound in her ears was in fact an approaching helicopter. Rufus dropped her and bounced away in fear, and crying, she shook with relief on the ground. Several rifle shots rang out, and the Magnaroo pack scattered in all directions.

Mercifully, she sank into unconsciousness, seeing an aboriginal teenager leap from the landing helicopter before darkness claimed her.

✳

"Miss . . . Miss . . . are you okay?"

Shaking her groggy head, Kimberly groaned. She hurt all over, and it felt like someone had bandaged her up. She opened her eyes.

Strapped into a chair in a helicopter, she saw the big smiles and friendly eyes of her rescuers. Every person onboard was indigenous, most of them quite young. The eldest was a middle-aged woman, the pilot.

"How you feeling, miss?" the boy repeated. "Don't worry, you're safe now."

"The . . . roos . . . ." she gasped. "Terry . . . Ken."

"They didn't make it." the pilot answered. "Damn devils killed them. The cars, wrecked. You're lucky we came along when we did."

"We didn't believe Terry when he told us." said a teenage girl, clutching a rifle as big as her. "Who would have?"

The Tredrea family owned one of the more successful stations near Yurla Crossing. Thankfully they had listened to Bob Filcher, and followed Terry's tyre tracks from Banross Station.

"We'll take you to Yurla Crossing, then we'll have to get the flying doctor out." Beatty Tredrea continued as she casually guided the whirlybird home. "You're pretty messed up, but you should live."

They made it back to town by daybreak. Another baking hot day had begun in the outback town, and the wind was already kicking up a lot of dust. Carrying Kimberly in a fireman's lift, two of the older Tredrea boys carried her from the airfield and towards Government House.

"Oh Jesus, no. Oh god!" Kimberly shrieked. Putting her on the ground, the boys hollered for help.

The streets of Yurla Crossing were filled with the dead. What was left of Bob Filcher lay face down in the red dirt, his legs and upper arms virtually gone.

Kimberly gagged when she saw the remains of the publican, guts split open and one of her arms several feet away, an unfired gun still clutched in her hand.

The windows of the store were ruined, and a massive hole gaped in the pub's side where something had smashed through it.

She stared in horror at the first Magnaroo, its ugly dog-like head level with the roof of the hotel. Spotting her, it swung forward on its arms and legs, its thick tail marking a line through the red dust. Hissing and barking at her, she saw it snap its sharp teeth. Loud breathing sounds surrounded her as dozens of roos emerged from hiding.

Closing her eyes, she drew herself into a tight little ball in the middle of the street. She did not want to look when she heard the screams and shots from the helicopter, the breaking glass and the eating sounds. She heard her two companions run for cover, heard their screams as they were run down and murdered.

She still didn't look as she heard the thumping sound of the roos giant feet, the hissing of their angry breath. A big foot rested on her, pinning her to the ground, and sharp teeth caressed her pale throat . . .

"Be ready," the CO told his gunner. It was dark, and the soldiers were getting nervous. "Fucking things can rip through the armour."

The tanks of the 3/9th were lined up across the Sturt Highway. The RAAF had been performing manoeuvres over the area, scanning for heat signatures in the nearby bush. The roo packs scattered whenever a plane flew over, and the bombings hadn't achieved much.

The killer roos were out of control and breeding rapidly. Having stripped the Outback of life, they were making their way to the cities.

One way or the other, another species was about to become extinct.

✳

GUNNING FOR A TINKERMAN

Lanyard was gunning for a tinkerman.

The hunt had taken him from Overland to Inland, an endless sunburnt landscape that made his eyes swim and attention wander. The only trees were those that hugged the dead watercourses, hoping for a big rain. Everything else was dust and twisted stone.

A strong wind punished his sails, and the rusty tube-frame shook under the strain. The wheels of the skiff churned up the fine dust and threatened to become airborne. Lanyard played the cords like a puppet-master, bringing in one sail while steering with his free hand.

Rounding a sharp bend in the tradeway, he saw it and swore. He yanked up the sails, hauling back on the choke-stick for all he was worth.

It was a grandfather of a serpent, curled up in the middle of the track. The snake had brought down the telegraph line, as they sometimes did when they were hungry or lazy. It knew people would come to fix the damage in a day or two, and waited with a patience honed by decades of blistering Inland summers.

The snake came for him, head low to the ground, drove forward, faster than a man could run, and it was all Lanyard could do to leap clear before its great coils were crushing the skiff. The tubular frame squealed under that immense force, and the wind-cart tipped over as the snake poured towards the man.

Sixty feet of muscle. Scales bigger than tea-saucers. Great fangs that could pierce an engine block. It rose up above him, ready to strike. In that final panicked moment Lanyard saw it had great gleaming slits for eyes, angry orbs which had seen a hundred years or more. It had been here before the settlers, might be here when the last of them died under these unwelcome skies.

Lanyard had a revolver out and squeezed the trigger quicker than thought, sending thunder into that death's head, rolling aside as the snake drove its fangs into the dusty earth. He got lucky and shattered one of those eyes into jelly. Another bullet into its tail as it fled, wounded, over the lip of the dry watercourse that hugged the tradeway.

He saw it slip up the other side of the dead creek, slithering into the bush and Lanyard knew he should chase it, make sure it was dead. Folks told tales about the snakes of Inland, that they were vengeful and crafty. He'd bled it, and it might follow him now, come for him some quiet evening. Perhaps it already waited up ahead, wrapped around an overhanging gum tree, ready to drop on him as he passed underneath.

"I'll take your other eye, grandfather," Lanyard called out, his heart pounding and nerves shot. Groaning against the weight of the motor mounted behind his seat, he pushed the skiff back onto its wheels. He had to leave, now.

The skiff rode on old bicycle tires, one of which the snake had bent out of shape. It was more than Lanyard could fix with his bare hands, but when he hoisted the sails and released the chock-stick it all seemed to work.

A hot wind punched at his sails, and he rolled along the road at a terrifying pace. He shot past a rusty sheet of tin nailed to a tree, painted to read BEWARE OF SNAKES.

"Good advice," he said.

*

He hadn't always been a hunter of men, and in a time he preferred to forget Lanyard Everett was once prentice to that most despicable of characters, a jesusman.

Bauer was an old man when he sniffed Lanyard out, one of

the last to walk openly under signs that brought death these days. Back then Lanyard was little more than a wretch on the wrong side of crooked, with his ribs showing and only the hope of a short and pointless life before him.

"We're not meant to be here, in the Now," the jesusman confessed to his new prentice. "Seems the Lord of the Crossing took a wrong turn. Or else this dust-bowl was his true destination, and a grander joke than I can understand."

Lanyard nodded, hating the man. This proved to be the first of many disappointments.

*

Lanyard knew that Thomas Cobbler, the tinkerman, was in this district, paying visit to the rough holdings that somehow existed between the towns.

The winds died off perhaps ten miles down the road, and the skiff rolled to a gentle halt. The flippant Inland weather had stranded him in the middle of nowhere, sails limp in the sticky air.

With a worried eye to the bush Lanyard checked the motor. He unscrewed the fuel cap, saw that the little tank was bone-dry. He had a flask of grain fuel and poured in about three-quarters of what he had, the trickle of liquid smelling something like rotgut moonshine mixed with kerosene.

Some folks drank the stuff, drunks who didn't mind going blind. When they got that desperate they were already dead.

The motor caught on the third try, coughing and belching blue smoke. This skiff was a marvel of scavenger engineering, bits of this and that cobbled together with spit and string. He threw the lever that connected the drive-chain, and the whole thing lurched forward.

"Don't die on me," he pleaded, watching for the snake; the motor chugged away. He knew that one day soon it would seize up, like all Before-Time stuff did.

Lanyard opened the throttle a little and made good time. He drew in all the sails, all but the tiny fore-sail which he watched for signs of fuel-saving wind.

There was a holding up ahead, some mad townsman keen to gamble against nature. The homestead was a shabby patchwork of corrugated iron and rust, ringed by rail fences which kept in a handful of sheep and the beginnings of a barn and stable. Some starving chooks scratched at a handful of feed scattered across the dead ground.

Lanyard steered the skiff from the tradeway and up to the shanty, passing a boundary of stones painted blue to stand out against the cracked red earth. That meant this place was protected by town-law.

He cut the motor and pulled back on the chock-stick till the wheels locked. Stepping out of the skiff he walked up to the shack, hauling a pistol out of his pocket which he held against the side of his leg.

A fella who must have been the farmer came out the front door, waving the business end of a rifle at him. His free hand had a dog by the collar, a half-breed native mutt which strained forward, slavering and growling. A bite from such could kill a man the slow way, his tongue black and back arched, throat scraped raw by desperate fingernails.

"Bugger off," the man said, swallowing nervously. "Nothing here for you."

Lanyard said nothing, just eyeballed the settler.

There was a wobbly windmill missing a vane, filling the silence with rusty squeals as it span madly, herald to an angry black cloud rolling in from the south. A line was strung out from the verandah, clothes pegged to it, shirts billowed like sails. A basket had been dropped to the ground, spilling linen onto the dirt where the ants crawled all over it. Probably left there by the farmer's sheila, likely some leathery old tart who'd seen too much sun. She'd be hiding inside the hovel, fearing any stranger if she had sense.

"You give me honest answers, I'll leave you be," Lanyard said. "I'm looking for a tinkerman, Thomas Cobbler."

"You find him, you send him here. The record player won't work, and me motorbike's seized up again," the farmer said. Lanyard tapped the gun against his leg impatiently.

"Look mate, I don't have time to muck around. Where is Cobbler?"

"You gunna kill him?"

Lanyard said nothing.

"You must be some sort of fool, mister," said the man. "You can't touch him. It's town-law."

Lanyard could see the man measuring the odds, waved the pistol to scare some sense into him.

"He's at The Folly. His windfarm," the man added. "You won't miss it, great mess of windmills stuck on a hill about fifty miles north. No water there worth boring for, but he's the tinkerman not you nor I."

Lanyard bartered with the settler for grain-fuel, swapped him a pouch of tobacco for enough to get him to the windfarm. All the while their guns were out and the mongrel snarling where it had been chained to the verandah post. Lanyard carried a sloshing jerry-can back to the skiff and casually topped up the tank, figuring if the farmer meant to shoot him he'd have done it by now.

He knew the type, this man would rather send trouble on for others to deal with. He left the settler unharmed and unrobbed, and by Now standards that was almost friendly.

Every now and then, Lanyard spotted bleed-throughs in the distance, a wall on its own with doors and windows, and once a melted skyscraper laying on its side like a great silver worm. There was a stretch of sealed road running parallel to the tradeway, complete with dead traffic lights and street-signs. Before-Time things made most folks nervous, even as they picked through them for scraps and trade. Had he the time, he'd have looked through himself, hoping he was the first to come along since they sprung out of the ground all twisted and funny looking.

Lanyard was more nervous than most around the bleed-throughs. There were sinister creatures lurking in the grey spaces between Before and Now, monstrous beyond anything this land could offer. They were often drawn to these thin places, eager to snatch those fool enough to linger there.

"Too many bleed-throughs round here," Lanyard mumbled, wishing he'd kept some tobacco for himself. He was dying for a smoke. He touched the motor with the back of his hand, felt it heating up.

There was a little breeze, enough to keep the skiff moving at walking pace, so he rigged up the sails and gave the old engine a rest.

When he saw a whole row of Before-Time houses, joined together and intact, Lanyard swore. He fumbled for his swag, reached into the filthy bed-roll and pulled out a shotgun wrapped in oilskin. He'd killed old Bauer for this gun, graven with mark and word of the jesus.

He could feel something there, lurking and watching him, not quite in this world but strong enough to break through. He felt all the usual signs, the crawling skin, throbbing joints and aching teeth. A witch.

Not much could harm a witch, but this gun could drive the life out of one. It gave him comfort to hold that great metal cannon, till he remembered that he had no shells left.

Lanyard yanked at the starter cord, ignoring the troubled whine of the engine and realised that the snake was the least of his problems.

He may have been a witch-sniffer and the last of the jesusmen, but Lanyard Everett wasn't fool enough to stay.

✳

"You're safe now," Bauer called up to the town-men, huddling behind what they thought was a safe wall. The jesusman held up the severed head of a mad jenny, still snarling and snapping with yellowed fangs at the old man.

Once people sang the praises of jesusmen across the Now, but a day came when people forgot their many good deeds. And they always, always remembered their one mistake.

"Another mob gone feral," Bauer explained after a frightened young lad brought them stale loaves and a handful of shrivelled turnips. Custom called for the towns to provision a jesusman and his prentice, but of late the fare had been poor, the gates always closed.

"But we saved them," young Lanyard said. He struggled with the shovel, trying to split the hard clay. The mad jenny screeched at him from under Bauer's boot, her rotting face consumed with bestial rage.

"These people, they've turned from the Jesus," and Bauer said this name with the old respect. "If I had good sense I'd leave these wayward daughters to slaughter their fool parents."

While Bauer set up a camp-fire and brewed up a soup that would hopefully soften the bread, the prentice kept at his job. When the hole was deep enough he lined it with animal bones, something to distract what was left of the mad jenny's head in the year or so it

— 136 —

would take to die. This would be the final resting place for a little girl stolen from her bed, an innocent soul made into something else.

"Here," Bauer said, throwing the head across the campfire. Lanyard caught it by the lank greasy hair, held it clear before it could take a bite out of him.

"Mark my words, lad," Bauer said, poking at the bubbling mess in his billy-pot. "This is what happens when folks start casting bones for Papa Lucy and the Lady Bertha."

The time of the jesusman had passed, and Lanyard had been recruited right at the end of their glory days, right before the word itself came to mean outlaw and dead man.

*

He spotted the snake when it lifted its great head above a rock, its body undulating as it crawled out of a dead billabong. Perhaps it saw the light of the midday sun reflected from his field-glasses; the enormous serpent sank out of sight, waiting for him to move on. Lanyard had driven till it was so dark he couldn't see the track, but now the snake was within a mile of his campfire. Grandfather must have been moving all day.

"I need a rifle," he mumbled. He'd scraped together enough tobacco crumbs to get a smoke going, a thin paper cylinder stuck to his bottom lip. It didn't help his nerves any. The smoke trailed straight into the air, telling Lanyard what he already knew, that there was no wind at all.

Tiring of the standoff, he tried to start the motor. It coughed once, twice, three times. Lanyard felt faint with panic. He pulled the ripcord, faster and faster. For a moment he thought it had worked, but it spluttered briefly and stalled.

"Come on, come on," Lanyard said. He lifted up the field glasses to see that the snake had abandoned its hiding place, was sliding across the baked earth towards the tradeway. It knew he was stranded.

He thumbed the focus dial on his field-glasses and saw the ruin of the creature's face, a great weeping hollow where its eye once was. Grandfather was furious.

"Start! Damn dust-bound junk." He ripped at the starter cord, again and again, the danger of the cord snapping outweighed by the approach of death swiftly gliding towards him.

Then there was the most beautiful sound he'd ever heard, the coughing and rattling of that bloody machine, and he was in the seat and racing away.

"Get stuffed!" he called over his shoulder. The snake kept pace with him for a few moments, but gradually the gap widened until he could barely see the creature, a tiny dot somewhere behind him, tirelessly pursuing him.

An hour later he saw the windfarm. Perhaps twenty or thirty windmills spun lazily atop a mesa, and the only way up to them was a steep switchback. He turned from the tradeway and took to the scrub, engine growling as he bounced across the rocks and through a field of spiky yakka. Lanyard had to get to the top of that mesa before the motor finally died, and hope he could drive off or kill the great serpent.

He hit the first incline, a stretch that looked like it had been blasted out of the rock with dynamite. On the first tight turn, the motor sounded crook, like a handful of ball bearings were bouncing around inside. Lanyard squeezed the throttle to full, and the engine missed a beat, almost stalled.

"Come on," he moaned. Shifting the steer-stick left and right, he tried to climb the skiff over the loose scree and around the grooves of water run-offs. He was about half-way up when the motor gave a final death-rattle. Lanyard was out and running, the skiff rolling backwards and flipping over to bounce back down the hill, spilling his gear all over the place. He spared a glance to see that the wind-cart narrowly missed the snake, wriggling up the side of the mesa.

Each breath burning in his lungs, Lanyard pounded up the pathway, praying that he wouldn't snap an ankle or slip off the narrow switchback and into the mouth of Grandfather. He stopped dead, right near the top. Some stupid bugger had blocked the path with a crazy mess of tiger wire and chicken mesh, nailed to a great wooden frame.

He swore, reaching for his gun. The snake would be on him in moments. It was tempting to put a bullet through his own stupid skull, but a last stand was more Lanyard's style.

Resigned to this end, he didn't notice the sound of the frame shifting, a footstep behind him. He almost put a round through the old man's head but he relaxed, smiled.

"Get in here, you stupid man," Thomas Cobbler said. "Bringing snakes right to my front door."

He helped the tinkerman shift the barricade back into place, and a few seconds later the snake was striking at it, great yellow fangs pulling at the mesh. The barrier wouldn't hold it long, and it ignored the sting of the tiger-wire. Lanyard made to shoot it but Cobbler put a hand on his arm, pulled him back.

"Save your bullets," he said. "I've a better way."

He threw a lever and the snake convulsed violently, smoke and sparks filling the air. Lanyard saw a thick black cable reaching back from the gate, to a messy network of batteries and the wires which ran up each windmill.

Cobbler turned the fence off. The snake fell from the wire, smoke pouring from its mouth.

"Grandfather, you look stone cold dead," Lanyard told the serpent, and the tinkerman looked at him strange. The limp weight of the monster snake dragged it down the hill, rolling and bouncing and smashing into rocks with horrific force till the last scaly coil vanished from sight.

"Electricity," Cobbler said, gesturing to the windmills. "Well, Mister Lanyard Everett. It's been a while, hasn't it?"

"It sure has," Lanyard said, holding his gun against the tinkerman's temple.

✳

He'd only been a year in Bauer's service when he murdered his master. One minute they'd been sitting around a cook-fire, and Bauer had been telling stories of people he'd once known. All dead now.

What with the camaraderie of camping in the outdoors and the prospect of the juicy critter roasting on a spit, Lanyard was almost surprised to find himself cradling a jagged stone in his hands. He leapt across the cook-fire, knocking the meat into the ashes, and wrestling with the old man he drove the rock into Bauer's skull again and again.

Finally the jesusman was dead, his face a bloody ruin, his body bent and broken across the log they'd both dragged over for a seat.

"I can't do it," Lanyard sobbed, the rock sliding out of his fingers. "Can't do it anymore."

During the struggle old Bauer had snatched up his jesusman's shotgun, a holy weapon the likes of which would never be made again in this world. But he was holding it by the barrel, not the stock. Even at his bloody end, it seemed that he was offering his prentice the weapon. A gift.

Lanyard had killed a man once before, but felt filthy with the shame of this cowardly act. He knew what was to come. An endless parade of monsters would still sniff him out, know him for a jesusman and an enemy. At that moment, Lanyard realised that this bloody freedom had truly brought him nothing.

Lanyard prised away the dead man's fingers, and gripped the enormous gun. It was heavy, and the gun felt cold and mean.

✳

"I can't fix it," Cobbler complained, throwing down a spanner with disgust. "Motor's burnt right out."

"Well you figure a way of fixing it, else you'll be towing me where we're going," Lanyard told him. He'd put the gun away hours ago, the threat established. He was much quicker than the old tinkerman and they both knew it.

"You bastard. I shouldn't help you. Snake will come get us both soon enough." There'd been no dead serpent down the bottom, just a bloody trail leading through the yakka.

"That's no way to speak to an old friend," Lanyard said, and the old man grizzled to himself and tinkered with the outboard. Finally he stripped the whole thing from its housing and dumped it on the ground.

"Useless," he said. "Just a wind-cart now, unless you got another motor in your swag."

Cobbler had a horse and buggy for when he did his rounds of the farms and the shacks, because "tinkermen know better than to rely on bleed-through gadgets". The animal was well-fed and strong; Lanyard decided it was his now. Cobbler went into the buggy, trussed tightly. His stores were full of tins scavenged by grateful settlers and Lanyard took the lot. He found and discarded the old man's rifle, a rusty old .303 that was missing the bolt, but with joy he pocketed a few shotgun shells found in the mountains of junk.

"Last I heard you were running grog to the natives," Cobbler said as they rode up the tradeway. "Gareth boot you out of his little enterprise?"

"Something like that," Lanyard said.

"A long way from Riverland to Inland. A long way to break town-law. You know they'll hang you for touching a tinkerman."

"I don't go into the towns much," Lanyard said.

"Who sent you?"

"Man with a bag of coin. Shut your mouth."

Lanyard kept the horse at a good clip, hoping that the snake was too wounded to follow at its usual mile-eating pace. Cobbler's horse was a fine animal, well-behaved and sturdy. He made sure to rest it several times a day, and gave it as much water as it could guzzle.

Lanyard had lashed the frame of the motorless skiff to the back of the buggy, its rear wheels bouncing along behind them. He'd too much attachment to the wind-cart to junk it in the middle of nowhere.

"Look there," Cobbler said. One moment they were looking on a stretch of cracked red clay, the next a misshapen slice of building pierced the earth, one corner of a broken gable pointing angrily at the sky. The pie-shaped section of building swayed but didn't fall. A bleed-through.

"Go on, you back-stabbing bastard," Cobbler raved as Lanyard halted the horse. "I hope it falls on top of you."

"You know, Cobbler, I'd gag you but I like the company," Lanyard said with false cheer. He felt wrong all over, and knew that this was a possible crossing point. There was the hint of something nearby, perhaps a distant pair of eyes watching.

"Paranoid," he said, but broke out the jesusman's shotgun just the same, primed both barrels. He now had one round left in his pocket and hoped it wouldn't come to that.

"Only a mug passes up good forage," Lanyard told Cobbler, and ignoring the twisted door he stepped through an open wall and into the past.

It might have been a book-store, or a library. Shelf upon shelf of books, here in the Now where one book was worth more than a man's life. Lanyard knew his letters but not much more. He grabbed a fat handful of books, tucked them under his arm.

"A bloody fortune," he said.

"Jesusman," he heard in his head, the mind-raping static of a witch. He dropped the books, pointed the gun left and right.

"You're a cunning one," Lanyard managed. It was almost there, watching him from its grey nest, in between all worlds and times. Hungry.

"Show yourself," Lanyard said. "I've mark and word and I'll shoot you deader than dead."

There was laughter, the witchy kind that made him want to tear his brain out of his skull, and then the sensation of the creature withdrawing.

✳

Lanyard spent many years trying to understand why he betrayed a good man. It might have made sense had Bauer been a monster, had he been anything but a doomed holdover from a kinder age. It was the most pointless of murders.

Perhaps it was fear that first set Lanyard on this dark path, from wretch to hero to killer. Fear of not living up to the old man's legacy, fear of an endless invisible army that he as a jesusman was fated to struggle against. Knowing that no-one cared anymore, that the jesusmen were finished.

Even then Lanyard must have known that he could not run from his master, any more than he could run from his own nature. Bauer's murder was a futile attempt to escape from himself.

All that was left to him now were lonely days, his only company the hungry monsters that came for him. Seems that Bauer had given him more than a gun, a trade to ply. He'd passed on this most certain legacy, the promise of a violent, lonely end.

✳

"There," Lanyard said, pointing at the beacon. The natives had crafted these by arts unknown, glass spires that littered all the lands from Riverland to Inland and perhaps further. By day they drew in the sunlight, and when night fell they lit the old ways. This spire was old, and gave a sickly red glow like the dying embers of a campfire.

A man was waiting there for them, and Lanyard knew he'd been checking the tradeway every night, just before dusk. A crooked man if ever he saw one, wearing a patchwork outfit of rags with a neat new waistcoat over the whole mess. He had a necklace of finger bones and gave them a gap-toothed grin.

"You Lanyard?" he said, and Lanyard nodded. The crooked man looked into the buggy, saw Cobbler all tied up. He licked his lips and rubbed at his crotch, and the tinkerman let out a terrified moan.

— 142 —

"Good, you brung him. Follow me," and the man picked up a rusty old bicycle from behind the spire. There was a little track running off from the tradeway, and the man pedalled down it, waiting for them at the first rise.

"You monster," Cobbler sobbed. "You're giving me to a crooked mob."

"I'd like to say it's just business. But I have my reasons, tinkerman. A little coin in the right hands and I heard whispers, that it was you led that town-patrol to us. There's blood on your hands, Cobbler."

Cobbler could say nothing because Lanyard was absolutely correct, he had crossed the wrong people and now it had caught up with him. Lanyard clicked his tongue and the horse walked forward, following the trail.

Their guide led them through a salt-flat, the trail punctuated by the occasional skeleton. There was no good land for miles, and no reason anyone would want to be here.

Except for the bleed-throughs. Lanyard had never seen so many. Before-Time buildings poked out of the dead ground at random intervals, but grew thicker and thicker until twisted ruins surrounded them. Wary, Lanyard lay the jesusman gun across his lap, watching for trouble. The goat track they were following sometimes ran across Before-Time roads, the horse's shoes ringing against the rippled bitumen.

As dusk gave way to night the big yellow moon made the ruins along the horizon look like a mouthful of crooked teeth. He could see campfires.

"That's our mob," said the fellow on the bicycle, eyeing off Lanyard's shotgun. "Better put your gun away mate."

They reached the camp, a collection of shanties and lean-tos on the edge of a great salt-lake, everything a curdled-milk colour under the light of that sickly moon.

The crooked mob eyed him off as he entered their turf, and they reached for home-made spearguns and what shooters they had. He could make about perhaps seven of them, wild folk living as far from town-law as they could.

"Where's your bossman?" he said. "I brung a tinkerman, like we agreed."

There was a man wearing the top half of a business suit, denim cut-offs and a cowboy hat on his head. He swung a cricket bat loosely in one hand. It was studded with cruel looking nails, stained with old blood.

"I'm Hat-Trick," and now he was close enough Lanyard could recognise the man. They'd met a few months ago, at an outpost that tolerated crooked men if they brought good trade.

"Got your tinkerman in the back," he told Hat-Trick, and the crooked men swarmed forward, hauling Cobbler out and laughing at his protests, mocking him for his tears. There was a great spreading wet patch on his trousers from where he'd pissed himself.

"Where's my money?" Lanyard demanded, and Hat-Trick pulled something out of his pockets, planted it firmly into his hands.

It was a purse, and with horror Lanyard realised it was made from a man's scrotum. There was the heft of coin inside it, but nowhere near the agreed amount.

"What is this?" he said.

"All our coin," said Hat-Trick. Lanyard felt the rage come on, had the shotgun and his revolver out in the blink of an eye. The mob made to rush him but Hat-Trick held up a hand.

"I've been through hell to get here. If you mean to cheat me I'll kill you where you stand," Lanyard said through clenched teeth. Hat-Trick laughed.

"Look around, you bloody fool. We've a fortune in forage. In the morning I'll let you take as much as you can carry."

Lanyard looked at the cannibals. One of them smiled, and in the firelight he could see that the woman's teeth had been filed into points. Common sense told him to leave now and count his losses. Greed won.

"I sleep light and I shoot quick," he told them. "If you would nibble on my toes, think on that."

He wouldn't drink or eat with them, turned down a plate of mystery stew which set the mob to laughing. He rolled out his swag and sat with his back against the wheel of Cobbler's buggy. They watched him nodding off, sharing little grins and whispers. He took one long heavy blink into sleep, but was awake with heart pounding. One of them was sliding towards him with a knife in hand, but the man dropped it into the dirt at the sight of Lanyard's revolver.

"Jokes. Just jokes," the man said with a weak smile.

*

The crooked men started as the ones who kept the true worship of Papa Lucy and the Bone-Man. Their practices were so repugnant that the towns turned them out, even as a sanitised version of the religion sprang up behind the thick walls.

The eating of a man became the eating of a suckling pig, wearing a child's clothing. The true believers still laugh at the townsmen now, rolling ox-tails for the Bone-Man instead of knuckle-bones. Something of the visceral nature of these new gods was lost, watered down by the civilised men who claimed these cults as their own.

So even as the crooked mobs tore up the countryside and preyed on lone travellers, Lanyard respected them. They were outcasts, much like him, yet remained true to their faith, which was more than he could ever do.

*

"I'm gonna start a new town," Hat-Trick told Lanyard in the morning. "For all their talk of laws and society, I know them other towns started out much the same. Just good forage, and a tough bossman."

"True enough," Lanyard said. "There's bigger crooks behind a town wall than anything out here."

They had Cobbler face down, holding down his arms and legs. One bloke was heating a great steel rod in a fire, until the end glowed cherry-red.

"Old days, in the Before, folks got together into villages and such," Hat-Trick told his crew. "They had blacksmiths, folks like our tinkerman here what kept everything working. Built all the stuff to keep the village alive."

He approached the man, pulled a sharp rabbit knife from his coat pocket. Cobbler saw it and screamed, wild-eyed, weeping, and begging for mercy.

"That blacksmith, most important fella in town. They needed his special skills just to keep the place going. Those villagers couldn't let him leave, not ever. They made sure he stayed, that he would serve his community for life."

It was over in seconds, but Lanyard fought the urge to vomit, made himself watch lest he appear weak. Hat-Trick hamstrung Cobbler, mutilated his tendons while the man screamed in agony.

The man with the hot steel rod cauterised the wounds, and another bloke bound them up with bandages crusted with lake salt. The file-toothed woman cradled his head, forced a good belt of grog down his throat. Cobbler spit up the first mouthful, but gratefully gulped at the booze. She let him have the rest of it, and he lay there sobbing and sucking from the bottle like a pouting baby.

"Can't have our tinkerman pissing off in the middle of the night," Hat-Trick said. "We've found cars, radio sets, 'fridgerators and such. That bloke's gonna make this place the envy of all the towns."

Lanyard was led to the bleed-through fields, a stretch of Before-Time junk bigger than any town. There was a car with the front half melted and poking up out of the ground like a headstone, two blokes scraping away with picks and mattocks to free it. As bossman Hat-Trick got first dibs on anything found, the deal was that Lanyard could cart off whatever he could fit in the buggy so long as Hat-Trick didn't want it first.

"You ever see anyone else around here?"

"Any fool sneak through my stuff ends up in the cookpot," Hat-Trick said, and Lanyard hid a smile. Witches didn't get eaten, they ate.

Lanyard couldn't feel anything sinister nearby, but the grey space between the worlds was thin here, thinner than paper. There'd be no trouble, no work for a witch to step through into the Now. It was only a matter of time.

He hauled out the murderous cannon he kept hid in the swag, and sure enough Hat-Trick eyed off the old double-barrelled shooter.

"There's jesus marks on that thing," Hat-Trick said. "I could haul you into a town, give you to a magistrate. You could make me very rich."

"Lawmen would take you too, crooked man," Lanyard said, scanning the warped buildings for movement. "We could end our days together, choking side by side on the gallows."

Nothing came for them, nothing but flies and dust as they poked through the ruins. Within an hour Lanyard had gathered a carton of smokes, a new shirt, some tins of food, and a book called "How to Win Friends and Influence People".

Lanyard was far from finished foraging, and a deal was a deal. He could fit a tonne of stuff in the buggy, and even intended to strap things to the skiff. He would leave this place a very rich man.

"Enough for now," Hat-Trick demanded. "You get one more forage after lunch, but then you leave."

They returned to the main camp. Lanyard could see a few other people now, filthy and haggard but not crooked men. A one-armed man was hauling a cart full of scrap wood for the fires, boards stripped from buildings and fences. A young girl was digging a latrine hole with a hand-scoop, eyes dark with exhausted terror. She was missing her right leg.

"Like any town, we got citizens," Hat-Trick laughed. "They pay us taxes to live here."

Most of these "citizens" were missing limbs. Lanyard eyed the cooking pot and decided he didn't want to know.

As his hosts ate their lunch, Lanyard hauled up a bucket of water from the soak, rank water barely worth drinking. He stripped off his shirt and washed himself for the first time in days.

"Nice tatt," someone said, and Lanyard saw it was the file-toothed woman, gnawing on a bone and looking at his leathery chest. At his jesus tattoo, a picture of a bleeding man bound tight, hands clenched into fists but for his pointer fingers, one to left, the other the right. BEFORE and NOW were writ under each hand.

"You're a jesusman," she said casually.

"I'm nothing," he said, wriggling into his new shirt. He'd gotten stupid, too tired to notice someone sneaking up on him. His pulse raced wildly.

"Fingerbone said you had a gun with that mark," she said, picking a scrap out of her teeth. "They all think you're toting the kit of some jesusman you killed. But my own eyes, they tell me you're the worst kind of fool."

"You keep your mouth shut," Lanyard said. "One word and I'll kill you first."

It was that moment that the familiar pains started, the throbbing inside his skull. There was a witch, real close, close enough to step through into the Now and make a meal out of him.

Trying to get a fix on the creature, he reached back for his shooter and that was the moment that the woman pounced. She wrapped her legs tight around his waist and worried at his neck with her sharp teeth, even as he rained blows on her head and smashed her nose with a fist. She drew blood and crowed with triumph.

The crooked mob were all over him in moments, kicking and punching and bearing him down by weight of numbers. When he came to, naked and bound before Hat-Trick, he knew that all deals had fallen through.

✻

The first jesusman to come for him after Bauer's murder was quick and strong, a man armed with naught but a sword-cane. He wore the image of the jesus across his leathery forehead and there was no mistaking him for anything else.

"Them I can understand, but why you?" the man had raved, and in a blur of movement he was so close with that sharp blade that Lanyard could see the cataracts filling his left eye, the scars covering nearly every inch of his skin.

The jesusman kept coming, even with a bullet in him, and buried his blade in flesh even as Lanyard put one final round through the man's temple. Lanyard barely survived the attack, nearly bleeding to death in a muddy Riverland street.

He found a revolver in the dead man's belt, and it spoke volumes of the contempt he must have felt for Bauer's murderous prentice. Not even worth a bullet.

There was only one more jesusman to attempt vengeance, before the pogrom and generous death bounties meant that the jesusmen had bigger problems than him.

✻

"A genuine jesusman," Hat-Trick was saying. "In our own town, no less."

Lanyard spat blood, nudged a loose tooth with his tongue. He'd had worse beatings. He could feel the nearness of the witch, content to watch for now from the safety of its nest.

"Some great work from Teeth, uncovering Mister Lanyard's dark secret," he said, and the woman gave a curtsey with an imaginary dress. Her face was a ruined mess, and it was hard to tell where his blood stopped and hers began.

"Now, the question on all our lips: what are we to do? What do we do with a jesusman?"

"Kill him!" one said. "Chuck him in the pot!"

"Make him a citizen and eat him slow," another said.

"Give him to me, I'll punish him enough," Cobbler said with passion, and the mob cheered. He hobbled over, ramming one of his crutches into Lanyard's stomach and spitting on his face.

"It was your kind what brought us here, you jesusmen!" Hat-Trick said, resting the tip of his cricket bat on the back of Lanyard's head. The weight of the willow pushed the sharp nails into his scalp. "Your dying man led us to the damned dusty Now. Not paradise, here. Our mob, the whole bloody human race having to pick through junk to survive, and it's all your fault."

He'd heard this rhetoric before, even believed it once. There was nothing worth saying, and perhaps in his heart of hearts Lanyard always knew it would end like this. The discovery, his brutal ending in some forgotten place. He was about to die, and mercy was a concept that never left the town-walls.

Hat-Trick hefted the murderous bat, held it high. He made to smash it into Lanyard's face, but pulled the bat up at the last second. Lanyard flinched and the crooked mob fell about laughing.

"You won't die that easy," he said. "You will beg for a bat in the face by the time I'm finished with you."

They bound his wrists with a loop of barb-wire and nailed the other end to a railway sleeper. A stretch of train track had bled through almost intact, like an obscene mouthful of teeth stuck sideways out of the ground and held together with a twisted belt of steel rail. Lanyard could see some of Hat-Trick's mutilated citizens shoring up the gaps, and knew this would be the basis for the town's walls.

They took turns to piss on him, and Teeth gnashed her horrid fangs near his privates. Hat-Trick would not let them harm him overly, and Teeth whined that he was ruining their fun.

"Mind your mouthhole around me," he said, a quick fist knocking her onto her bony arse. "I say he suffers long and hard, like every bloke who followed the jesus out of the Before."

They gave him nothing to eat or drink, and Lanyard baked all day, naked and red raw beneath the burning sun. They left him a rusty saucepan full of piss, all they intended for him to drink. He held out into the chill of night, but even he knew that he'd eventually give in, anything to stave off this crippling thirst.

"I'll have you eating manflesh inside of a week," Hat-Trick said. "This is just the beginning of a most delicious death."

They left Fingerbone to guard him, and the gap-toothed cannibal said nothing throughout the frosty night, just pointed his home-made speargun and dozed beneath a filthy old poncho.

"Will you take my fingers?" Lanyard croaked as the sun rose. "Will you wear them around your neck?"

Fingerbone looked at Lanyard, and nodded for yes.

They set him to working for forage, digging out the old car that Hat-Trick had his heart set on. His muscles ached from the honest rhythm of the work. The heft and swing of pick and mattock drove him on, through pain and thirst and heat.

No water when they called it a night, nothing but the pot of stale piss waiting by his post. Another guard, some crooked man without a proper name, who kicked him in the ribs when no-one was looking. Teeth drank grog with the man by the light of his little fire, her nasty little eyes watching Lanyard the whole time.

He would die of thirst tomorrow, if he survived the night. Lanyard found himself looking at the piss-pot, made himself tip the urine out before he was tempted.

"Not give you lot the satisfaction," he said through a dry tongue and leathery mouth. Somewhere between sleep and death, Lanyard felt a cool stream of water pass his lips, gulped greedily at the waterskin.

"Hat-Trick's got a temper," he heard the guard say. "Don't want the jesusman dying under my watch."

When he finally felt the witch step into the Now, Lanyard was almost grateful.

✳

Drink helped a little, but Lanyard Everett found himself drawn more and more to violence, to risk. Every time he got the shakes, or had one too many dreams about the demons he'd seen in Bauer's service, he'd throw himself into a fight.

He gambled, stole other men's sheilas, exploited the natives, shot his enemies before they could shoot him, and soon he found that the criminal underworld could accommodate a man of his temperament.

But always there were the dreams, and the certain knowledge during his waking hours that bad things were real and quite often nearby. And that he was the only person left who could do anything about it.

＊

"You bring anyone with you?" Hat-Trick asked again. He'd beaten Lanyard black and blue after discovering the shredded remains of one of his mob. There wasn't much left of the man.

"I didn't have to bring anyone," Lanyard said through a fat lip. "You bring trouble, just by being here. Witch trouble."

In dust Lanyard had tried to etch what wards and marks he knew, but when his guard saw that he swept them away, fearful of jesusman magic.

"Witches," Hat-Trick snorted. "More of your jesus lies. We follow the word of Papa Lucy here, cast his bones and do all the custom. We're watched over."

"Papa Lucy," Lanyard laughed. "Your crooked god won't guard you against what's out there."

The cannibals went for vengeance instead of sense, gathered into a great pack to hunt for the killer. They left Lanyard to his exhausted slumber, and he woke up to look into the eyes of the crippled girl.

She'd fashioned herself a crutch out of scrap wood, and limped over to give him more water when the crooked men had left the camp.

"You need to run," she said, picking at the wire twists that bound his hands. They'd bent it with pliers, and she couldn't budge it. She tried till her fingers were pricked and bleeding.

"Please take me with you," she said. "They've done bad things to me, and Hat-Trick said they're gonna eat me a bit at a time until I'm just a torso that they pass around."

The end attached to the post was hand-twisted, and between them they unravelled the wire around the nail. She helped him stand, got him moving.

"Where's my stuff?" he said. She shrugged, didn't know. He needed the shotgun, fast. The witch would feed on stragglers, and then it would come for him. They didn't like groups of people, and now that the crooked men were gone the danger was very real.

They passed the new workshop that had been made for the tinkerman, a lean-to surrounded by piles of Before-Time junk that they wanted him to fix. He was working on some gadget and looked up to see Lanyard moving towards him, murder in his face.

"Help!" Cobbler hollered out, a second before Lanyard whipped him with the loose end of the wire.

"Shut your mouth," Lanyard said and gave him an absolute belting. "Get me out of this, or you'll get another."

With shaking hands, Cobbler fetched a set of tin-snips, sheared through the barbed-wire. Lanyard felt the circulation return to his hands, winced at the deep cuts that the jags had left.

The posse had taken the tinkerman's horse, and there was only a bicycle and a broken motor-bike left in the camp. He would have to leave the girl.

Ignoring her cries, he ransacked the dwellings of the crooked mob. He found a sharp rabbit knife but none of his own stuff, pulled on some filthy clothes that had seen better days.

"Seems our jesusman is resourceful," Hat-Trick said as Lanyard emerged from the hut. The crooked man was on horse-back, pointing his own shot-gun at him. Lanyard's eyes were drawn to the yawning black of the double-O, briefly wondered if he'd see the flash before he died.

Before Hat-Trick could squeeze the triggers the horse reared up and threw him. Lanyard never thought he'd be happy to see the enormous grandfather snake, but as it sank its fangs into the horse he blessed every broken scale on its battered body. Against the odds, this enormous creature had found him, despite being shot at, electrocuted, and battered to within an inch of its life.

Lanyard snatched the shotgun from the limp hands of the crooked man, groaning and winded from his fall. The snake was curled around the twitching horse and hissed at Lanyard, ready to strike but wary of the enormous shooter.

It was only the arrival of the crooked mob, hollering and firing at the serpent which saved him. The snake held its ground, lashing out at any who came near, till it bristled with spears and bullet wounds.

From where he stood Lanyard spotted his old skiff, parked behind Cobbler's workshop. He ran for it, snatching the girl on the way. The cannibals were too busy dealing with the enormous snake to stop him.

He lay her down in the spare seat and stashed the shotgun in back. He was messing around with the rigging and sails when he felt the barrel of a pistol in the back of his head.

"You're taking me, not her," Cobbler said, and at the tinkerman's frantic urging Lanyard lifted the girl out, left her sobbing on the ground. Cobbler threw his crutch into the back and climbed in, ordered Lanyard to move.

The canvas sails rippled in the breeze, and as he pushed the skiff out onto the salt-pan the breeze became a strong driving wind. But not quite quick enough, and even as the little wind-cart darted across the flat salt-crust the snake was in pursuit, only pausing for a moment to snatch the girl into its mouth.

"Snake killed them all," Lanyard realised, which certainly explained what Thomas Cobbler the tinkerman was doing holding some dead man's pistol.

"Move this damn thing!" Cobbler said, looking over his shoulder. "Make it go faster."

With one smooth motion Lanyard heaved Cobbler over the side, and freed of the extra weight the skiff went much faster indeed.

✳

Despite his fractured apprenticeship, Lanyard knew enough to do his job. This world did not need a soft and loving shepherd, did not need a man of letters or even a man who could preach. The old morality was long dead, and the words of the jesus less than the dust he'd given them to live in.

There were creatures out there, supernatural trespassers that needed killing. He could sniff them out, make them regret the moment they trod in his world. It was a purpose, one that lifted him above being a common thug. He'd finally accepted this destiny.

He was always afraid, and often alone. But the last of the jesusmen did not need the approval or help of others. Lanyard would cheerfully kill a man over a bag of coin, but the monsters he began to murder as a community service.

He had become the last jesusman, perfectly suited for this cruel new age.

✳

He had bigger problems than the Inland snake. A witch came for him the next night, openly and without fear. Lanyard had his jesusman's gun primed and had already scratched the marks and wards into the dust when the creature sat down by his campfire, just outside of his protective circle.

"You've nothing to fear from the snake," the pasty-white creature told him, in that strange static that was halfway between voice and thought. "We fed from it, my kin and I. Every last scale, every scrap of its gizzards."

"A shame," Lanyard said. "It was honest enough, in its own way. Wouldn't say the same of your kind."

It shifted forms, like runny candle-wax. The creature had become something like the dead cripple girl, but mature, lush, a vision of the future robbed from her by Hat-Trick's crooked mob. She had both her legs, and writhed by the fire, laughing and moaning seductively. Lanyard shook his head, every nerve urging him to murder the foul creature.

"I've been sent to make you an offer, jesusman," the witch said, shifting into the form of Teeth, her foul head snapping at him from the end of the grandfather serpent's body. "We would have a settlement in the Now, and seek truce with the last of the jesusmen."

"No truce," Lanyard said. "When I have enough kit to do the job, I will return. I'm fixing to murder you, you and your whole bloody mob."

"Fool," the witch snarled. "You will never rest. We will haunt your dreams, hunt you by day and by night."

"Your friends might. But you won't."

Lanyard emptied both barrels into the monster, the report scaring a flock of cockatoos out of a nearby tree and into noisy flight. Even as the witch dragged itself across the ground, whimpering and trying to open a door to somewhere else, he hammered the life out of it with the wooden stock of that holy gun. When it finally lay silent, stinking of rotten meat and stale piss, he heaved the slippery beast into the fire.

Lanyard stacked wood around the body of the witch, and sat up throughout the night to watch it burn. When he slipped into an exhausted slumber, his dreams were still.

✳

ROLLING FOR FETCH

When Whip went skeg, he arranged a meet with a back-alley butcher, a coin-friend whose pockets rattled with illegal meds. When the coast was clear the gear was brought out of hiding. First, it was the stained hack-saw, slow, but much neater than an axe.

The amateur surgeon cauterised the stumps with an old oxy-set while his chums keep lookout for the pol', throwing the feet over his shoulder for the dogs to snap up.

The best surgeons claimed that they could do the chop and fit a skeg with a rig in five minutes or less, but Sad Pepe's personal best was seven minutes even. Anything else was either boasting or butchery.

The main struts of a skeg rig eventually fused with the shin-bone, but the first month or so it was just stainless steel pegs and wires, driving Whip's immune system nuts. He'd been dosed with dirty nano-work, old cancer-killing stock bred into a dubious cure-all. A nostalgic fallacy, given the filth on the street and the clip-clop of horse shoes on asphalt.

The drive train went underneath the muscle itself, something like the innards of an old clock, a mesh of gears and cogs. Then the winder cranks, one in each leg, protruding between the *peroneus longus* and the *tibialis anterior*, reminding the world that anyone mad enough to actually go through with this was not a human now. More a wind-up toy with a death-wish.

Finally, a pair of wheels were connected to the bottom of the rig, hooked up to the drive-train dangling from each bleeding leg. The most popular option was a pneumatic tyre with knobbly grip, one foot in diameter, filled with smart-gel to ward off punctures, magic goop to heal over little nicks and tears.

Good suspension is a must.

When Whip survived this procedure, shook off the inevitable infection, unlearnt the life-long art of walking and earnt his gangdanna, he had the right to call himself a skeg.

*

Whip never stopped rolling. He slept upright like the horses he'd once curried, rolling around in slow circles, motivators clicking as the tension slowly bled from his rig. The constant ache in his legs became a dull absence, and even the lowest gears began to struggle as his muscles and tendons relaxed.

For that moment, Whip was nothing more than a cripple, a tottering freak with several kilograms of metal and rubber protruding from his mutilated legs. Dawn was his least favourite hour.

Whip knelt down, winding the cranks, feeling the first delicious tickle as his muscle fibres stretched. He redoubled his efforts, until every muscle from the hip down burned with tension. Motivators humming, he could feel the potential, and Whip danced on the spot like a Lippizaner in dressage, testing the rig. He was ready to roll.

Five years in from his own chop, and Whip was a world removed from the stable-lad he'd been. His legs were enormous, twin trunks of muscle, and his only concession to decency was a filthy kilt. His hair and beard were a knotty tangle, partially hidden beneath a gangdanna.

An arc of goth-print rose above his navel, the ink rainbow pasted across his abs reading NEVA STOP ROLLIN'.

Whip usually went lookout, keeping an eye on his mob, tonight kipped out in a run down park. The abandoned edges of the old burba were best for skegs, and the pol rarely visited, save to scope for looters.

"Reveille, you dozing dogs!" Whip shouted, scooting through the pack of dozing freaks, clipping his wheels against theirs. Cursing, his mob met the dawn, grumbling and winding their own leg cranks. Some of them hit the go-powder, passing around a paper funnel and drawing in that magic dust through red-ringed nostrils.

"Don't sob so hard for a bed and a pair of shoes, me grumpy chums. You all wanted this life," Whip laughed, rolling down an ancient and rusted slippery-dip.

"Yeah, but I didn't want Lord Whip crowing every dawn," young Rabbit said, and the mob whistled and clapped.

"Alright, you bunch of sooking babs, we're off to the metro," Whip said through a wide grin. "I've got an inkling that there's good fetch at Jona Smif's today."

They rolled through the inner burba, a mob just over a dozen strong, laughing and jostling and darting through the morning traffic, baker's nags and the last of the crap-carters. Whip rolled at the front, legs sweeping and motivators whining, working up through the gears until he was somewhere between a canter and a gallop. When a milkman cursed them for spooking his horse, Whip rolled backwards, pointing to his tattoo and staring at the man, daring him to go for the switch.

The man looked away, swallowing his outrage, and Whip laughed. The rest of his mob whipped past the cart like hornets, fly-wheels whining, and the old nag jerked around in its harness, terrified by the noise and the speed of these butchered men.

The fetch-house of Jona Smif was a squat lean-to, cheap like the man himself. The mismatched fibro shell was connected to the power and best of all, the telling-phone. Smif was the real deal and all the mobs knew it.

"Look there," someone said, and Whip saw another skeg mob, sprawled across the footpath like feral dogs. He didn't know their gangdanna, and didn't care. They'd staked out Smif's joint, and he wanted it.

"Roll on now," Whip told them. "Or grief."

One of them arced up, a wirey little bruiser with a mouth to her. Skeg women were a hard kind, nothing feminine left to them after they swapped their feet for wheels. She launched into a string of foul language, and so it was grief that they chose.

The mobs circled each other, testing and baiting and waiting for one to make the first move. The street cleared of walkin-folk in seconds. This new mob had strength in numbers, but some of them looked new to their rigs, and Whip reckoned on them not being worth squat in a rumble.

They did for them, but not before their mouthpiece pulled some ballerina move, clocking Rabbit in the head with one of her wheels. Such flexibility he might have appreciated under different circumstances, but the skinny kid was left shaking the pain out of his brain-pan as the other mob rolled on.

"Can't even see straight," Rabbit said shakily when he stood, and Whip swore. He was the quickest skeg rolling under his gangdanna, and knew the metro better than any of them. They would have to work double hard to make up for his thumped noggin.

Then the first jobs came in over the telling-phone, and Jona Smif was out on the stoop, handing out chits and haggling over the fetch-fee.

"This one's right urgent," he said, "Plans or summat, got to be before the suits within the hour."

Grimacing, Whip knelt down and took the chit out of Smif's hand. He was the only one who could do the fetch, but he didn't know the area as well as Rabbit, who seemingly had all the shortcuts carved onto the insides of his eyeballs.

He poured on the speed as he rolled to the pick-up, a munici depot. To Whip's eternal shame, he got the address wrong. He rolled around, thumbing through his old road-book and cursing, finally hitting the right depot.

"Quick now," some daft desk-jockey told him as he stuffed the rolled sheaf of paper into his pack. "You're right late."

There'd be hell to pay if he muffed this, and Jona Smif might not pony up with the fetch-fee. Always a first time for everything, but Whip didn't have to like it.

Not paying attention as he read his grid-guide, he moved through the horses, steam-carts and bicycles by instinct but didn't see some poor lady making to cross the street. He knocked her onto her broad backside, sent her groceries flying.

He might have hung around and helped her pick up if he'd the time. As it was, the minutes were falling by and he was right late.

A wave of apology was the best he could give as he kept rolling, but this was seen by a polizei, who turned the klaxon on his coughing steam-bike and gave chase.

"Stop, skeg!" the chubby law-lark yelled through a loudhailer. Whip spared them a glance, and saw the pol in the side-car cranking on a wireless tellingphone.

"Never stop rolling," he said to himself.

Head bent he laid the power on, sweeping his legs and working through the gears until the motivators screamed and whined like they would fall apart.

He pulled away from the pol, and took a cunning left through a cramped street-fair. He flipped the bird and laughed at the pair, who turned their great sputtering machine around and took off with an angry roar.

"Left you damn fools in my spin," he laughed.

But it was far from good. The law was probably staking the main roads, and he'd have to sneak through the curly little alleys and lanes to get to the drop-off.

"Never muffed a fetch, not gonna start to," he panted, rolling on. It was the best time he'd ever made, scraping his arms on brick when he took those tight turns too fast, knocking over bins and such, and he rolled into his drop-off, right on the knocker.

He was panting like a race-horse, covered in scratches and sweat, knowing that the pol would be watching for him all day. He stepped into that office, locking his wheels and clumping awkwardly across the carpet floor, jerking the plans out of his pack. Tossed them onto the counter and made as to leave.

The young lass behind the desk cleared her throat. Whip thought she might be about to tell him off for leaving wheel marks on the carpet, or to accuse him of being late with the drop.

"Come here, skeg," she ordered him, a sneaky little smile on her dial. He was a handsome lad and got his fair share of attention, figured her as another fool girl love-mad for skegs. She was Vietnamese, a pretty girl dressed plain, with a laddish bob-cut and wary eyes.

"You're a fair lass," Whip said, leaning on her counter and giving her the once-over. "But you've no wheels, and I'll only break your heart."

"You forgot your docket," she said, stamping it DELIVERED and sliding it across the counter. "Well, don't let me keep you."

✳

Early next morning, Whip left his mob, went off on his own business. He went to the munici offices, lurked around by the fruit sellers and water-haulers, waiting for the morning rush. The horse-trolleys and bicycles began to arrive from the burba, spilling walkin-folk into the metro for another day of coin chasing.

He saw her, the girl from yesterday. She stepped from the back of a horse-lugged bus, looking a little bit lost in all the chaos. She couldn't spot a street-sweep and made to cross the street anyway, pulling up the hem of her dress, eyeing the growing sea of horse dung with disgust.

Whip saw his chance, and in a flash he cut across the traffic, sweeping the lass into his arms and depositing her safely on the far side of the street. It was all over in a moment and she barely had time to blink.

"Get lost, skeg," she growled, glaring up at him from somewhere near his navel. He stood there on the sidewalk, motivators quietly humming as he watched her walk into the building.

He was out the front of her office the next morning, and swept a path across the street for her, him who'd never lifted a broom in his life. He fixed to deliver all the fetch to that building, and would only do those runs, smiling at her as she drove her DELIVERED stamp into the dockets with great force.

Day after day he bothered that poor girl, and weathered her scorn, noting that she still did not send for the pol. He learnt that her name was Anh. One day, she gave him the dried leftovers of her bánh mì and a hello. Some weeks later they were standing at her front doorstep and she still hadn't told him to nick off.

"Well, goodnight I guess," Anh said with some surprise, and shut the door in his face. But she didn't slam it, and Whip counted this as progress.

"Will you bring me a sandwich tomorrow?" he shouted through the keyhole.

"Maybe," came her muffled reply.

✳

They began a deliciously slow courtship, and it was the same old story, told with different parts. Once it was skin or religion, but the modern scandal was a modified, daring to step out with a "classic" human. The mixed couple of the day, greeted with finger-waggling and disgusted whispers in the salons.

He brought Anh to meet his mob, the most important thing in his life meeting the previous most important thing. Some of the lads were a little bit sore, and while no-one gave her grief, you could see their disgust. The great Whip, brought low by some piece of walkin-folk fluff.

"This is ridiculous," Rabbit whispered to Whip. They were rolling slow through a quiet part of the burba, letting Anh keep up with them. She was in one of those feet-strapping rigs, legs all awobble and many a time upended on her arse. The skeg only laughed the once, until Whip unpacked his fists and got a beating out.

Some folks take to wheels, some never get the knack, but Whip knew she'd never fall in love with her wheels. She'd never get the chop, not even for him.

✳

They were meandering, following the canals. It was a Sunday, and with the barge-masters in church and the usual tangle of horses a-stabled he could get a good run along the banksides, the slow rhythm of the metro streets stilled during God's hour. Anh didn't care much for church and skeg never went, nor were expected to.

Anh clutched to Whip's back as they drifted down the street, her legs wrapped around his waist. She'd given up the feet-rig as a bruise-maker and a bad idea.

"I love you Anh," he blurted out, fooled by the romance of the setting. He couldn't see her face, but felt her arms tighten around him. He instantly regretted saying it, but went on. "I can't hold it in any longer, I love you and I want to be with you."

"Whip," she said. "Whip, you're a good boy. But it won't work. We should end this."

He slowed, let the wheels spin, the gears work down, and then finally he rolled to a stop. He felt her arms relax, and she slid off his back.

"So that's it then," he said, not asking. "We're different, so you just give up. I'm not a thug on wheels, you know that."

"No, Whip. It's not about that," but her voice gave, and they both heard the lie.

"It is. I don't care that you're walkin-folk, that the lads give me a ribbing over you. I don't see feet, I only see you."

"I won't go through with it," Anh said suddenly. "I won't—my feet—"

"I don't want you to get a rig," Whip said. "You don't belong in that world."

"But that's it!" she said. "You don't belong in mine! Do you think I want to show my skeg boyfriend to my neighbours, people from work? I'll probably get fired."

"For seeing a skeg?" he snorted. "Right."

"It happens. They sacked some girl in accounts, she wore his gangdanna as if it didn't matter. She had her hand in the till, supporting his mob."

"Who cares what people think? We can make it work."

"We can't! You—you're not normal," Anh cried.

She ran, and he let her go. He'd run out of words anyway. Whip rolled alone for a long while, just looking at the filthy muck floating along the canal.

He rolled here and there, gave his rig an absolute flogging. It began to sink in that this was a goodbye of sorts. He'd never move this fast again.

Whip was going to need a lot of money.

✳

Next day Whip pulled Rabbit aside, asked if he would go as his second. Death-run, high stakes.

"No Whip, oh no," he said. "Whatever trouble you're in, it can't be that bad. Let your mob help you out, we're your brothers. Don't do this."

"I want you as my second. I'll go alone if I have to."

Loyalty was its own currency in skeg circles, and so they rolled. This death-run was being held in a warehouse, spotters on the roof to watch for polizei. Whip's mob didn't usually hold much truck with this, figuring it was a sport for washed-up skegs in need of fast cash.

All for the rich folk in need of excitement, those willing to pay skegs to strap on blades and have at one another. An underclass of an underclass, these warrior skeg were often seen on the roll, all hacked up with scars and that mad gleam in their eyes.

"She's not worth it," Rabbit said. They were sized up for blades, great sharp cutters strapped to their forearms. They had a handle in the middle, like the hated baton of the pol. Whip and Rabbit were to race around the pallets and barrels and other junk they'd arranged into an obstacle course. Another pair of skeg would come for them, legs pumping and sharp blades swinging.

"We should roll on," Rabbit said. "Who cares what these mongrels think?"

"Well, we're here now," Whip said.

"I'm so scared I'm about to piss my cullottes."

Whip ran his blades against each other, the sharp edges going *snikt!* "Look at yonder skegs. We can take them."

They'd been matched up against a pair of menacing shapes, just beyond the circle of flickering torches. The odds slated onto the bookies" chalk-boards put them at very long odds to even come out alive. Their opponents were sparring against each other, blades flashing and clanging, very quick.

"Please Whip," Rabbit begged. "We don't need to do this. They're gonna kill us."

"I need the money!" Whip snarled.

"Why? You don't need lodgings, and your rig looks fine to me. All you need is food and go-powder, and we can spot you if you're short. This is madness."

"I need an operation," Whip said, and would say no more.

Someone blew a whistle, and they were herded into the makeshift arena, prepped for the death-run. The crowd were right up to the torch-line, howling and waving their betting slips in the air.

"Money's no good if you're dead," Rabbit said.

"Go then, you pink puss. I'll do this without you." Not unknown for a seconder to pass on a death-run, but solo fights were fine. He'd go toe-to-toe with their chief cutter for half the purse.

"She's not worth dying for," Rabbit said, and threw his blades down against the cement floor. The mob booed and laughed and threw their empties at the lone skeg.

"I need you now Whip, brother's got to watch a brother's back," Rabbit yelled, a half-empty bottle nearly hitting him in the head.

After a moment of indecision, Whip closed his eyes with a grimace, pulling off his blades. The pair traded punches and abuse with the crowd the whole way to the door, and barely made it out of that place. A trio of skeg tried to jump them in a back-street over their voided wager, but Whip took a beating to them with a fury Rabbit had never seen.

The next day, Whip vanished.

*

Rabbit had been as far as Anh's front door once, and knew the way. She answered the door when he knocked, had it sitting on its chain.

"Oh. What do you want?" she asked. Her face was lined with worry, eyes reddened from crying.

"I'm worried about Whip. Have you seen my brother?" A moment's pause, a heavy sigh. She unchained the door.

"Come in," she said. He locked his wheels, moving clumsily over her wooden floorboards, trying not to knock the knick-knacks and ornaments over.

"Through here," she said, ushering him into her living room. He could see Whip sitting down in an arm-chair, facing the window. The curtains were parted and he must have been looking out at the stars or the moon or something. A kerosene lamp flickered on the sideboard, giving a weak light to the room.

Rabbit clambered awkwardly across the tatty old rug, and when he saw Whip he gasped. His rig was gone. Completely gone. They'd pulled the boxes and gadgets and gears out of him, separated the steel struts from his shin-bones. Where his legs had ended in stumps were a pair of feet, pale and held on with thick black stitches. His new feet were marble white, except for the ends of his toes, which were a worrisome dark colour.

"The doctors grew these in a tube, took a bit of my hip bone. First time it's ever been done," Whip said, looking at Rabbit from the chair where he rested. Anh fetched him a thin blanket, which she put across his lap to hold off the winter chill. He looked weak, worn out. Rabbit stood there, towering over him in his rig, and Whip seemed less than a man, something broken and wasted.

"Why did you do it?" Rabbit whispered.

"We disgust them," Whip said. "We fetch and scurry for those walkin-folk, and they admire us but there's envy too. How a skeg can roll so very quick, while they must toddle down the road on their feet."

He waggled the pale flesh, as if making some sort of point. The lamp ticked and hissed, and Whip was quiet, contemplating the lumps of meat tacked onto his legs.

"Did it work? Can you wriggle your toes?" Rabbit asked, and Whip bit his lip. Finally he shook his head no.

"Spend all of my coin on the feet, but didn't have enough to pay the bills. The doc did a rush job. Reckons they're gangrenous now." He sounded calm but something in his face spoke of panic and worry.

Rabbit offered to pony up enough coin to get him back into a rig, knowing that he'd decline the offer. He wasn't skeg now, could not accept charity from those he'd cut out of his life.

"Well, goodbye then," Rabbit said, and the last he saw of Whip was a broken figure hunched in a chair, keeping a silent vigil as his feet slowly killed him.

*

Some years later, Rabbit caught a bus, quietly nodding off, lulled by the hum of the hydrogen engine warbling underneath him. It still took some time to traverse the old metro, but it was market day, the streets choked with nags hauling ancient carts. Mostly a show for the tourists nowadays.

A courier sped past on a sleek little scooter, its exhaust puffing water vapour, and climbed up onto the footpath when the horses proved too slow.

He did not see any skeg rolling today.

"Nostalgia is a thing of the past," he told the nun seated opposite, who did not even look up from her romance novel. Snorting, he waved his hand above, fumbling for the stop-cord, and reaching for his cane he stood.

Rabbit left the lonely bus-stop and walked into the cemetery, limping and leaning heavily on the stick, but walking. The stone he was looking for was modest, with a tiny plaque. With some difficulty he knelt before Whip's resting place, his new feet throbbing.

"Roll on, my brother," he said, and finally laid his gangdanna down.

BUSKING

I didn't see it, the moment that it all happened. I was in the zone, with five balls in the air and I'd just added the sixth. I was looking up, trying to maintain the rhythm of my juggling, and I remember seeing a pigeon flying overhead, and then suddenly the bird wasn't there.

"That's odd," I said, and found myself alone. Randall Strip was deadly still, and all the people had gone. Just gone.

Nothing left of the world but piles of clothing, knickers and hats and boots and socks. Randall Strip looked like the floor of Tegan's bedroom. Everywhere there were little mounds of leftovers, where moments earlier the mall had been thick with people, shopping, living and laughing.

I dropped that sixth ball then, nearly dropped the other five. I wanted to get off my unicycle and run like hell, get to a phone and make sure that my kids were okay.

I got a real bad feeling just then, like someone was squeezing my heart in a fist. There was a sharp tang in my nose, something strong. Iron. Rust. The stink of something dead and rotten. My head throbbed, my joints ached.

Everything seemed to be—well, less there. I was viewing the world through three pairs of stockings, and the light was getting dimmer.

So I went out the way I wanted to. I kept juggling. I'd only dropped that first ball, and even though I got the wobbles I stayed upright on the unicycle, five coloured spheres twirling through the air.

The bad feeling went away. I didn't die. I figured it was a very good idea to keep doing my act.

*

I wasn't the only one left. By the front of Toy-Castle I could see Creepy Bob, and further along was Graham, playing in his usual spot by the fountain.

"Don't stop!" I called out, my voice echoing against the glass of the shopfronts. I don't mind telling you, it was eerie. There was hardly any noise at all, just the faint strains of Graham's guitar, when normally you couldn't hear yourself think during the lunch rush. A gust of wind picked up someone's hat, one of those ridiculous pork-pie ones that were back in fashion. It rolled and bounced and came up against a walking frame with a pair of pantyhose caught on it.

"What's going on? WHAT THE HELL IS GOING ON?" Creepy Bob yelled, his gruff bluster betrayed with a touch of squeaky hysteria. Even as I slowly pedalled towards him, balls arcing from hand to hand, Bob was finishing a balloon animal. Good, he'd figured it out too.

"I don't know, Bob," I said, wheeling back and forth as I kept my balance. All I wanted to do was get off the damn unicycle, but I didn't know if I could do a dismount without losing my balance and fouling up my juggle. I'd never been able to manage it before, and if I dropped those balls I was dead.

I was close enough to read his T-shirt now, bright green with BALOON BOB! printed across it in fluoro yellow letters. The printer had misspelled it, and heaven help you if you mentioned this.

"Did you feel it, Anna? When you tried to stop?" he said, hands shaking as he set the balloon sculpture on the ground. It was a giraffe, and the breeze pushed it down the mall, bouncing and turning and drifting. He didn't pause, pulling another balloon from his pocket and blowing into it.

"I think we're safe. We just gotta keep doing our thing," I said. I risked snatching two balls out of the air and putting them in my pocket, while I kept the remaining three going in one hand.

I had a brief moment of dizziness, but whatever had done this was impressed with the one-handed juggle. I faked a brief yawn as I did during my act, and the horrible feeling went away completely.

I knew then that something was messing with us. Something intelligent and malevolent, and it was linked to several hundred people disappearing in a split second.

"Follow me," I told Creepy Bob. He was Creepy Bob due to an unsubstantiated busker rumour. Word on the street painted Bob as a convicted paedophile, or a suspected paedophile, or abused by a paedophile or something. Whatever the truth, Bob was not right in the head. He nearly lost his busking licence one day, when he snapped at a little girl and made her cry.

"Take the fucking balloon! You ungrateful little shit!" I'd heard him yell at the kid, and we didn't see him for a month after that. No-one knows where he went, and no-one knows why the city allowed him back after *that* outburst.

I wouldn't let him near my kids; but even so, us buskers gotta stick together, especially in a time of freaky weirdness. I was willing to overlook Bob's personality issues in the face of this spectacular clusterfuck.

We went to Graham's spot, by the fountain. I kept flipping balls back and forth, and Bob was working on a balloon bicycle. Graham was ghost-white and I could see his knees shaking from here. He had an electric guitar plugged into a little amp, and continued to pluck away at the easy-listening rhythms that got him tons of change. "CDs for $10" the card read, taped to the inside of his guitar case.

There was a ring of empty clothes around him, and one set of clothes halfway between the edge of the invisible circle and Graham. A coin lay just beyond the outstretched sleeve of a child's jacket.

"Anna, what's going on?" Graham asked, voice choked with fear. A tear slid down past his too-cool stubble. "What happened to everyone?"

All I could do was shrug and juggle.

*

Graham was a lovable guy. Not enough that I wanted to arch my legs around him and risk another kid, but enough that he could warm my heart and make me smile. He always knew what to say, even when someone not only broke my heart but also a rib or two. I hated to hit him up for loans but I knew he would gladly give what little he had. Graham was a soft touch, and that's why he was playing folk music in Randall Strip and not doing something better with that talent of his.

On this the worst day of my life, I asked Graham if I could borrow his phone. He shook his head.

"I'm sorry, love. I lent my phone to Keller."

Keller was his drug dealer. He wasn't getting his phone back.

"Goddamnit, Graham, I need to call my kids!" I said. Another moment of dizziness and the stench of imminent death, and I quickly balanced the fourth ball on my nose while flourishing the other three balls in a high looping cast. I need to bring my other hand in to do this, and one quick movement later I had a four-ball cascade going.

"What about you, Bob?" I ask. "Have you got a phone?"

Bob's fat face was red, and he was starting to run out of puff. A menagerie of rubber animals was floating down the strip, bumping into each other as the breeze took them away.

"Piss off," he said. "I don't have any credit left."

"C'mon darling, don't be like that," I said, wanting to vomit on the inside. "I'll pay you back, honest to God. It's important."

The world had ended and he was worried about his phone credit. Creepy Bob wasn't exactly a "big picture" kind of guy. I gave him my most winning smile, even as my rubber spheres soared into the heavens. He looked at my tits again and I wanted to brain him with my unicycle, but I needed that phone and grinned like an idiot.

"Okay," he said, and with half a balloon dog clenched in his left fist he drove his right hand into his pocket, fishing around for a long moment.

"No," he moaned, and staggered like the mean drunk that he probably was. For a long moment, Creepy Bob looked less there. I saw Tegan do something like this with a photo on the computer once, sliding the contrast bar between all black and pure white. Somewhere in the middle was the correct picture. Even as Bob began to fade, he produced a battered Nokia.

"What's ... the number?" Bob asked, and I was horrified. I didn't want him speaking to Tegan or Jay, but worse, he was almost transparent. The stupid fat fool needed to tie some more balloons before he vanished.

"Quick, the phone!" I said. "Throw it to me!"

He was on one knee and clutching his chest by then, so the throw went a little wide. It was all I could do to pedal madly one way, and as I leaned out for the phone I lost my balance. I fell off the bike seat and came down hard on one knee. As the dizziness claimed me I bounced to my feet, my hands moving in that beautiful place beyond conscious thought, beyond worrying about bills and people-snatchers and Parent-Teacher Nights.

Even as the unicycle bounced and crashed into Graham's guitar case, sending change everywhere, the death-veil lifted. I had Bob's phone. I had it tumbling and arcing through the air as part of my juggling act and I hadn't dropped a single ball. Even I had to admit that was a pretty neat trick.

*

Going back to a one-handed cast (three balls) I punched my home number into Creepy Bob's phone. There was full signal and two-thirds of the battery life left.

"Come on!" I said as the phone rang, fearing the worst, imagining a twin set of hand-me-downs scattered across an empty living room. "You'd better be home."

Tegan was fourteen going on thirty, and was sneaking out more than ever. She'd only left Jay alone the once, though, and caught blue murder for that.

The phone went to the machine and I waited impatiently for the beep: "This is Anna—Tegan—And Jay! You know what to do!"

"TEGAN, SO HELP ME GOD YOU'D BETTER BLOODY PICK UP THIS PHONE!" I screamed down the line. "I ought to tan your bloody hide! You're meant to be home!"

It was easier to think of her running around with her no-good mob of mates, somehow alive despite all this. I prayed that she was just up to no good. And then I thought of Jay.

"Jay, sweetheart, Jay, pick up the phone," I begged, tears sliding out of my face and blurring the balls, the life-saving smudges going up-down-up-down.

The answering machine cut out. No-one answered.

"Are they okay?" Graham asked, and I pressed my lips tight, bit down on the hysterical screams that wanted to rise out from my gut.

I tried for the cops, and when the number rang out I knew it was a waste of time. In my mind's eye I could see the station, peaked hats and gun belts tangled around office chairs. I jammed Bob's phone into my pocket.

"Hey! Give that back!" Bob panted. He popped the balloon in his hands and fumbled for another one. He gave me a death-glare over the green rubber sausage as it grew out of his mouth.

"My kids might phone me back," I said. "Tegan's smart enough to punch in that reverse-last-number-thingy."

"Your little slut's dead, like all of these other bastards," Bob said, wrestling with an inflatable alligator. He set it free. "Give me back my fucking phone."

Graham started playing *Smoke on the Water* and a moment later cried out with pain. He reverted back to the mindless drivel that people paid to hear.

"Guess it doesn't like Deep Purple," he said. I'd pulled Bob's phone out of my pocket, more worried about Graham, when the fat weirdo snatched it out of my hand.

"You'll keep, Bob," I said. "How dare you say that about my little girl? You're a sick piece of work."

I knew Bob was right, but prayed that he was wrong. I was terrified for my kids, and there was absolutely *nothing* I could do.

We performed in sullen silence, the three unhappiest buskers ever, the only good news being that I was back on my feet and not having to work my leg muscles staying balanced on a unicycle.

Even so, I was getting dead tired. Going by the Hainsbury's clock, I'd been juggling for nearly three hours straight. Creepy Bob was looking like a heart attack on legs, each puff taking longer than the last. He made three giraffes in a row, until a burst of sudden pain from our invisible tormentor forced him to change it up a little.

I began to worry about Graham's hands. He claimed once that he'd developed arthritis in them, one of the reasons he puffed and injected and snorted whatever he could lay his hands on. If his hands became crippled claws, unable to pluck at the strings . . .

If dear sweet dependable Graham vanished, I wouldn't be able to go on. I tried to think of other things. I thought about the average day in Randall Strip. It was renowned for buskers and street theatre. I found it hard to believe that only three of us had survived. On a good day there were twenty or more acts going, all along the strip.

I shared this thought with the guys.

"We should try and find some of the others," Graham said. "We might find a way out of this."

"Do whatever you want," Bob said. "I don't give a rat's fat arse."

Graham couldn't go with me, being plugged into his amp, and Bob was just a fat, lazy shit. I began to head up the mall, alone. I felt a little bit sad when I passed Edith's newspaper cart and saw her crumpled dress (okay, she was a troglodyte with no teeth but she had a heart of gold) so I kept my mind off this by doing some backcrosses and a few body throws to change it up a little.

Little balls looping, up, down, through my legs, behind my back and up again. I had never, ever, juggled so well. When your life is on the line I guess that's motivation enough.

I kept moving up the strip, and when I saw Eric I got more than a little excited. He was by the flower cart today, leaning on the wall but definitely alive—and there.

Eric was a sword-swallower. He'd been on TV once or twice, and was very good at what he did. Let me set the record straight: those guys do *not* use collapsible blades. Not the proper sword-swallowers anyways. It's all about keeping the body in a perfectly straight line—the mouth, the throat, the oesophagus and stomach. You have to suppress your gag reflex. Gently insert the object, and don't move. This is the whole secret, more or less.

Eric had three swords in his gullet, and was sliding in a fourth. Something was terribly wrong here. Instead of his usual flourish, he was sliding the blade down in fits and starts. He made a choking, gagging sound.

Then I realised. He'd been doing this for three hours straight. Without a break. I don't know how much sword-swallowing the body can take, but he must have been dying for a glass of water and a rest.

"Eric!" I called out, and when he saw me he blinked, shocked. He began to pull the fourth sword out, gestured for me to come closer.

"Eric, you can't stop," I said. "You'll go like all the others." I was looking around for a bottle of water or juice. I could free up one hand and give the poor bloke a drink at least.

He had the sword all the way out of his mouth, and I screamed. The blade was running with blood and spit bubbles and chunks of something were stuck to the point.

"Oh God, Eric, get them out of you," I said. "I know you can juggle a bit, you can do a two-man juggle with me. Please, Eric!"

He coughed again, a wet muffled sound. He had tears running out of his eyes, and his face was going from white to grey.

Then I realised. He'd stopped performing, and humanity's killer had no use for him. He was going to vanish right in front of me and there was nothing I could do.

"Quick, Eric!" I was frantic; his skin looked like tracing paper, his veins little clear tubes with the dark of bone clearly visible behind them. I had a five-ball one-hand juggle going, trying not to hurt him as I pulled at a sword with my free hand.

I wasn't quick enough. He vanished, and the swords dropped, ringing out as they struck the pavement, bouncing and clanging and getting tangled up in his dirty pants, which were full of shit and blood.

✳

I had to find the others, if any were left. I'd seen the look in Eric's eyes as they turned to water and air and then nothing at all.

I didn't know why the buskers were spared from this mass vanishing. I had a lot on my mind and juggling tends to keep you in the now.

"Anna! Anna!" I heard someone say, and couldn't believe my eyes. It was Lewis, the three-card Monte guy. He had his little card table set up out the front of Mega-Books, hands flicking left and right as the cards moved quicker than most eyes could follow.

The city wouldn't let him operate this heist the traditional way. Lewis was permitted to make tips from amused tourists, but he was forbidden from hustling people the way his granddaddy had.

"Keep your eyes on the cards, my friends. I run a good honest game; the card is on the table but you gotta keep your eyes open!"

he said. I could see that he was getting a little tired, but he was flicking the cards back and forth like nobody's business. I guess he had the least strenuous show out of all of us.

I stood close to one side, flipping away in a double crossover. There is no way that Lewis would have let me juggle so close to him if it wasn't such a weird day. Very territorial, that man.

"Are you okay?" I asked, hoping not to throw off his banter. But whatever was doing this seemed more interested in his card skills, and he continued to flick the cards around as he turned to me.

"Sugar, I am on fire," and he grinned, and I felt it too. There wasn't much else to say about our situation. Sure I was scared, but I was pulling out tricks I hadn't tried in years. The average punter didn't push you this far, didn't demand the very best you had. It was only your next meal on the line, not your very life like it was today.

"Anna, check this out," Lewis said, and stopped shuffling. He looked straight ahead, to the empty spot in front of his table.

"Pick your card, friend!" and damned if one of the cards didn't push itself forwards slightly. *Something was really there.* Lewis flipped the card over to reveal a six of spades.

"Sorry, friend. Like another shot at the title?" and without pausing he got back into it, shuffling and singing and bantering away.

"Damn hoo-doo been playing my game for three hours straight," Lewis said. "Most folks get bored by then, wander off and get a balloon for their kids from Creepy Bob."

"It's like a child," I said. "No-one else has the attention span to watch a busker for hours on end. You're right, Lewis, the punters always move on."

I told Lewis about the other two by the fountain, and about Eric. He pretended to be sad, but I could see that a primal part of Lewis was satisfied. He'd wanted that pitch by the flower cart for years, and now here at the end of things he'd gotten this most useless of wishes granted.

"I can't leave my spot, Anna, but I suppose you can bring the others here."

"Don't stop," I warned him, and he nodded. I didn't think he would, but I didn't want another death on my conscience.

✳

There were no others left. I walked from one end of the strip to the other, my forearm muscles starting to burn up from the constant motion of the juggle.

Creepy Bob, Graham, myself and Lewis. That was it. The whole rest of the human race might well be dead or gone or even invisible. We just didn't know, couldn't stop to find out.

"I can't move, Anna," Graham said when I suggested we go to Lewis. His guitar was electric, and he couldn't carry the amp and play. He sometimes brought his battered old acoustic, the one covered in Dead Kennedys stickers, but he'd sprung this setup from the pawnshop and missed it so bad he had to busk with it. Today of all days.

Being a single mum might have made me superwoman, but even I couldn't heft that thing with my free hand and continue to juggle. My whole centre of gravity would be out, and the balls would drop to the ground a second before I did.

"What's the point of all this?" Creepy Bob said. He looked very, very ill, and his face changed to a dark purple colour every time he huffed into a balloon.

"We've just got to worry about surviving," I said. "If we can keep going, we'll live."

"It's like Space Invaders," Bob said, and I was mystified. He was all out of puff and couldn't explain this remark.

"Do you think it's *aliens* doing this?" I asked.

"I think I understand what he means," Graham said after a long moment. "Bob means that you can't win at Space Invaders."

"You can hold out for ages," Bob said, rubber squeaking as he twisted a balloon into the shape of a dog. "You can hold the aliens off for hours and hours. But eventually you'll stuff up, and then you die. Game over."

No-one spoke. I'd broken out into a sweat and my arms were twin pivots of hurt. Bob sounded like a racehorse on its last legs, and Graham was starting to screw up his tune every now and then. He always managed to recover, but with every minute he looked more frantic, trapped.

We hadn't acknowledged it till then—and damn Bob for being right. It really was only a matter of time. How long could we keep this up for? I could feel a pressure growing in my bladder, and knew that I would need the toilet soon. I was thirsty and tired, and soon I'd need something to eat.

Eventually we'd need to sleep.

"He's right," Graham sobbed. He was crying, head forward and his fingers moving slower and slower on the strings. It was about two hours later on the big Hainsbury's clock. "Everyone Saves!" it read. I was somewhere beyond time and sense, and the sun had moved a long way across the sky.

"Just give up, you useless junkie," Bob laughed. "Do us all a favour and stop playing."

"What's wrong with you?" I yelled at Bob. "Are you trying to get someone killed?"

"My hands really hurt," Graham moaned. He was playing like a complete amateur, his timing was all out and he kept missing notes. I could see the wet slick of blood on the strings.

"The way I see it, we're all dead here," Bob said. His lips were cracked and dry, and he licked them with his white slimy tongue. "I don't know if it's the Rapture or some sort of crazy nerve-gas shit. But if the single pleasure left to me is to watch both of you fuck up and die, then I'll take it."

"You're sick, Creepy Bob," I said, and he flinched.

"No-one calls me that, Anna. No-one." He took a step towards me but I backed away, never missing a beat as I juggled a four-ball half-shower, switching the fourth ball from left to right hand over the classic three-ball cascade. I didn't even *know* I could do that.

"I see what you're trying to do," Bob raved. He wore a nasty smile, as if he'd uncovered my greatest secret. "You're trying to wear me out. Well, you won't win. You'll never beat me."

"You're on your own, dickhead," I told him. "I'd rather hang out with Lewis than spend another minute in your company."

"Fine, go," Bob said. "I'll just keep motivating young Graham here."

So I stayed, as he knew I would.

✳

"I'm running out of balloons," Creepy Bob said. He fetched another balloon out of his pocket, added it to the balloon top-hat that he was making. He sat it on his head.

"Good," I told him. "The sooner you're extinct, the happier I will be."

I could see a spreading wet patch on Creepy Bob's trousers and realised that he'd just pissed himself. The way my bladder was swooshing, I wasn't far behind him. Heaven help the first person who needed to take a dump.

I'd taken to bounce-juggling, just to reverse the motion of my poor tired arms. It was all about dropping the rubber balls, hitting the ground in a pattern and catching the bounce.

Graham's music was sounding atrocious, and he tensed up, seized with a sudden burst of pain. The monstrous force was making another attempt on his life. He responded with a quick burst of Greensleeves and his silent killer retreated.

"Go on, just give up!" Bob said. There was an off-white froth running from the corners of his mouth, and he was popping more balloons than he was inflating.

Graham's music was sounding tinny, and I realised that his little PA was running out of power. It had been sitting in a pawnshop for weeks, and I'd seen Graham load the thing with mismatched and half-used batteries sometime before that.

It died a moment later, and his mute pluckings meant nothing. He couldn't be heard over the bubbling of the fountain.

"Graham, no," I said. He was a junkie, a lost soul. He always followed the path of least resistance, always away from pain. I'd known him long enough to see him quit at just about everything.

He switched off the PA, pulled his guitar over his shoulder and set it down gently. He sat on the lip of the fountain just behind him.

"I'm sorry, Anna," he said, and fell back into the water. A moment later his clothes were drifting in the bubbles, empty of that beautiful, foolish man.

"It's just you now," Bob said. "Just you left."

I didn't waste words on him. By some miracle Bob was still alive, still breathing. He'd sat down on the flagstones, dizzy from blowing up balloons, but he kept at it. The only thing driving him was the hope that he would see me die.

"Adios, dickhead," I said. "I'm off to check on Lewis. Don't wait up." I made good on this threat, and started slowly walking up the strip, the three balls shooting between my legs with every step. I refused to play Creepy Bob's evil mind games today.

It didn't feel like there'd ever been a time when I wasn't juggling. I was convinced that I'd popped out of my long-suffering mother with three rubber balls in my fat little fists and they'd been moving in my hands since day one.

"You can't do this, Anna," Bob said. "Don't you walk away from me!"

I heard him get up, heard his drunken dead-man shuffle. He was coming for me, the rubber balloon squeaking in his hands as he twisted it. I knew he'd try to bump me, try to throw me off my rhythm. I moved a little faster, hoping that I wouldn't miss a beat.

He was panting, shuffling. He could not run quick enough, and I relaxed. I heard him hit the ground like a sack of shit, heard some balloons pop, and I knew that Creepy Bob would not be getting up. I didn't spare him a glance, and somehow it seemed fitting that he should die alone and unremarked, as I had always suspected he would.

When I saw one of Lewis's cards blowing down the strip, I knew I was the last one left. From here I could see the overturned card-table and realised that even the killer of humanity could get bored with three-card Monte.

*

I was juggling alone in the middle of Randall Strip, surrounded by a sea of designer clothes and hidden little treasures. I spotted a fake hip joint and what I guessed might have been a pacemaker, though what would I know? I'm a juggler, not a doctor.

"I'm gonna die," I said to myself. "I'm really about to die." It still didn't seem real though. I could just drop the balls, sit cross-legged on the ground and wait for it to come. From everything I'd seen today, I was really just delaying the inevitable.

But I couldn't stop. That was basically suicide, and I was made of stronger stuff. I would never, *ever* give up. Even though my children were most likely gone. Even though everything really hurt, and I was alone and terrified.

I'd wet myself some time back, beyond dignity and with no need for privacy. I wanted to get on my hands and knees and lap at the little pool of piss, draw in some moisture to my parched mouth, but I made myself walk away before the temptation grew too strong.

It was a gift from my kids that brought me to the truth. I've always been good at those Magic Eye pictures, and Tegan and Jay bought me a book of them for the Mother's Day just gone. You know the ones, where you kind of unfocus your eyes, look through the picture, and then you can see a dolphin or a sailing ship or whatever.

It was then, even as I flicked the balls higher and higher, combining a bounce routine with a high-cast, that I saw them. Only in my peripheral vision, and only when I did the Magic Eye thing. The first time was almost by accident; I was tired beyond all reason and staring into space as my arms, distant fulcrums swinging in some other galaxy, flicked the balls back and forth.

Nothing but shapes, they were. They were clear and small, like a fuzzy jelly about the size of a child. And they were everywhere, climbing on everything; and all around me, capering and waving what might have been limbs.

I'll be honest, this spooked the living shit out of me. Where I had been numb to exhaustion a second before, the adrenaline kicked in with a vicious efficiency that left coffee for dead.

I dropped another ball just then, and I could see one of them reaching for me. A fuzzy stub of a limb brought a flash of pain and the sense that my brain was shutting down, even as my body vacated the premises.

It only brushed against me for a moment, but the important thing was that I saw it happen this time. These little fuckers were critiquing my act, in a very personal manner. I didn't know if they were ghosts or aliens or whatever. At this point, a label really didn't matter.

If this was Space Invaders, the aliens were about to touch the earth. I couldn't keep this up for much longer. I would stuff up my rhythm, drop ball after ball until these little freaks got bored with me. And then I'd be toast.

Juggling is my first love, but it's not to say I haven't dabbled in other performing arts. I had a bag of goodies in the spot I'd staked out earlier this morning. I led a large group of the creatures back to my pitch, hurling what now felt like massive fiery planets from hand to hand. When I'd set up here it had been in a whole different universe, one where people didn't vanish and where I'd be home cooking tea by now.

They'd killed my kids.

One long, tired blink, arms on automatic, and I was standing over my gym bag. It was packed full of anything I might need, depending on the competition and the mood of the crowd. I had rings, clubs, a couple of knives (though I'd cut myself badly once and didn't think I'd ever be able to juggle blades again) and something that might just even the odds for me.

"Thank you for your patronage!" I called out, and snatched the remaining balls out of the air. I bowed. "If you'll bear with me, I have an even greater trick to perform for you! Please, a moment to prepare myself!"

They knew about banter, from listening to Lewis do his card tricks. I held my breath, waiting for the painful shocks, but they did not come. I looked up and unhinged my eyes by staring through a nearby lamppost, and sure enough they were waiting, watching me.

I dug through and found my firesticks, and poured some lighter fluid over the wicking on the ends. Flipping the top of my Zippo, I held the flame to the wicking and with a bright hot flash the sticks were live.

That got their attention. I could see them moving around, agitated and very active. They weren't happy about this latest development.

I began to twirl the sticks, great figures of eight, behind me and around me. I moved in swooping circles, driving the critters back. Every now and then one of them tried to touch me, but they couldn't get close.

They were hesitant, unsure of what to do. Whatever these things were, they were scared of fire. And I had plenty of it.

Returning to my gym bag, I dropped one of the sticks onto a pile of nearby clothes, letting it burn good. The flames began to spread, keeping me safe for a moment. I pulled out the bottle of isoparaffin oil and drew in a mouthful of the stinging liquid.

It's also known as white oil, and it's the fire-breather's best friend. They came for me as I was kneeling, but before they could touch me I breathed out, letting a fine mist of the oil pass through my burning fire-stick.

I will never, ever forget the sound of their screams. They burned like paper, quick and clean.

*

I'm burning everything.

They're terrified of fire and stay away from anything that has the stink of ash. Everywhere I travel, I'm torching houses, setting forests aflame, razing bookstores to the ground.

I don't know where they came from, or even what they are. All I know is that they took my babies away from me, and they must pay.

As far as I know I am the last woman alive, the last human. All that I've got left is the desire to roam the world till I grow old, doing everything in my power to kill these little fucks. I'm laying down some serious arse-kicking vengeance, just like Sigourney Weaver in *Aliens*.

God, how Tegan loved that movie. I miss my babies so much that it hurts.

Every night I sleep next to a strong fire, with a spray can in one hand and the Zippo in the other. I have my Magic Eye book for eye exercises, and one photo album for the memories I'm trying to keep. This notepad too, till the day the memories hurt too much when I might just decide to start a fire with it.

I might be the last person on Earth, but I've got them on the back foot. This will be my final and greatest performance.

WHEN THE CHEERFUL MISOGYNIST CAME TO TRUE TOWN

The rocking of the tram lulled Imogen into a light doze, the bloated sun baking her through the scratched glass of the windows. She'd spent the morning at the beach, hoping to shake the heat of the day, and her hair was reduced to a salty tangle, her swim-suit already dry.

The cracked bench seat drank her sweat, and her skin peeled off the vinyl as the tram rounded a long curve. She stirred, and found herself leaning up against a stranger, all white teeth and brown face.

He nodded down at her politely, and went back to reading a battered old thesaurus, flicking the pages with nicotine stained fingers.

This place is full of benevolent idiots, Imogen thought. *Just once, I'd like an adult conversation.*

Anything but this.

Always they watched her with that same guileless smile, with blank eyes framed in a serene expression, sometimes a confused one. These empty-heads somehow kept True-Town working, doing rote tasks, masquerading as complete human beings.

She thought about Raoul, and gnawed at her fingernails. The last time she'd seen him, the minotaur was kneeling over her bed, stroking her hair gently.

"I'll be away a short time," he'd said, and when she stirred from sleep he was already gone. That had been weeks ago. Raoul had never gone more than a day or two without contacting her. Until now.

The minotaur didn't believe in phones, and she'd tried all the numerous ways of contacting him. Yelling into the empty goldfish bowl, writing on the battered note-pad by her bedside, even flushing these notes down the toilet.

Her last message to the minotaur had been less than kind, and even as the scrap of paper burnt in the ashtray she'd regretted writing it.

This idyll in True-Town was driving her loopy.

I will hide you in a place of logic and currency, Raoul had promised her. He'd omitted certain truths, but that was his way. So eager were True-Towners to gobble up any scrap of knowledge, Imogen had lived quite comfortably for the past six months in this faux Algiers.

Grocers would trade food for random factoids, and she often ate at the finest restaurants on the waterfront, literally singing for her supper. Beatles songs always went down well.

A sound penetrated her thoughts, a slow rumble that she didn't notice at first. It grew until the tram shook around her. Something blocked out the sun, and Imogen felt a shiver. She sat up, pressing her nose against the window, and her heart sank. Looming above the white city-scape was an enormous ship. A living, breathing monstrosity, a city on rollers and wheels, driven by a cacophony of sails, engines and zeppelins.

The Cheerful Misogynist had found her.

Imogen yanked on the emergency brake and braced herself as the tram shuddered itself to a squealing stillness. Even as the other passengers were cheerfully picking themselves up and rubbing away bruises, she was out and running through the bazaars and sun-baked plazas.

"Quick, go," she said to a moon-faced young man, piling into the back of his rickshaw. She gave him her address, and for payment she sang several verses of "If You're Happy and You Know It Clap Your Hands."

His face split into a broad grin, and the rickshaw driver twisted the throttle, launching the rickshaw into traffic. Settling against a stack of thin pillows, Imogen worried at her nails, wondered what she was going to do.

The arrival of the enormous party-ship meant a world of trouble. Raoul had crossed *The Cheerful Misogynist*, going back on a deal he'd found less than favourable. Now the ship was hunting the minotaur, and anyone dear to him.

✻

Imogen ran up the stairs and drew short. The front door to her apartment was half open, the frame splintered where the lock had been forced.

They've found us, she realised, heart pounding.

There was no crime to speak of in True-Town, and thus they had no use for law enforcement. The laws were gladly followed by even the most simple of residents. Imogen was on her own.

She rummaged around in her satchel, looking for something to use as a weapon. There was a hairbrush, receipts, sunblock, even a small backgammon set. Digging through the junk, she found a collapsible police baton. Closing her fingers around its rubber grip, Imogen flicked the baton to full extension.

Advancing in the guard position as Raoul had shown her, Imogen nudged open the door with her leading foot. She frowned. Sitting at her little kitchen table was Aurora Luca, the deposed and now reinstated captain of *The Cheerful Misogynist*.

He wore the peaked captain's hat, on top of an open Hawaiian shirt and khakis. He still bore the scars of Raoul's rage, deep gouges in his chest and stomach. A small loop of intestine was visible.

"Imogen Mithras," Luca said, his broken face curving into an awful smile. "You've given us quite the run-around, girlie."

He had laid out her favourite tea set, with two cups. Steam drifted out of the kettle, and he poured.

"I'm still unsure of the local custom. I'm told the Algerians favoured mint tea for breakfast, and coffee for evenings. I've decided on tea."

"Fuck you, Luca. Get the hell out of my house." Imogen slid forward, baton shaking slightly. She stepped across the threshold, across the mosaic Raoul had brought in from Pompeii, from the old One-Way-World. CAVE CANEM, it read in faded letters, the coloured tesserae depicting a long dead guard dog.

Bad dog, she thought.

"Put down that ridiculous night-stick," Luca said, sipping his tea with relish. He set the cup down, sloshing tea into the saucer. "We've matters that need settling with your guardian."

Luca put two items on the table. The first item was a large horn, curved and yellow. The point was incredibly sharp, and difficult to look at. It was one of Raoul's horns, the one they'd tricked him out of.

The minotaur had been halved in more ways than he cared to admit.

Next to this, Luca put a thick sheaf of papers, bound in red legal tape.

"Raoul still owes us his other horn," Luca said, "and we've been to court. It was found against your master *in absentia*. This is a lien, ordering restitution."

"You broke the bloody deal," Imogen said. "I was to be hidden on *The Cheerful Misogynist*. You made me a prisoner."

"Now you're just splitting hairs," Luca said. "Hand over Raoul. There's nothing stopping my ship from crushing this lunatic asylum into white dust."

"He's gone, and I don't know where. Not that I'd tell you, you rotten shit." Imogen backed away slowly, baton raised. Luca stood, rounded the table. Shuddering and gagging, his eyes rolled back into his head. Seeming to stare at her through that veiny whiteness, he lurched forward.

"Give me what is mine," Luca said, now speaking in the voice of the ship itself. She felt the weight of a million tonnes of creaking wood behind his words, knew that if it caught her, she would suffer every sort of indignity. She'd never leave the bowels of that unholy place.

Stepping back over the mural, she struck the tiles sharply with the tip of the police baton. Even as the shell of Luca closed in, a figure rose from the mosaic, a dancing cloud of tiles and ash. It grew in seconds, until it resembled the shape of a large animal, filling the doorway.

The dog-thing stood between her and Luca, snarling at the man, its broad jaw lined with jags of coloured glass and stone. Its heaving sides were clad in scales of bright tesserae, and it stank of smoke, pulsed with an intense heat.

A little flavour of Pompeii, Raoul had explained.

As she turned and ran down the stairs, she heard the guardian launch itself into the ship's puppet. The ship itself screamed in ear-splitting pain above the city, even as the pair wrestled and tore at each other behind her.

Raoul had designed the guardian to take out just about anything, but she knew it had only bought her a minute or two at best.

Luca's threat to destroy True-Town had not been idle either. As she ran onto the street she saw a thousand sully ports and hatchways open along the hull of the vast city-ship, howitzers and trebuchets emerging, even a missile or two. *The Cheerful Misogynist* held for the moment, a breath away from wiping True-Town from the map.

I've doomed all these people, she thought. *Helluva time for Raoul to nick off and have a holiday.*

❊

Even as the howitzers boomed, Imogen began a barrage of her own. Over the whistle of the shells, she told the old man every dirty joke she knew. When the explosions got closer, she began swearing like a sailor.

Wiping away tears of laughter, the man waved at her to stop. Pausing only to remove a brace of chickens from the spring-catch behind the seat, he pushed the bicycle into her hands.

"Merci beaucoup," she said. Huffing down the street, she pedalled as if she was in the Tour. The edge of the barrage had caught up with her, and *The Cheerful Misogynist* started to smash apart True-Town. Buildings were pulverised, and great slabs of masonry fell from the sky.

She took a quick peek over her shoulder. The man who sold her the bike was already a smear on the cobble-stones, his chickens running free. An onlooker was trying to catch the birds, even as bombs fell around him.

There was an unholy roar, followed by an explosion that knocked Imogen clean off the bike. What might have been a cruise missile had just destroyed her apartment building.

Bricks and mortar rained all around her. She reached for the bike in the cloud of dust, coughing, praying that the debris wouldn't just cave in her skull. She pedalled blindly, smacking into rubbish bins and skinning her knuckles when she got too close to a wall.

She thought of all her belongings, the house that Raoul and she had made here. Everything destroyed, or buried in the rubble. Aurora Luca had bested the dog-guardian, and was back on board his monster ship.

So the missile was clearly a *fuck you*.

Imogen was out of the dust now, and marvelled at the sudden silence. Looking back at the boat, she saw that *The Cheerful Misogynist* was trying a different tactic. It rolled forward, crushing buildings underneath its treads.

Thousands of figures launched themselves from the high decks of the boat. They descended on the white buildings of True-Town, and Imogen was sure they weren't there for the falafels.

Shapes filled the sky, and soon she could make these out. Parachutists. Hang-gliders, racing zeppelins, World War I bi-planes. Something that might have been a gondola, suspended by a flight of huge swans.

Imogen had spent over fifty years (in subjective time, she was barely out of acne) imprisoned on the boat. Passengers were typically psychopaths, fetishists with very specific requirements, or folks who would get in on a murder if it was phrased as part of the entertainment program.

"Get inside!" she shouted at the people on the street. "Don't just stand there!"

But the people smiled at her words, and pointed at the excitement in the skies above True-Town. Visitors, about to set the whole place to the sack.

She pedalled until she saw spots in front of her eyes. Behind her, she heard the first scream, the revving of a chainsaw. Above, a bi-plane was strafing the marketplace with a Vickers machine-gun.

Muscles aching, she raced through this place's mirror-version of *Bab El Oued*, and fell huffing against the wall of a fisherman's hovel. Lost and disoriented, it took Imogen a few minutes to find what she was looking for.

A potter's shop, complete with wheel and small kiln. She'd befriended the potter, an old *pied-noir* with few teeth and an excess of conversation. The shop-front was empty, and Imogen was thankful for small mercies.

"Raoul, I've had enough of your nonsense," she said, slapping a handful of clay onto the bench. "You'll help me whether you like it or not."

She worked the clay into an approximation of a minotaur shape. A doll that fit into her hand, complete with horns.

Digging into her satchel, she found what she was looking for. The hair-brush that she used to curry Raoul's fur, still there from that one time he'd caught the tram to the beach with her.

"If this doesn't work, I'm all out of ideas," she muttered. Plucking a few hairs from the brush, she pushed them into the figurine with her thumb, smoothing the clay back over.

RAOUL MITHRAS, she scratched into the clay with her thumbnail. She marked it with what magic she'd been able to glean from her guardian. Opening the kiln door, she popped the clay minotaur into the heat. Imogen cranked the heat to maximum.

She gave the clay five minutes, twitching the curtains nervously. Judging by the smoke outside and the distant screams, the edge of the riot was close now. Once, a rhinoceros went charging down the street, a length of intestine draped around its horn. A trio of men were hunting it on motorbikes, and they themselves hunted by a sabretooth tiger the size of a house.

Standard behaviour onboard *The Cheerful Misogynist*. The sack of True-Town had begun in earnest.

Imogen paced around the kiln, fretting and gnawing at her nails. Luca had her scent now, and nowhere in True-Town was safe. She peeked through the curtain, and watched in dread as a gaggle of party-goers filled the street. They broke windows, kicked in doors, and stole as much booze as they could carry. Wherever a True-Towner was found, the fool was dragged out into the street, and murdered to the tune of laughter and vuvuzelas.

It was just shy of four minutes when Imogen popped the kiln, snatching the clay minotaur with a pair of tongs. The figure wriggled and waved to her, gesturing frantically.

"Oh, I'm such an idiot," Imogen said. She'd forgotten to carve her miniature Raoul a mouth. Even as she hunted for a craft knife, she heard a ruckus next door, the screams as the ship's passengers beat a family to death.

Tucking the clay Raoul in her satchel, Imogen ran to the back of the shop, pushing through the curtain that hid the potter's house from customers. Testing the back-door, she found a deserted alley.

Loping through the mud and human waste, Imogen wished she hadn't left her bicycle out the front of the shop. She fetched out her extendable baton, and with her journeyman's sorcery she tried to imbue it with speed and power.

"That'll do," she muttered to the figurine. "Any more and I'll probably turn it into a celery stick."

The clay figurine was waving desperately, trying to communicate something to her. Imogen shook her head at the attempts, unsure of what Raoul was trying to say.

The minotaur ducked into the depths of her satchel, and finally emerged with an old ballpoint pen, and a receipt. Gripping the pen like a quarterstaff, the minotaur scratched and struggled, the pen seemingly dry. Imogen took the pen from the clay bull's grip, squiggling a dozen circles till the ink began to flow.

CASBAH, the bull managed to write.

"Do we have to go *there*?" Imogen moaned. "Gotta be a better option."

The pen was truly dead, and further attempts at written communication proved fruitless. Raoul pointed emphatically towards the centre of True-Town, and once to where a watch might sit on his little clay wrist.

"Alright, alright. Don't drop a cow-pat."

✻

There was one authority figure to be found in True-Town, and Imogen sped towards him on a stolen motor scooter, one eye to the towering menace that filled her rear-view mirrors.

Desperately trying not to hit anyone, she weaved through the twisting laneways and traffic-fouled streets. At one point she abandoned the scooter, the road too blocked to continue. Running up a rubbish strewn set of steps, she found herself facing a reasonable facsimile of the Casbah proper.

This resemblance only lasted until she passed through the outer archway. What should have been a wafty maze of seraglios and shaded gardens was a log-jammed mess of One-Way-World culture.

Bowling alleys. A full scale greyhound track. An upmarket

island marina, flanked by empty McMansions. Movie sets, shopping malls, even an open menagerie that seemed to operate on Darwinian principles alone.

This was the home of the Juggler-King, custodian and warden of True-Town. He'd done his level best to make his surroundings as ridiculous as possible.

"Heaven help me," Imogen muttered, scanning a large and ever-changing location map. "Alright, let's find the idiot in charge."

ROI DE JONGLEUR declared a little flag, slowly moving around in a section labelled TROU DE PÊCHE. Imogen identified a shuttle service that would transport her across the vast interior of the faux Casbah, and in short order she stepped out of a bus and straight into a thick wetland. Pushing through thick reeds, she spotted the leader of True-Town in waders, fly-fishing in an enormous lake.

"Oh bloody hell," Imogen said, remembering her high school French. "Of course he has a personal fishing hole."

"Bonjour," said the Juggler-King, smiling at her. He doffed a floppy hat full of flies and lures. "You are scaring away all my fish, but I can forgive the sudden appearance of a pretty girl, no?"

"Sir," Imogen said through gritted teeth. "We are all in deep deep merde. An enormous evil boat full of sickos is destroying True-Town."

"This will not do," he said, reaching into a stand of reeds and pulling out a boat. "Come with me, my darling. I will hear all of your words, and make a bold decision at some point."

Scowling, she took his hand and clambered into his boat, trying not to fall into the water. Dipping the oars, the Juggler-King winked at her, whistling a jaunty tune as he drove the boat forward.

He twisted the oars just so, and she found herself in a drawing room, the hard bench beneath her transformed into a love-seat. She was wearing a dress that was layer upon layer of frills. Clad in a mass of gold cloth, leering and right in her personal space, the Juggler-King was doing his best Louis XIV impression.

"Do you mind?" she snapped, and he sat back, pouting.

"Suit yourself," he mumbled. "What is it you were wanting? Not that I care."

"Well, you should. *The Cheerful Misogynist* is killing everyone!"

"Ah! *Le Misogyne Gai*. A fine vessel. Have you sojourned upon her?"

"Far too long for my own liking," Imogen said. "My family and I have a grievance with the boat. Stop that!" she said, slapping away his wandering hands.

"Try that again, and I will pop you right in the regal nose. As I was saying, they have been hunting Raoul and I, and . . . "

"Wait. Raoul? You are Imogen, no? You are the ward of the Mithras bull-man, yes?"

The man was lying. Imogen could read his eyes, saw that he knew full well who she was. She extracted the clay figurine from her satchel. The bull pointed at the golden buffoon, and drew his hand across his own throat.

"Forgive me, mademoiselle," he said, smiling sheepishly. "I was meant to deliver this to you some days ago."

Digging into his ruffled shirt, he pulled out an envelope, marked IMOGEN MITHRAS—PRIVATE. She recognized Raoul's messy scribble. Imogen snatched the envelope, enraged.

IMOGEN, the letter read.

AM ATTEMPTING TO MAKE GOOD ON THE HORN ISSUE. MAY HAVE FOUND A WAY. SORRY FOR TELLING YOU LIKE THIS, BUT WHERE I GO, YOU CANNOT FOLLOW. GO TO THE JUGGLER-KING. HE CAN HIDE YOU SAFELY IN WHAT PASSES FOR HIS CASBAH.

ALL MY LOVE,

RAOUL.

Clutching the letter in her shaking hands, Imogen began to pace the room. She stood before a merry little fire-place, tempted to snatch up the poker and drive it through the Juggler-King's jovial face.

"I needed to know this right away," she said, voice dangerously calm. "This is all your fault, you dangerous lunatic."

"Forgive me, little one. But Raoul was wrong to tell you this," the Juggler-King said cautiously. "Where he goes, there is no way you could help him."

"You know where he is?"

He paused, licked his lips nervously.

"Raoul is trying to kill himself."

✳

"Don't you dare," Imogen said, gripping the clay minotaur tightly. A fat tear dripped from her chin and splashed the doll. The miniature of Raoul had given up on trying to communicate in pantomime, and it clutched her thumb just as tightly.

"I don't know what sort of mess you're in, but I'm going to help you," she told the figurine. The tiny minotaur merely shook its head mournfully.

They were on the Juggler-King's personal shuttle bus, speeding into the depths of the Casbah. The tunnel shook slightly as a barrage of cannon fire smashed into the city.

She shivered in her courtly dress. It was getting very cold. The bus pulled over with a sickening lurch, and the doors opened to reveal a vast glacier, an endless stretch of dark ice birthed under an alien sky.

"We will be safe here, little one," he told her. "Let that ship do what it will."

"What the hell are you doing?" Imogen cried. *"The Cheerful Misogynist* is gonna roll right over the place."

He led her out onto the ice field, and the bitter cold flooded through her instantly. Seeing her shiver, the Juggler-King dressed them both in seal-skin slickers, called up a dog-sled.

"I've got a place," he said, pointing vaguely somewhere ahead of them.

It turned out to be a ski-lodge, as imagined by someone who'd never set foot in one and perhaps only read a description once. It was an angular mess of log walls, animal skins and fireplaces.

"I can speak more freely here," the Juggler-King said, curling up around a drinking horn filled with eggnog. "It will take some hours for that ship to reach us."

"Those people are dying," she said, shivering in front of a fire.

"Oh, Imogen dear. Did you truly believe I was running an asylum for the simple? How you say, a sheltered workshop?"

"Raoul said they had been affected by the Crossing. It had driven all the knowing out of their heads."

"A small lie," the Juggler-King said. "There is nothing true about True-Town. Just a home I made for my dolls, sweet puppets too dumb to see their own strings. I do love them so, but they are not real."

"Not real?"

"Raoul never told you?" At Imogen's blank look, the sorcerer continued. "When we snatched the One-Way-World from Yahweh's fingers, we—we broke it."

"You broke *Heaven*?"

"We have done our best with Yahweh's scraps, but this Severed Garden we have made? It is mostly ice and darkness. Everything else? Flim-flam. Legerdemain."

Imogen had spent most of a century in Raoul's land. She'd seen many strange things, mixed with gods old and new. The thought that most of the place was a magic trick made her feel light-headed.

She helped herself to a big stein of eggnog, and twitched open a curtain. Beyond the cheerful glow of the fires and lamplight, the glacier and the darkness were absolute.

"Oh, some parts of the Garden are real," the Juggler-King said. "That evil boat, certain territories we have crafted. But underneath our pretty palaces," and here he drained the drinking horn dry, "we are the lords of ice and failure."

"I don't care," Imogen said. "Yahweh can use this whole place for an esky. I need to get to Raoul, right now."

"Ah," the sorcerer said. "You will need more than your *voudoun* magic to find him. He treads through time and the stars, dances through the ruins of Yahweh's great work. The last time I tried to see where he was going, his footwork gave me a headache."

Imogen set the clay figurine of Raoul down on the smorgasbord. It plucked a knife from the nearest ham, and started to carve letters into the wood.

STAY HERE, it wrote, before Imogen knocked the knife away from it.

"Enough! I'm not going to sit here and wait for you to *kill yourself*! Stop being such a fucking idiot."

She flicked the clay minotaur in the forehead, knocking it onto its backside. When it got up and groggily ran for cover amongst the food, Imogen had an idea. She'd achieved one half of a sympathetic magic with the doll. She could actually hurt Raoul via the link, wherever he was. If she could reach him, he could sure as hell reach her.

She snatched up the figurine, and then the knife. She drew the blade across her palm, smearing the bull doll with her own blood. She felt the magic make a connection, a laggy bond that stretched to wherever Raoul was.

"You want to die? Fine. Maybe I'll join the club."

She moved to the centre of the lodge, where a bed of whole trees blazed in an enormous trough. It was a Scandinavian firepit, extrapolated to godly proportions. Getting as close to the edge as she could bear, she looked down on a bed of white-hot coals.

Now the bull-doll was beating against her grip, hammering her fingers with his tiny fists. Despite that, he was assaulting her with a mass far beyond his size. Each blow felt like the fall of a hammer, and it was all she could do to keep her grip on the clay figure.

"You've got a choice Raoul. Bring me to you, or watch me die."

Then she ran for the edge, leaping out into the inferno. Even as the Juggler-King shouted for her to stop, she was falling, burning, before passing through the flames and into elsewhere.

*

One moment, everything was searing, the next Imogen stumbled onto an endless glacier. It was near to perfect darkness, interrupted only by the tiniest of cook-fires. A sled of supplies, a bedroll, and looming over her, a one-horned minotaur god with a fury in his eyes. She fell to her knees, panting and blinking.

"What were you thinking!" Raoul shouted. He seemed worn, his fur crusted with jags of ice. The point of Raoul's remaining horn seemed to throb with an intensity here, in contrast to the sawed off nub of the horn that he'd surrendered to the Cheerful Misogynist.

In a heartbeat she was up and hitting him, kicking his tree-stump legs and swearing up a storm.

"Don't worry about killing yourself, arsehole. Let me help you." When she'd stubbed her toes blue, she fetched out her enchanted baton, and cracked him in the shins. By the way he hopped away and held her at arm's length, she could tell *that* was hurting him.

"You're always running away," she cried, smashing his fingers when he tried to grab for her. "But I never thought you'd be running away from me."

She cracked him once more for emphasis before the fight fell out of her. The baton dropped from her limp hands, and then she was wrapped in Raoul's arms. Imogen sobbed, tears and snot freezing all over her face. Her face was glued to the minotaur's fur in a wholly undignified way.

"Don't hurt yourself," she whispered. "Please. Don't you leave me."

"You couldn't understand," Raoul said gently. "I never wanted you to see this."

"There's nothing to see. You're coming back with me."

"I will," Raoul said. Imogen had been spoiling for a fight, and his rapid acquiescence threw her. Raoul led her over to his campfire, dished up a rude stew he'd been cooking.

"When the Juggler-King told you that I was going to kill myself, he was correct. Semantically correct, or near enough as makes no difference."

Imogen blinked, the spoon forgotten in her hands.

"I need to kill myself. Not, not myself. Him," and here he pointed towards the horizon. "I need to pay my debt to the *Cheerful Misogynist*."

"You're not making any sense."

"Okay. This gets difficult. I've been travelling throughout the Garden, peering down different . . . vines? Branches? This isn't your One-Way-World—there are ways to slip around time."

"I get it. I've been eighteen for about a hundred years. Don't school me, dude."

"We are a whisker away from the end of the universe. Over that horizon is a version of me, one that has limped through to this last age."

"Oh."

"I'm about to kill my future self. Imogen, dear heart, you won't like who you're about to meet."

＊

"We have a loose consortium. Most of us leftover gods, pooling our strength. Given enough uninterrupted time, we think we can fix the Severed Garden."

The minotaur and the girl were trudging across the dark ice, barely visible in the gloom. There were no stars left, no moon. Nothing but their shadows, and the swinging glow of Raoul's gas lantern.

Below them, the endless glacier glowed faintly—a fraction of a lumen, just enough to make out the horizon. The only interruption to the horizon was a set of jagged ranges, and Raoul steered them towards it. If the lamp were to fail, Imogen thought she'd be able to see just enough to shuffle forward, a pair of shadows against all that sickly green ice.

"So, you can't give your horn to the ship."

"Exactly. We're barely holding on as it is. I'm at half strength now, but with both my horns gone? My home will fail, and my part of the project will falter. Then the next god will stumble under his burden, and then others will quit."

Raoul stopped talking, but the glacier around them spoke volumes. They began to climb up through a bumpy rise, passing between icy spires. What she thought was a jagged range had once been a great city. She could just make out a series of colonnades, facing the broken jag of a skyscraper long crushed by the weight.

Beyond the broken city, there was a light. A bright blue glow, almost obscene against all that darkness.

Imogen slipped and scrabbled, thwarted by her attempts to conjure up spiked boots. Her magic was weak here, with the Severed Garden all but choked of life. Each step was hard won, and soon she was sweating, even as the glacier beneath robbed her of heat.

There was a faint humming sound ahead, as if a million flies were arguing. Raoul doused the lamp, and hiding behind a frost-encrusted cenotaph, he gestured for Imogen to join him.

She stole a peek around the edge of the memorial, and her jaw fell open. In what would have been a public space, something had created an ice amphitheatre, now a bowl in the lowest park of the ruin. Rows of seating ringed the centre, and these were filled with the dead. Tens of thousands of bodies, more ice than bone, silent attendants to the monster within.

The middle of the amphitheatre was a cavernous space, filled with mounds of bone that were more like small hillocks. In the middle of all this desolation was a throne, a raised mess of concrete and exposed rebar. It was wreathed in blue flames, as if a gas outlet was constantly purging into the atmosphere.

"Aether," Raoul whispered. "He's been hoarding it."

Seated in the throne was Raoul's future self, an enormous minotaur almost three times the size of the version she knew. He was all hard edges, shaggy with fur that was more like steel wool. Where Raoul might have slouched in a chair, this apocalypse king sat stern and upright on his throne.

His horns were great curling things, and this was the cause of the buzzing, humming sensation. This close, and it felt like drills were grinding into all of her teeth. The points of these were painful to look at, and hummed their own challenge at the blank sky.

Each curled horn was like a cornucopia, an electrical coil, a spring compressed to an impossible tension.

"What the hell do you become?" Imogen whispered. "Do you kill all of those people?"

"I don't want to talk about it," Raoul muttered.

"Well, don't fight him."

"I have to," Raoul said.

"Raoul, don't."

The minotaur knelt down, gave Imogen a sad smile. He snuffling Imogen's forehead with his snout. He licked her temple gently with his broad cow's tongue, three times.

"Forgive me, my dear. But I have to forget about you for a while."

Too late, Imogen realised the magic that Raoul had worked upon himself. As he staggered away from her, the days fell from his thoughts, all memory of their trek through this final land. Raoul's discarded thoughts squirrelled back into her own mind, and left her head throbbing.

Blank-faced, Raoul stumbled out of cover. Future-Raoul stirred from his trance, and regarded his past self with a nasty smile. Where Raoul's eyes were kind, brown melt-pools with eyelashes that parted legs, this end-times Raoul was a twisted thing. His eyes were as black as the sky above, reflecting the blue flames that licked around his seat.

"I HAVE BEEN EXPECTING YOU," he rumbled, in a voice that shook ice from the ruins. "I REMEMBER STANDING THERE, IN YOUR SHIVERING SKIN."

Raoul climbed over the outer walls of the amphitheatre, crushing through the husks of the long-dead. Imogen watched in horror as Raoul approached the throne, his sole horn little defence against such a monster. He took the shortest possible route through the frozen amphitheatre, unintentionally drawing those dark eyes away from Imogen's hiding spot.

Raoul doesn't remember me coming here with him, she realised, eyebrows wrinkling as she wrapped her mind around the non-linear concepts of the Severed Garden. Causality and paradox were concepts left at the threshold of the One-Way World, and the rules of the Garden were usually in flux.

So future-Raoul doesn't realise I'm here.

"Did you enjoy your slaughter?" Raoul asked, gesturing at the mounds of bones. "Did it bring you peace at the end, Moloch?"

"HO. YOU NAME ME WELL," Moloch said, and gestured with a hand that was more claws than fingers, waving at the death around him. "I WAS RIGHT TO EAT THEM. NOW I SIT VIGIL, AND SHALL WATCH THE END OF ALL THINGS."

Imogen had always known that Raoul was an amalgam of many gods and spirits. She remembered something about Moloch from the Bible, some horror tale about child sacrifice and fire. Whatever Raoul had become in these end-times, he'd done so with his usual brute style, and literal adherence to his source texts.

He'd been born as Mithras, and spent an era as a dozen different gods before becoming the Raoul she'd fallen in love with. It made sense that he was mutable, could change identities with each era.

Moloch she did not like.

"I'm just disappointed," Raoul said. "To think, that I become an Aether-hoarding murderer. You know that stuff is bad for you."

Moloch snorted then, a shade of Raoul's familiar laugh. But the amusement soon passed, that alien stare returning.

"YOU THINK TO DEFEAT ME, AND CHANGE THIS," Moloch told Raoul. "BUT THIS TIME, I WILL CHAIN YOU IN ICE. YOU WILL WATCH THE FINAL MOMENT AND WEEP WITH ME."

Moloch stood then, an unfolding mass that dwarfed the approaching minotaur. He left his flaming throne, crunching across the bone-middens. A beast on the hunt, and nothing more.

A cord of blue fire connected Moloch to his throne, and the nimbus danced over his furry limbs. *Aether,* Raoul had named it.

The buzzing sound reached maddening levels, and Imogen felt like she was about to faint. Raoul ran forward, but he seemed unsteady on his feet, shook his head as if clearing away a horde of invisible flies. Imogen watched in horror as Moloch closed the gap, murderous horns held low.

Raoul reached into his vest, pulling out a vuvuzela. He honked away on the ridiculous instrument, as if attempting to level Jericho. Imogen saw the sigils etched on the plastic horn with ink, felt the strong influence of the Juggler-King. It was true *jongleur* magic, a ridiculous raspberry to dispel Moloch's considerable defences.

But the secret weapon had no effect. Moloch came on relentlessly, and then the two bull-men were rolling around in the ice and bones, clashing their horns together, trading punches that would kill anything less than a god. Finally Raoul lay beneath Moloch's hand, eyes wide as he struggled to free himself.

"I REMEMBER THAT TRICK," Moloch said. "IT WORKED WELL, THE FIRST TIME."

The enormous beast lifted something from the mass of fur on his chest. It was a yellowed skull with a chain threaded through the eye sockets. Even from a distance Imogen could feel the sympathy between the skull and the abandoned vuvuzela, and knew it could only have come from one man. The late landlord of True-Town.

"MY TALISMAN TASTED SO SWEET, AND HOW HE BEGGED AND SANG AND TRIED HIS TRICKS. AND SO, NO, HIS LITTLE TRUMPET WON'T WORK TODAY."

Moloch's horns hummed and sang another insane note, on some scale beyond human comprehension. Reeling from the sound, Imogen watched in horror as the enormous bull-god lifted Raoul by the throat.

He touched Raoul's feet to the ground, as if planting a seedling. The ice came at Moloch's bidding, flowing upwards like putty. Soon Raoul was encased from foot to throat in a sheath of crystal-clear ice. The cold was swiftly overcoming him, and the minotaur struggled to breathe against the weight of his prison.

"NOW, YOU WILL WATCH WITH ME, YOUNG SELF," Moloch said. "THE END IS UPON US."

Even as the lumbering beast returned to hold vigil on his throne, Imogen sprang from cover. She crept through the terraces, hiding behind the long dead whenever Moloch looked her way.

"DO YOU SEE THAT?" the beast rumbled, and Imogen flinched. But he was looking skywards, rapt. She picked her way around the amphitheatre till she was behind the throne. Wincing every time a bone cracked underfoot, she crept closer, finally crawling forward on hands and knees.

"I can't see it," Raoul said weakly.

"NOT THERE. THERE."

"Oh."

She saw the two minotaurs staring skywards, at nothing she

could see. To her eyes, it was nothing but the deepest night above them.

Imogen made for the base of the throne, hardly daring to breathe. She kept brushing against empty containers of every variety, recent additions to the field of skeletons. Soft drink bottles, fuel cans, big oil drums.

Each of the abandoned containers was labelled with AETHER 100% — EXTREME HEALTH / TEMPORAL WARNING. Dribbles of a glowing blue liquid pooled in the bottom of each one, and the stink was unbelievable, somewhere between ammonia and sulphur.

Maybe this is power in the Severed Garden, Imogen mused. *Some sort of fuel.*

Where piles of bone gave way to the ramshackle throne lay a belching apparatus, the chuggings of its engine easily drowned out by the mad chatter of Moloch's horns. A great vat of the fluorescent slurry, surrounded by more empty containers. A tangle of pipes and hoses led from the open vat, reaching up to the top of the throne. Above, the pumped Aether burned straight from the hose, fuel to sustain Moloch long beyond his unnatural existence.

Trying to breath through her mouth, she poked around with the chattering pump, trying to find a way to stop it. She couldn't understand the ancient machine, so futuristic that it had no power source that she could comprehend.

"LOOK NOW, FRIEND. THE FINAL HOUR IS HERE."

Raoul's head lay slumped forward, and he was no longer even conscious. Moloch sighed in annoyance, and slid from his throne to cross the courtyard.

The Aether nimbus was trailing behind him, burning strong and pure. Imogen poked frantically at the workings, hoping to switch it off somehow.

She tipped out her satchel, hoping to find something useful. Dead biros, the baton, her hairbrush. Backgammon pieces and the make-up she'd tired of wearing in True-Town.

A box of matches.

Even as Moloch slapped Raoul across the face and swore at him, she struck a match, hand shaking. She dropped the match into the bones at her feet. The second match didn't take.

She felt it above. Nothing dramatic, just a lessening of the weight of the night, the sense that the world was a little less there than it was a second ago. The perfect darkness found a way to get a little bit darker.

Imogen was wondering if the end of the universe was going to hurt when the next match caught. She tossed it in a flickering arc, dropping to her face as the Aether caught with a great WHUMP!

The pipes blew, the hoses split, and with a puff of blue-grey smoke, Moloch was no longer surrounded by his nimbus of protective power.

He turned in disbelief, watching as Imogen stood up. Moloch came to her slowly, a pained look on his face. He'd aged visibly in moments. The humming from his horns stuttered, and a crack began to show in one.

Above, the darkness was wavering like a mirage, and it seemed like the roof of all existence was inches away from simply falling in.

"IMOGEN," Moloch rumbled. "I HAVE NOT SEEN YOU IN A MILLION YEARS. YOU I REGRETTED EATING MOST OF ALL."

"Up your nose with a rubber hose, buddy," she said, flicking the police baton out to its full extension. The enchantments were still holding on the weapon, and she ran rings around the failing giant. She cracked away at Moloch's shins and reaching fingers, even once across his snout when he tried to take a bite out of her.

Between the physical assault and the failure of his sorcery, Moloch simply laid down on his side, huffing pathetically. He looked up at Imogen then, an animal sacrifice resigned to death, and for one quick moment she could see a familiar expression, a hint of the Raoul that he'd once been.

Imogen beat his brains out.

✳

The baton was bent now, so Imogen went at Raoul's ice casing with a chunk of cement. It was slow work, and her arms ached from the effort. She worked frantically, unsure of how far away the collapse of the universe was.

"Come on, horn-face. Wake up. Please!"

Raoul looked dead, head slumped against the ice collar. Sobbing, Imogen ran for the sled. Raoul had a bone-saw in his sled, the tips dipped in the tell-tale blue of Aether. She hacked away at Moloch's horns, and in seconds the saw parted them at the roots.

With her remaining strength, she dragged one of the enormous growths across the ground, crunching skulls and other dessicated things underneath its weight. Imogen pushed the tip of the horn to the ice casket, and found herself praying, hoping, visualising the ice away from her best friend.

She felt the hornets in her mind, the barest flicker of that mad cacophony. But it was enough. The ice receded, and Raoul Mithras slumped to the floor.

He wasn't breathing. He was cold to the core. The universe was ending above her, and it seemed appropriate.

"Please," she said, and honked away on the Juggler-King's vuvuzela. "Please help us."

Even as the world sank into a slick toffee, the sky running like black tears, a door opened to elsewhere. A hand reached through, gloved and clad in a ridiculous sleeve, and swept girl and minotaur through with no effort at all.

The Juggler-King slammed the door shut, and the awful feeling of non-life went away. They were in his ski-lodge. Imogen crawled over to Raoul's wet body, trying her best to perform CPR on a huge bull-man.

"It is no good my dear," the Juggler-King said, peeling her away from Raoul. "Too late for that."

"No. No it is not too late. You save him or you shut up."

"*Sacre bleur,*" the Juggler-King sighed. Even as Imogen howled grief into Raoul's chest, the sorcerer staggered over under the weight of one of Moloch's horns.

He connected the sawn off end to the nub where Raoul had severed his own horn. In moments the horn grafted itself together, the curls and great length slowly deflating until it matched Raoul's other horn.

The minotaur drew in a deep breath, and sat bolt upright. Imogen tumbled to the floor, sobbing deeply.

✳

When *The Cheerful Misogynist* came to True-Town, it had expected a battle with the reclusive Raoul Mithras. Tricks from his sorcerer ally, and some sort of injury at the hands of his inventive foster-daughter, Imogen.

But when it rumbled to a halt by the Juggler-King's lodge, it was faced openly by the trio. The minotaur, held upright by the girl and the sorcerer. "Take your damn horn," Raoul shouted. With the last of his strength, he hurled an enormous horn at the ship like a spear. It lodged itself deep in the wooden gut of the boat, and it shrieked like a fish on the hook, a most terrible sound.

The wounded ship withdrew into a distant part of the Severed Garden, even as various lawyers on board conceded that the minotaur had followed the letter of the agreement and delivered One (1) Outstanding Minotaur Horn.

✳

"Don't you dare lift anything," Imogen scolded. They were at the newly rebuilt terminus, the only passengers on the next train. Raoul was too weak to attempt far-travel, and despite the Juggler-King's insistence that they stay, all parties were glad that this arrangement had ended.

"I liked True-Town," Imogen said.

"Me too," Raoul said. "Amazing attention to detail."

They watched the white city through the windows, marvelling at the speed with which the Juggler-King repaired his buildings, repopulated the bay with boats, the docks and marketplaces with people.

"Are you going to tell me how you found me?" Raoul said carefully. "How you brought me back?"

"You can never know," Imogen said, taking a mint julep from the drinks cart. She saluted him, all the while praying that he never remembered taking Imogen to see Moloch. If he remembered her being at his side, and that memory travelled through the ages . . .

"It doesn't make sense," he muttered. "I was defeated. Yet here I am, with—with his horns."

"Do you think you can fix things?" Imogen said, changing the subject. She remembered the ice that lay just below the façade of sun and sand.

"I've learnt some new tricks," Raoul said, raising a hand to his repaired horn. "It will take a long time, but we shall repair the Severed Garden, the last splinter of Yahweh's blessed Eden."

She watched the minotaur for a long time, wrapped in her own dark thoughts. Even as the train lulled Raoul into sleep, Imogen remembered Moloch, and shivered.

✳

GOGGY

The little boy had been asleep in his booster seat, lulled by the endless drive. He could only dimly remember a house and a yard, and then nothing but driving all day and night, pointing at shapes in the dark, Mum-Mum screaming. Always being hungry.

He was woken by shouting, and a door slamming. Then came the shaking hands on his safety straps, and even as he stirred Dad-Dad picked him up, set him gently on the road-side. The boy reached up his arms, high as he could, but no-one would give him a cuddle, or pick him up. His parents got back into the car, closing the doors. Lips trembling, the boy began to sob.

Then they drove away, showering him in stones and dust.

The boy screamed at the sight, florid little face bunched up into a ball of terror. Tears and snot ran onto his dirty yellow one-piece, the one with the picture of a duck on the front.

"Mum-Mum!" he cried over and over, reaching out with his fat little hands.

Just past a ruptured tyre and an empty fuel canister, they'd quickly dumped a messy pile of his toys. Duck-Duck, his yellow bath friend. His blocks, fallen out of their pail, and well loved books scattered all over the verge. The boy clutched Ted-Ted close, sobbing into his worn fur. They'd left his sippy cup on top of the tyre, barely two fingers of warm water all that they'd spared him.

He was scared, and tottered a few steps down the road, following the car. Seized by a fresh wave of outrage, he threw himself onto the road, shaking and crying and slapping the packed gravel with his hands. All he could see was endless scrub, the road that stole Mum-Mum and Dad-Dad, and the hot sun shining straight into his eyes.

Twigs snapped, and the boy sucked back his tears, absent parents forgotten. He stared wide-eyed at the other side of the road. Emerging from the bush were a pair of long heads, ears twitching. Sinuous necks followed, rough red fur and solid muscle.

Kangaroos.

"Dat. Dat!" the boy said, pointing at the animals. He got to his feet and began to waddle across the loose gravel. The kangaroos swept forward using their forearms as pivots, long legs swinging through, tails dragging through the fine dust left from countless cars.

"Gog. Gog-goggy!" the little boy squealed with delight. He was pointing and reaching for the nearest roo, a broad toothy smile splitting his tear-streaked face. He was thinking of Gog-Gog the family dog, last seen skinned and turning on a spit over a sad camp-fire.

The kangaroos closed in. Had he been a little older, the boy might have recognised the unusual size of the creatures, the blood-shot eyes, the mangy fur. Leaning in close, the nearest roo snarled, its lips curling back. Sharp yellow teeth, the deep hollow of its gullet. Its breath stank of rotten meat.

"Goggy?" the boy whispered.

EVERYTHING IS A GRAVEYARD

Everything stopped in 1976.

The Festival Centre hunched on the banks of the Torrens like a cement barnacle, silent of arias. Now, it was a place best avoided. The Apollo Stadium no longer rocked out to bands like Status Quo, Queen and AC/DC. Anzac Highway was broad and empty, and it led to a pristine beach at Glenelg, long untouched by thongs.

Rundle Mall was only ever opened to eager shoppers for a few months. Now, it was a mess of broken glass and rubble, burnt buildings interrupting the façade like rotten teeth.

Across the Adelaide Plains, tiled roofs baked in the sun, gutters long since clogged with leaves and muck. Hills Hoists sagged and span in backyards, still wearing the rags of cricket whites and pinafores. Above, the TV antennae lay dormant, coathangers scratching at the sky with futility. There was no more *Number 96*, no more *Dick Jane Show*, no more *Channel Niners*. Nothing but silence on the airwaves.

The Holden factory at Elizabeth was a lonely place. Shells of cars still sat on the production line, quietly rusting in the dark. Once, great machines used to roll out into the lot, roaring monsters of metal and glass. The Kingswood for dad, the Monaro if you were a petrolhead. A Statesman if you had money in the bank.

Everything stopped in 1976, so when a cherry-red LJ Torana blasted across the corpse of Adelaide, it was like a loud fart in a church.

Gretel was squeezed in behind the steering wheel, foot to the floor. She was a big girl, and had to have the driver's seat all the way back. Working through the gears, she wove the muscle-car through the ancient wreckage littering South Road. Abandoned cars, burnt cars, cars wrapped around cement stobie poles.

The Torana danced through the wreckage like a dressage horse, and Gretel rarely had to slow down, navigating the forest of dead cars by memory alone. Sometimes she thought of herself like an ancient sailor, and pictured the wrecked cars as a dangerous reef she knew off by heart.

When she'd restored the LJ from three different wrecks, Gretel dropped in a big 3300 engine. It chewed through the fuel like a pig, but the power and speed of this machine was unrivalled. It was the same basic set-up that Peter Brock once used at Bathurst, and nothing had a hope of touching her.

In the beginning, some of the other rovers got around on motorbikes. Anyone with a brain in their head put as much metal around them as they possibly could. No-one bothered with the bikes anymore—and these days, anyone with a death-wish never had to wait too long anyway.

Gretel was headed north, through the city and onto the trading post at Port Wakefield. No cargo today, just a passenger run. A very important man was waiting for her there, and she had to bring him back to Stanvac in one piece. As per usual, Gretel was running early, so she decided to organise some trade for herself.

"What do you think, Mog?" Gretel asked the cat. Draped across the dashboard, the tomcat of questionable parentage opened one eye, closing it again with disgust. He continued to soak up the sun from the hot dash, sliding across the vinyl when Gretel turned from the main road. Mog didn't even stir.

The Torana growled through the side-streets of some broken suburb, and Gretel looked for a likely place. The new supermarkets like the Bi-Lo were too big, long picked over. Dangerous to enter now.

Houses were too depressing to enter, and just as unsafe. If you were gonna get out of your car, it might as well be worth your while.

She pulled over, smiling. It was a corner store, and yellowed signs offered everything from milk to mixed lollies. While someone had kicked the door in, none of the windows had been smashed.

"That's usually good," she told Mog, who ignored her. Fighting her way out of the driver's seat, she left the motor running, just to be safe. The Torana rumbled like a beast at bay. Looking into the backseat, Gretel considered the big .303 she took on roving trips, but left it behind. She wanted a hand free to snatch up anything the looters had overlooked.

Gretel fished out the service revolver from her pocket. Her dad's .38, well-worn. At close range, it could kill the damn things, but she'd need to be quick.

Never longer than thirty seconds. Booting the door all the way open, she swept the shadows with the gun, heart pounding till she thought she might be sick. No movement, no sound. Good. Gretel picked through the leftovers, stuffing her pockets with the dregs the previous looters didn't think worth taking.

Canned dog food. A jar of Vegemite with the seal intact. Cigarettes. A dirty magazine. Gretel smiled some more, and opened the door to the street.

That's when the hairs stood up on the back of her neck, and she froze. She'd just seen a movement out of the corner of her eye. Everything was still now, but she knew what was about to come.

Shooing Mog away from the dash, Gretel lay down the pistol where she could reach it. She quietly slid into the car with as much grace as she could muster. Making sure the windows were up, she kept her eyes straight ahead.

There. Behind the billboard advertising Chiko Rolls. She saw the barest shadow where it clutched to the back of the sign. A twitching ear. The barest sliver of a questing nose.

Gretel contemplated reverse, but then she dropped it into first gear. Slowly she brought up the revs, felt the torque rock the car from side to side. The wheels fought the hand-brake, and a cloud of smoking rubber began to fill the street.

"How do you like that!" Gretel shouted, punching the steering wheel. Mog hissed from the passenger seat. "Let's play a game of fucking chicken."

Then she dropped the handbrake.

The Torana roared defiance, and shot forward like a red blur. At the last moment Gretel yanked the steering wheel left, then right. She passed underneath the billboard, glanced back as a dark shape fell from above.

Then they were drifting, sliding sideways, and then she fought the car back under control, fishtailing all over the street. Mog settled down, back to sunning and licking himself.

In the rear-vision mirror, she saw a monster pace the street, howling and frustrated. Bigger than a big dog, all claws, teeth, and bad attitude. It gnashed its enormous jaws, and Gretel knew that it could peel apart the steel skin of a car, quicker than anyone ever managed with the jaws of life.

"Fucking drop-bears," Gretel said.

✳

On the highway to Port Wakefield she could often get the Torana up to 120 km/hr or more, but here and there she had to slow down to get over the cracked tarmac in one piece. Just past Two Wells, there was a one kilometre stretch where the road had been washed away by a flood. Many years since the councils had rumbled out with their yellow machines, keeping the roads in good nick.

It was safe out here, more honest. No cars blocking the way, nothing but shitty land and open road. Either side of the highway was a salty marsh, barely interrupted by anything bigger than a box-thorn. The drop-bears had nothing to hide behind, nothing to pounce from.

The folks at Port Wakefield took no chances. Packs of drop-bears still made it out this far, ribs showing and hungry for any meat they could get. At first the traders made do with a barricade of tyres and junk, but now their camp was surrounded by a big wall. Besser bricks, filled with cement and steel rods, rendered over with more cement to give the bears nothing to grip.

Times were good out here.

Gretel guided her car through the steel gates, nodding to the boys tending the fire. The smoke from burning tyres was rumoured to keep drop-bears away, but Gretel had shredded through enough tyres while roving to know that this was wishful thinking.

"Can I go for a ride?" one of the boys asked. He stared at the car in awe, only heaving another retread into the fire-barrel when one of the guards yelled at him. The boys had scarves around their mouths, and sweated from their labour. She put their age as perhaps eight or nine years old.

"Maybe later, kid," Gretel said. She tooted the air-horn as she passed by, and the strains of *La Cucharacha* announced her arrival. Soon a small crowd of kids kept pace with her, watching as the red muscle-car purred into the trading camp of old Port Wakefield.

A row of petrol stations flanked the road, ruins now. There wasn't a drop of fuel left in the place. Around here, they'd gone back to old ways. Horses, buggies, whatever livestock had been saved from the drop-bears. By the jetty, tin dinghies and sailing boats lay at dock. Survivors from the Yorke Peninsula enclaves and even as far as Port Lincoln, come east and south for the good trade.

Gretel parked the car under shade, next to some cob-webbed fuel pumps. She took care to lock up, and left the window down a crack for Mog. Even now when people would kill each other over a litre of fuel, working cars were worth stealing. She almost pitied the poor sod who interrupted Mog's sleep.

The trading camp was the fullest she'd ever seen it. Buggies refitted with car tyres were lined up by the dam, horses hobbled within drinking distance. Fishermen hawked their catch under canvas stands, and another group had just arrived through the north gate, people pushing wheelbarrows from God knew where.

They haggled furiously, survivors trading for food, for old world forage. These days, entertainment traded well, and Gretel found a man missing several fingers, hawking records out of a milk crate. She took a moment to swap her forage for a bottle of scotch, and talked the scarred man out of a Johnny O'Keefe album.

This might break me even for this trip, she thought, and knew she was kidding herself. They kept her debt in a neat ledger back at Stanvac, and the trades never quite matched the fuel she went through. She looked back to her car, admired the bright red paint, the authentic shark gills and rims.

Totally worth it.

Gretel saw the contingent from Alice Springs, over by the livestock pens. Dozens of feral camels were fighting over a water trough, honking and jostling in the sun. After their long journey south, the cameleers were relaxing in their rough camp, a tarp keeping off the worst of the sun.

The outback men were tanned almost to leather, filthy from months of travel. They had a game of cards going, and a jug of flat beer passed from calloused hand to cracked lip and so on around their muttering circle.

When they noticed Gretel approaching, the men talked in low voices, and someone chuckled darkly, like a crow. She knew the words they were saying to each other, even if she couldn't hear them yet. Fat. Ugly. Broken nose. Comments about what she'd be like in bed, and then they'd rib the lowest man in their pecking order to have a go at the big girl.

She stood in front of the desert men, eyes narrowed, lip curled. Someone gave a low whistle, and she felt her bull neck tense up, felt her hands clench into meaty fists.

"I'm looking for Purdie," Gretel said.

"Well, fuck me," one man said. "You look like a fridge wearing clothes."

Even as the cameleers fell about with laughter, one of them got to his feet, smiling broadly. Gavin Purdie, Deputy Prime Minister of Alice Springs. He touched his battered Akubra with his index finger.

Gretel nodded curtly, fighting down the urge to wade into the group, breaking noses and bones. It must have shown in her eyes, and Purdie's broad smile fell.

"Show some fucking respect," he snapped at the others, and the laughter fell back into a low crow murmur, the quiet whisk and slap of cards at play. Purdie offered Gretel a smoke, and she pushed the pack away.

"Let's get to business."

Purdie shrugged, poking the crumpled pack back into his shirt pocket. He led her over to the brace of camels.

"Take a good look. You'll need to vouch for these in Stanvac," he said. "Good stock, plenty of meat on 'em."

Gretel had no idea about anything outside of a car's engine bay. She nodded, pretending to understand as Purdie talked about their operations, the number of beasts they could bring south.

"Once your lot get us the fuel to run our trucks, meat from Alice will feed the entire country," Purdie said. "Mostly camel, but we've got pigs, sheep, some cows."

"Bears ever get into them?"

"We watch our stock day and night," Purdie said flatly. "Anyway, the drop-bears are carking it left and right. Stupid things are starving out, girlie."

"Still thousands in the city," Gretel said. "Only takes one to rip off a man's head."

"The bears are finished," Purdie scoffed. "Time we took everything back."

*

"I used to have one of these when I was a lad," Purdie said for perhaps the tenth time. He was eyeing off the steering wheel, the eight-ball gear-stick, everything polished and kept as new. "Six cylinder LC, and it ran like a horse. Toffee apple coat, fat rims. Dropped knickers every-time I revved the old girl."

Gretel said nothing. When the man wasn't drooling over her car, he was keeping a careful track of the twists and turns she took, which roads were cleared of wrecks and which were deliberate logjams of trucks and buses. Adelaide was a maze now, and the closer they got to Stanvac, the more convoluted the safe passage got.

There were between three and six safe ways for cars and bikes to get through the southern suburbs. But only one way for the fuel truck to get through, a safe road cleared of ambush points and anywhere a bear could drop.

Bastards like Purdie had tried to nick the fuel before, whether enroute to Port Wakefield or south to Victor Harbour and further.

"I haven't even seen a working car in almost ten years," Purdie said. "Every lick of fuel up north, gone. We're down to riding horses, push-bikes, walking around like a miserable pack of mongrels."

Gretel said nothing.

"Big engine like this, must take a fortune to keep it running. You making enough scratch to pay your bills, girly?"

Gretel narrowed her eyes, and Purdie laughed.

"You must be greasing a rich cock just to fill the tank. Or you owe more to that mob than you can ever repay. Don't look at me like that, I can't see how else you do it."

"Purdie," Gretel said in a measured voice. "I swear to God I will throw you out and let the bears have you."

That shut him up for almost a minute.

"Now girly, I want to know something, and I want the truth out of that fat gob."

She gripped the steering wheel hard, knuckles tight.

You play nice, thunderthighs, the Foreman had told her that morning. *You represent us today. If this trade goes wrong, don't bother coming back.*

Tight-lipped, she looked over at the man from Alice. Waited for him to say his piece.

"We've heard stories. That the fuel in Stanvac's running out. Your mob aren't just ekeing out the supply, they're almost tapped out."

Gretel shrugged, downshifted as she slalomed through a precisely fashioned "car-crash". She didn't even have to tap the brakes to get through the intersection. Purdie held onto the ceiling, face white as they came within inches of a burnt out ambulance. The speedo read 80km/hr.

"Jesus, love," he gasped. "Don't fucking kill me."

Gretel said nothing. Mog slid around on the dashboard, glaring murder at the stranger who dared to sit in his car. Soon the chimneys of the oil-refinery came into sight. Port Stanvac, dominating the cliff-face like a cluster of medieval turrets.

It was still fifteen kilometres to the facility, made into twenty by the crafted approach. If Port Stanvac was the castle, the approaches were well-designed curtain walls, capped by "barbicans" of overturned vans. Here were carefully hidden ambush points, caches of weapons in case the mob up north decided to make trouble.

"Would it kill you to make some conversation?" Purdie said. "Can we at least play some music?"

He pointed to the 8-track player, a notion that Gretel had quickly disabused him of early in the trip. The tapes sometimes jammed, and she didn't want to waste any of them on this sleazy cowboy king.

You play nice, thunderthighs.

A heavy sigh fell out of her, and she pointed to the glovebox. Purdie popped it open, and his eyes nearly fell out of his leathery old face.

Almost fifty 8-track cartridges lay neatly stacked. AC/DC, Black Sabbath, Aerosmith. Pink Floyd and Frank Zappa. This collection alone was worth more than she'd made in the last three months of roving.

Eventually Purdie selected *Hotel California* by the Eagles. The lonely strains of the song's protagonist echoed through the pristine sound system, and it suited Gretel's mood as they wound through the final approach to the Fuel Council's stronghold.

"Goddamnit," Purdie said when the tape snapped halfway through. "I ain't heard that song in almost twenty years."

"Now you're never gonna hear it," Gretel said. Yanking out the broken cartridge, she threw it out of the window and into the ruins of the old world.

Even as the Torana negotiated the turns of that metal maze, the cartridge bounced onto the cracked asphalt once, twice. Quick as a flash, a drop-bear broke from hiding, pouncing on the broken tape in the hope that it had snared a mouse.

It spat out the plastic in disgust, and stared at the disappearing car. Several of its fellows emerged from the wreckage, all mange and pronounced ribs. Even the smallest of these was the size of a big dog, with eyes that spoke more of hunger than common sense.

They followed the car, a huge pack of drop-bears that didn't even bother lurking in the shadows now. There was the stink of Man up ahead, all soot and engines, meat and sweat. It was time to eat.

*

"Hope your mob has got something cold to drink in there," Purdie said. "I'm as dry as a nun's nasty."

They were at the gates of Port Stanvac, waiting for the guard to turn off the power and open the gate. The facility was surrounded by so many chain-link fences that it looked like a prison—and of course these were all electrified at night to keep out the bears.

For fifty feet beyond the outer fences, the earth was scorched, fused with fire. Only the scars of surrounding houses and factories remained, every brick long since carted away. Nothing left for a hungry bear to hide behind.

Guards paced a scaffolding walkway behind the inner fence, rifles and crossbows at the ready. At fixed points the defenders had raised flame-throwers, jerry-rigged from hoses and pipes that led back to the fuel-tanks. Others paced the courtyard with home-made Owen guns. Teams with Alsatians checked the fences, watching for any drop-bears attempting to tunnel underneath.

In the middle of this considerable defence sat the refinery itself. A mass of tank farms and cement silos, pipework and gantries, with rusting catwalks connecting everything. Looming over the site, the old brick chimney, now fashioned into a guard tower.

On top of the catwalks and gantries, a small town had grown like a rusty tumour. The survivors of Stanvac had made their rude home of tin shanties a safe distance from the ground. Below, thick tangles of barbed-wire, caltrops forged from sharpened rebar, and more dogs.

You had to be rich to live up there. Gretel wasn't, and didn't.

They swung the gate open and waved her through. It was close to dusk now, and the entire compound would be on a high alert for bears. Even as the sun slid down towards the ocean, teams were lighting the first of the fires. Whumping generators lit a chain of spot-lights, and the beams crept from shadow to shadow, daring a drop-bear to make a run.

Gretel saw how Purdie took in the town defences, the thicket of guns that weren't just there to keep the drop-bears out. She hadn't fully appreciated the need to make this trade in Port Stanvac, but as she saw the bravado evaporate from the desert man's face, she understood.

Fuel was power, and power was coveted. This was all a show for the hick from the bush, a little theatre to keep him in his place.

She pulled over in front of the refinery, and tooted a defiant *La Cucaracha* to let the boss know she was back. They sent an elevator down from those lofty heights, three men working the big winch that lowered the cage.

"Come on," Gretel said. "The Foreman's waiting."

They entered the lift, an old shark-cage refitted for this purpose. Gretel heard the winchmen curse her from above as they wrestled with the big ratchet. Of course she wasn't a ballerina, but they'd moved heavier loads than *her*. They paused twice during the ascent, as if to make a point. Beside her, Purdie had broken out into a sweat, and clenched the rails for dear life.

"What is it?" Gretel grunted at him. "Heights, confined spaces, or me?"

"All of the fucking above."

This was the home of the Fuel Council, and all whom they favoured. As they entered the maze of catwalks, Council guards relieved Gretel of her pistol, and the enormous Bowie knife hanging from Purdie's belt. She was little better than a contractor in the Foreman's eyes, and hardly to be trusted.

Here, the Fuel Council lived in what passed for luxury now. Pinball machines rattled away in one room, and a record player blared Sherbet's "Howzat!" from somewhere deeper in the complex. Fans fought the heat, and did little but blow an everlasting cloud of marijuana and tobacco smoke from one room to another.

Girls with ganja-blank faces lay on pillows, half-naked and numb to everything. Others were on the go-powder, and whizzed about on roller-skates. Everyone was drunk, stoned, or both. Every night a brawl broke out in the Council's sky-town, and barely a week passed without some idiot falling over the railings and breaking his neck.

Gretel and Purdie were ushered up another set of stairs, towards the highest point of the complex. They'd reached the fat tube of the chimney, rooms bolted into its sides with enormous brackets that *just* held on. It was just shy of thirty metres high, and up here, you could see Adelaide laid out from north to south. Huffing up the spiral staircase, Gretel appreciated the view of the bay, saw the oil tanker still rotting in dock far below the cliffs.

Last delivery from a dead world, she mused, and wondered how long the Fuel Council could milk that for.

It was the highest room, with only the crow's nest above it. The Foreman held court here, and rarely ventured down even to the lower levels of the sky-town. The other rovers said that he'd been nipped by a drop-bear once, and was deathly terrified of the things.

Rumour had it that he'd been a spanner-jockey once, back in the old days. Now, the Foreman ran Port Stanvac like a feudal warlord. More than one person had died at a word from his lips, plummeting from the towers, or doused in fuel and torched in the courtyard.

Purdie climbed the stairs, exuding patience and a stockman's calm. Part of Gretel hoped the deal would go sour, just to see what would happen to the man.

A set of plastic shop-strips kept out the flies, and Gretel pushed past these to enter the Foreman's house. The master of Port Stanvac sat in a folding chair, his feet in a plastic wading pool full of water. He wore a kimono over grimy footy shorts, and a shark-tooth necklace was almost lost in his thatch of chest hair. From throat to crotch, his torso was hashed with old scars. Deep, and roughly Y-shaped, as if an animal had attempted an autopsy on him. His eyes were bugged out, glassy. Needles and spoons littered his tiny throne room.

"Gretel, Gretel," he shouted suddenly, flinging out his arms. "Light as a fucking petal."

"Boss," she said. "I brought Purdie."

"Mister Purdie, do come in. I trust my Rubenesque rover delivered you in comfort?"

"That she did, Mister Foreman sir, I—"

"Derwent."

"Derwent, I want to get down to brass tacks. We've got a lot of livestock to move. Prime Minister says to offer meat for fuel. Ongoing trade. For as long as your supplies can hold out."

"Heh. I've heard those rumours too. We're bone dry, running on fumes. This place," the Foreman gestured wildly, kimono sleeves flapping, "will be a ghost town inside of six months."

Purdie stood in front of the drug-addled boss, hands hitched in his belt. He stared down the Foreman with the contempt of the country man for his soft-handed urban cousin, until the latter broke into laughter.

"We've got years' worth of fuel, Mister Purdie. Years. It's simple mathematics. Once there were over a million of us in this fine state. Living, working, driving our cars to and fro. A fuel stoppage would grind the place to a halt within the month. Rationing, the whole box and dice, right?"

Purdie nodded.

"And now that the drop-bears have chewed the place down to the stubble, how many cars do you see driving around now? A few thousand? No? Less than a few hundred?"

There were fewer than a hundred working vehicles within a day's travel, and everyone in Port Stanvac knew this. Because this was the only fuel to be had between the Nullarbor and the eastern seaboard.

"We are still processing crude oil from that tanker. Production is at a fraction of what we can do, because we don't need to make much fuel. Even getting your cattle trucks on the road won't make a dent in our reserves."

His one tactic gone, Purdie simply nodded. Alice Springs wasn't going to roll over Port Stanvac that easily.

"You, tell me what you saw," the Foreman said to Gretel. "Do they have what they say they have? Camels and some such? In good nick?"

"Yes," Gretel said.

"Good. You, fuck off," and he pointed to the door. "And you, pull up a chair."

Gretel left the two important men to their trade deal, and prayed that the creaking shed would shear free of the chimney, plummeting straight to the ground. The image made her smile, even as she huffed and sweated and made her way back downstairs.

✳

"What will you give me?"

"Hmm."

The Bursar poked around in her trade goods. He considered the bottle of booze, examined the record for scratches. Gretel had even broken her own rule, and a half-dozen of her precious eight-track tapes lay on the counter.

"Fifty Stanbucks for the lot."

"Don't insult me, Don."

"Fine. Go somewhere else then."

She got him up to fifty-five, and he wrote the figure down in his ledger. She saw that her page was still well into the red, and that it hadn't even covered the fuel she'd used for that trip.

"I was driving on Council business. You can do better than that."

"Deal was, you could forage on that tank. You need to start bringing in some trade, girl. Or we are going to have to get nasty about this debt."

"I can pay my bills," she said, leaning on the counter. The wood groaned underneath her weight.

"So pay them."

She left the Bursar's warehouse before the Council heavies could throw her out. Behind the wire-mesh barrier lay a fortune in loot, which grew with every squirt of petrol and mouldered in the dark.

Gretel panicked, wondered what she would do next. There was no other option but Port Stanvac, not if she wanted to keep her beast of a car on the road. She owed more money than she could hope to repay, and they'd let her hang herself, one tank of petrol at a time.

If the Bursar told the Foreman just how the books were looking, he'd probably stake her out for the drop-bears to munch on. Or cut her hamstrings, and put her in the fuck-shack to pay off her debt.

I just need to talk them out of one last tank of petrol, she decided. *And then I will get the fuck out of here.*

Gretel drove away from the Bursary, rumbling across the courtyard. She made her way through the outbuildings, the poor part of town. These people paid away a fortune in loot for a spot on a cement floor, for days of back breaking labour in the plant.

Flush against the inner fence was the rover's shed. A workshop from the old days, this was home for the dozen or so scavengers who ran the roads in Stanvac's name.

Gretel guided the Torana into the bay she'd claimed as her own, settled the car square over the pit. She saw that everyone was in from the road, and the shed rang with spanners, arc-welders, and colourful language. She climbed out of the car, and Mog disappeared into the shadows on his own errands.

"Look out, here comes ten tonnes of fun," someone shouted, and she responded with her middle finger. Someone laughed, but in a good natured way. She'd earned her place here.

There was Percy, an old poof with a FJ panel-van and more miles on his face than anyone. "Wog" Carlotto had his HQ Monaro halfway through a service, blower out and oil everywhere. Louis and Mick were Ford men, with a Mark II Escort and XB Falcon respectively.

Others she was less friendly with, but no-one was stupid enough to fight her anymore. It was easier just to work on your machine, tell bullshit stories about what you'd seen on the road, and leave the "psycho butch" alone.

At the thought of leaving this place forever, Gretel felt despondent. This was the only world she knew, but it was time to start over. Maybe she'd make it up to Coober Pedy or even Alice Springs, work in an enclave. Dream of some place where the siphoning was good and the drop-bears all starved out.

Gretel moved through the dank corner that passed for her bedroom, quietly scooping up belongings and stuffing them into a bag. The sum total of her life came to some tools, a handful of dirty clothes, toys from when Mog was a kitten, and a dog-eared copy of "Picnic at Hanging Rock". Last month, she'd traded in her mum's jewellery box on a full tank, and the promise of enough trade to get the heirloom out of hock.

They tore up her slip when she couldn't pay, moved a number over to the bad side of the ledger. Her debt was growing, eating up everything she was, nibbling at her future.

"Thinking of leaving us, love?" someone muttered at her elbow, and she was ready to come out swinging when she realised it was only Percy. The world had given him little more than wrinkled skin, a twinkle in his eye and a thick white beard. But still, he had moments of kindness. He'd done a turn as Father Christmas a few years ago, when this place still bothered with such things.

"Just doing some washing," she said, slinging the bag in through the driver's window. He nodded in understanding, and nudged a tin forward with his foot.

"All I can spare you," he said, and was gone before Gretel realised he'd left her five litres of super. She smiled, and her heart broke just a little more.

The rovers lived much like a commune, and boosted the nightly stew delivery from the "commons" cart with their own collection of scavenged tins and condiments. Wog broke out a backgammon set—this was the game of choice in rover circles.

Gretel staked a cartridge of Richard Clapton, and lost it to Mick on her second game. When the moonshine jug passed around their circle, she passed it on without touching the potent muck.

Tonight, she needed her wits about her.

Gretel helped Wog put the head and everything else back into the Monaro. When he turned the key it roared like a dragon, and the big Italian smiled.

"Got a run tomorrow to Victor Harbour," he said. "You want to come with?"

She'd ridden shotgun—literally—for Wog before. Plenty of drop-bears on the southern run. He paid well, and it was *fun* to ride in the big HQ. Even if he listened exclusively to disco.

She looked over at the Torana, the way the red paint gleamed in the flickering lamplight. She'd started off as a spanner monkey, then gone on runs. Got a taste for the life, the feel of thousands of horses under her right foot. She shook her head.

"Suit yourself," Wog said.

"Got another job on."

He nodded. She'd only gotten that Port Wakefield run because everyone else was out on the road. Everyone knew Gretel was on the outer, but none of the rovers realised just how badly.

"Take my advice. You're not a driver who forages. You're a forager who drives."

Gretel nodded. It was far too late for advice.

Mick played some Slim Dusty on the record player. The fences were quiet that night, apart from one rifle-shot, and the *whoof* of burning fuel as the guards cooked a drop-bear that got too close. Over at the sky-town, a party was in full swing, complete with the sounds of laughter, breaking glass, and vomit raining onto the cement far below. Soon, a Council runner came to the rover's shed, already the worse for wear with grog.

"Foreman's invited you all upstairs," he slurred. "Big trade deal just went down. Drinks and ganja on the house, fuck-shack for free."

That got the rovers moving. It wasn't often the Fuel Council opened the liquor cabinet to the ground dwellers. In moments the shed emptied, laughter and horseplay following the men towards the elevators.

Percy paused in the doorway, nodding at Gretel. There was nothing left to say. Soon she was the only one left in the workshop, and she couldn't believe her good luck.

First, fuel up, she thought. *Then I nick enough food to see me well away from this place, and talk my way past the gate while the party is in full swing.*

Easy.

She took a quick stroll across the courtyard, enough to see that the plant bowsers were still under heavy guard. Over at the Bursary, the lights still blazed, and shadows could be seen moving inside.

Taking turns to attend the party, the guard seemed to be running at about two-thirds full strength tonight. But the search-lights still swept relentlessly, and the gates were buttoned up tight.

Heart sinking, she returned to the workshop. Her Plan B was less than honourable, but she was desperate now.

She moved from bay to bay with her siphoning hose and jerry-can. If she was caught doing this, all bets were off. Rover justice was just as fast and brutal as anything the Foreman could mete out.

Cracking open the Wog's petrol tank, she drew out a little over two litres down the garden hose. Percy added another litre to his recent donation. Mick and Louis added two litres each, and she moved down the line, taking just enough that the others wouldn't notice.

Even as Gretel crouched behind the last car, shaking a few more drops into her jerry-can, she heard footsteps, someone entering the shed. She froze. If they found her back here . . .

The steps echoed closer, but then stopped. The visitor turned, paced along the row of vehicles. As if looking for someone.

"Gretel. Gretel!" a man shouted. It was Purdie. He sounded three-sheets-to-the-wind drunk, and she risked a glance around the car, saw him swaying on his feet. He'd lost his hat somewhere, and was barely able to see, let alone walk.

She pushed the jerry-can underneath the car, made sure to hide the siphoning hose. Standing up slowly, she walked out of the other rover's bay, as if she had all the reason in the world to be poking around another man's machine.

"There you are, sweetheart," Purdie slurred. "You're missing the party."

"I don't go up there if I don't have to," Gretel said, nodding in the direction of the sky-town. "So, what is it?"

"You. You've got something that I want," the man crowed. He stared at her with glassy eyes, and grinned, as if sharing a confidence.

"Not interested," Gretel said. "Go to the fuck-shack."

"No. Oh, no no no. I'm talking about *that*."

He pointed to her car. The cherry-red LJ Torana with the 3300 engine, the car of her dreams. The beast she'd restored with her own two hands, had gone into a mountain of debt over. She had a rapport with this car, and just as she'd saved its life, it had often saved hers.

"You have got to be fucking kidding," she said. "That's my car. It's not for sale, dickhead."

"Well, that's not up to you," Purdie said. He spent a long moment looking at the Torana, admiring the polish, the shark-gill cut-outs, the rims that Gretel buffed to a shine whenever she came back from a run.

"What are you talking about?" Gretel said. A cold fury rose from her core, threatening to take over everything. The big man from Alice was looking at her car with the same fuck-eyes a man gave a beautiful girl, and Gretel didn't like it one bit.

"They've called in your tab," Purdie said. "Your bossman said he's done with you. Should have heard the things he was planning to do to you, girlie." He shivered for effect, smiling broadly.

"But don't worry, Gretel. I talked the man around. He wants to keep me happy, see, and now I've fixed everyone's problem. You're debt-free, Gretel."

Her chest squeezed tight at the words, and the fury bubbled over, sending a cold fire tickling through her body. Her hands were fists, and just like that she was in a place beyond common sense.

"When I leave tomorrow, I'm leaving in this. This is my car now."

Purdie leaned in through the driver's window, popped the hood open.

"This whole machine is a credit to your skill," he said, leaning on the edge of the engine bay. "Bloody immaculate."

The sight of the man leering over the car, *her car*, was more than Gretel could bear. She sobbed, and staggered away, shaking her head. *She'd been so close.* He continued to enthuse over the car, oblivious to her heartbreak.

"There's a place for you in Alice," Purdie said, fiddling with the distributor cap. "Come with me, and I'll put you to work on fixing our trucks."

Brushing against a trolley, Gretel was blinded with tears, and her hands fumbled through the detritus of oil cans, a socket set, needle-nose pliers. Finally, her hands closed around what she was after.

"What do you say, girlie? You'll have a better future up there with our mob. You might even find a fella. Miners get pretty lonely, heh."

She sidled up to the engine bay, weeping openly. He ignored her, more interested in his new toy, and she stood behind him snuffling, said his name quietly.

"What?" he said, annoyed, and turned around just in time to catch a 24-inch spanner across the face. He crumpled backwards in a mess of blood and teeth, and grabbed at the car blindly, moaning, fumbling for something to defend himself with.

Gretel hit him again with the spanner, and this time she knocked all the fight out of the man. He sagged across the front of the car, coughing and sobbing and dripping blood and spit all over everything.

"You want the fucking car?" Gretel shouted. "It's yours!"

She slammed the hood down on his head, once, twice. By the third time, Gavin Purdie wasn't moving anymore.

*

A thousand eyes watched the refinery that night. They stayed just out of reach of the bright lights, wise to the tricks of Man. Hunger bred canny, and only one of the runts broke cover, dead and charred before he could reach that first fence.

The moon was full tonight, and so the beasts moved slowly, bellies flat to the grass. They got as close to the fence as the weak eyesight of Man allowed them to, and looked for a way in.

They'd hunted in packs before, but never to this scale. They possessed the rudiments of tactics, as all predators do, but their slow advance wasn't the action of a regiment. It was a body of ants, of locusts, rolling forward, following the path of least resistance. They had reached a critical mass, and had to operate to new rules.

Back in the old, familiar world, they'd been at the top of the food chain. Apex predators, fierce and unopposed. One of them alone could take out a Diprotodon, a creature half again the size of the cows of this world.

At their lead was a scarred old beast, one of the last to be drawn through the veil of time. The younger ones, pups who had only known this soft world, feared and respected this one. He followed the mesh fence patiently, sniffing at the watching guards, heeding the stink of their guns. There were others behind these shepherds, hundreds of soft throats, braying and playing stupidly in the night.

The *Thylacoleo Carnifex* was an ambush predator, designed for maximum damage. It had a bite comparable to any of the big cats, with teeth that could shear through bone. The marsupial lions had operated well in the Pleistocene era, and did even better in this one.

A favoured tactic was to drop on their prey from above—they just weren't built for speed, for chasing anything over a great distance. The Men clutched at their tools, dubbed the invaders "drop-bears", and told jokes to salve the cosmic joke of this invasion. For all their godlike skills, the bald creatures of this time had died by the millions.

The scarred beast ignored the three main fences of the refinery. They were too well kept, and Men were in place, watching for their approach. The drop-bears were wary of the guns now, scared of the whistling arrows and crossbow bolts. These days, they had to earn their meat the smart way.

Finally, they'd circled the whole fence line, and the battered old veteran looked out on the bay, animal eyes considering the moonlight on the water. All of this had been covered in a glacier in his time, and in the depths of his hind-brain, this barely-realised anachronism made him angry.

The old drop-bear slipped over the cliff's edge, clutching at the chalky clay with his sharp claws. It was a long way down to the sharp rocks, and the rusting hulk tied to the pier looked like a leaf on a pond.

He fought for purchase, slipped and scrabbled across the cliff-face. The fences ended in a cluster of tiger wire and barbed strands, and it was necessary to climb down for several metres to get around the sparking, dangerous tangle. Behind him, another drop-bear attempted the crossing, and another. One slipped and scratched at the air for purchase, mewling the whole way down.

The cliff-face was sheer, and the current lodgers of the refinery had designed their fortification like a Tintagel. Only a token fence stood here to keep out anything stupid enough to scale the cliff. The wire-mesh was patchy, long worn to rust by the salt in the air.

The old drop-bear made it down and around the edge of the fence. He climbed up over the lip of the cliff, eyes narrowed as he took in the lights, the sounds of so many Men.

He ran for a gap in the fence, the thrill of the chase rising in his heart. For one brief instant, the scarred old beast felt no hunger, felt nothing but the most primitive urge. Slay, eat, repeat.

He was halfway through the wire before the electricity killed him. Others bounced from the barrier, charred and plummeting into the black ocean below, but the old bear shuddered and shook, joined by others who tried to claw through similar gaps.

Under the weight of such a sustained assault, the electric fence finally failed. Soon the bears were pouring in through gaps in the fence, and whole sections of rusted mesh crumpled under their weight.

The few guards watching in that direction were drunk, the rest absent. Above, the party continued, oblivious to the horde of drop-bears swarming into their midst.

The stereo thumped out Skyhooks" "Ego is Not a Dirty Word", the fuel barons fought and fucked, and the pinball machines rang out into the night like a chorus of dinner bells.

*

Gretel stood by the front of her car, numb with shock. She staggered past the remains of Gavin Purdie, slipping in the blood. She fell heavily to one knee, even as a spray of vomit fought its way past her lips.

She got to her feet to see Wog Carlotto standing behind her, mouth open, the backgammon set forgotten in his hands.

"Wog . . . I—"

"What the fuck," he whispered. "What the fuck did you do?"

"He was gonna take it," she cried. "He was gonna take my car."

Wog stared at the mess, gagged when he saw the caved-in head, the mess of brain and skull splattered all over the front of the Torana. Even as Gretel fussed around, trying to wrap the body in a tarp, Wog stood back, arms folded.

"This is on you," he said. "We can't protect you."

She wiped away a rope of snot from her face, nodded.

"You know I'm going to have to tell the Foreman. You killed the big man in our shed. In *our* fucking shed! You fat fucking idiot!" Wog threw the backgammon set across the workshop, kicked over buckets and toolboxes and anything that got in his way.

"It was an accident," Gretel said, numb to Wog's abuse. She began to mop up the blood and gore, and quickly gave it up as a waste of effort. It would take her hours to clean the murder scene, time she didn't have. Dragging Purdie's body to one side, she used the mop-water to sluice his life-fluids from the front of her car.

There was a scream from near the sky-town, long and loud. They both flinched at the sound. The party was still in full swing, and there was laughter, the sound of smashing glass.

"You fucked up, Gretel," Wog finally said. "I'll give you five minutes to pack up your shit and go. No more."

"Thanks," Gretel said. Wog merely shook his head, leaving the shed without saying another word. In moments, Gretel had the fuel-can in the boot, stuffed her bedding into the back-seat, and walked around the shed with a beating heart, jingling her keys and whistling for Mog.

"Come on, you stupid bloody cat," she whispered. "We've gotta go. Quickly!"

Finally the battered tom appeared, dragging a dead rat into the shed. He dropped it at her feet, rubbing at her legs and proud.

"Sadly, that's not the most disgusting thing I've seen tonight," Gretel said. She hurled the cat into the car by the scruff of his neck, and got behind the wheel.

❋

When Wog Carlotto finished telling his story to the Bursar, the man pressed his lips together, picked up the phone. A dedicated line to the sky-town, cobbled together from spit and copper wire.

"Derwent," the unsmiling man said into the handpiece. "The fat rover killed Purdie. In their shed. Of course his mob will find out. Forget the trade. Trade's fucked now."

"Yes boss," he said finally, and hung up the phone. He clicked his fingers, and the Council goons instantly sprung from their slouching game of cards, all leather and spikes.

"You boys, grab your gear. Rover," and here he looked to Wog, "you're coming too. Boss wants her alive, but not too much."

Thus commandeered, Wog accepted the cricket-bat that the Bursar pushed into his hands. He was philosophical about this turn of events. Friends became scum at the drop of a hat, and the bossman filled up the cars and kept them in food.

The hard men crossed the compound, only to see the Torana blast out of the shed, wheels chewing up the dirt. Gretel was headed straight for them.

The thugs scattered, but the Bursar stood calmly in the glow of her headlights, a crossbow raised. He contemplated the difficult shot, but at the last moment he smiled, stepping aside.

The Torana roared past the jumped-up pawnbroker, missing him by inches. The muscle-car punched through the first set of gates, shearing through the locked gate as if it was made of tissue-paper.

"Looks like you rovers are about to earn your keep," the Bursar said to Wog. "Party's over."

Gretel had reached the outer gates now, and made no sign of slowing. The guards sprayed her car with twinkling rifle fire, only jumping away at the last moment. The LJ Torana ploughed through the electrified fence, leaving a tangle of wire and steel in its wake.

Wog smiled. Clear as a bell he could hear the strains of AC/DC's "Jailbreak", blasting out of Gretel's Torana, echoing out into the still night.

✳

"I want her in chains," the Foreman screamed into the phone. "I'll feed that fat slut to the bears, one toe at a time."

He slammed the phone into the cradle, breaking the Bakelite handset. Storming over to the squawking record player, he threw it out of the nearest window. The sound of the Bay City Rollers continued for one long second, until the portable player exploded on the cement far below.

He was greeted with a chorus of complaints from the party, and came out swinging. He sent the girls back to the fuck-shack, one with a bloody nose. A ground dweller protested about being sent back downstairs, and the Foreman tossed him over the railing to make a point.

He herded a posse of drunk gunmen to the armoury, press-ganging the rovers and anyone else too slow to hide from his fury. He handed out all of the good gear, scavenged from police stations and the RAAF base. Assault rifles, mortars, a light machine gun, a bazooka, sniper rifles that could hit a shadow on the moon. Weighed down with this arsenal, the Council shooters staggered towards the elevators.

Only half of the winch-men could be found, the others drunk or comatose. The lifts descended with maddening slowness, and with bug-eyed junkie fury the Foreman screamed his frustration out into the night.

"Wind quicker, you fuckers!" he shouted. "She's getting away!"

Scanning the horizon for signs of Gretel's escaping Torana, the Foreman didn't notice the silence below. Guard-posts unmanned, the first flicker as an outbuilding went up in flames. Big shapes darting through the shadows.

"You lot, we're going in your cars," he told Percy and the other rovers. "You know all the squirrelly ways she might run. If that bitch of yours gets away, you'll share her punishment."

"Gretel?" Percy said. "What's she done?"

"Speak again, and I'll nail your tongue to your forehead," the Foreman said, and that was as democratic as he got.

The cage cars reached the ground. The Foreman herded his army towards the rover shed, pistol whipping anyone too slow to move.

"Don? What are you doing, you grizzled old knacker-guts?" he said, squinting through a heroin haze as the Bursar ran across the compound, waving his arms frantically.

He heard the first scream. A growl, interrupted by a gunshot and turning into a yelp. When he heard the yip of drop-bears on the hunt, the Foreman turned around slowly, and his heart sank into the depths of his greasy shorts.

Drop-bears in their hundreds, running loose in his refinery. The livestock screamed and pressed against their fences, bleating and helpless as they were slaughtered in their pens. The ground-dwellers were being hunted from building to building, and he saw a drop-bear snatch a young boy out of a shattered window by the neck.

The Foreman felt his balls contract, dry-reaching as his worst fears were realised. They were everywhere, foxes in the hen-house. The guards on the outer fences were only just now realising the danger within, training their guns and flamers inward.

Then those around him were yelling, shooting in every direction. A wave of drop-bears was leaping from a nearby roof, snapping and growling. At least a hundred of the beasts, and they'd crept to within thirty feet of him before anyone noticed.

The Foreman moaned with terror, emptying clip after clip of bullets into that horde. Someone's gun jammed, and in moments the unfortunate man was covered in bears. They dragged him beneath the refinery, and the man screamed as he was eaten alive.

In the chaos, someone loaded a rocket into the bazooka tube. It skimmed above the drop-bears' heads, and almost instantly punched into a fuel silo.

Man and beast alike were knocked prone by the explosion. For one moment, night became day, and the Foreman saw the sheer number of monsters who'd crept through his fences.

Then a second fuel tank erupted, and another. A pipe leading towards the tank farm cracked under the heat, and if that went up . . .

"Run. Run, you idiots!" he shouted. Perhaps half of the people who'd stepped out the elevators moments ago were still breathing. The Foreman made a bee-line for the Bursar, who was waving and shouting from just outside the rover's shed.

Behind them, some of the drop-bears began to scale the elevator ropes, drawn to the smell of those hidden in the sky-town. The winch-men were too late to draw the elevators back up, and ran for their lives.

The fire was in the pipes now, and in one sickening moment the fuel bowsers and generators all went up. Some of the guards on the fence became flaming marionettes, their flame-throwers erupting in their hands.

"Get inside," the Bursar was shouting, and rover and gunmen alike ran into the shed, piling into the motley collection of hotrods and muscle-cars.

"She did this," the Foreman said, shaken and sweaty. He needed his gear badly, but the best drugs were under lock and key in his room, high above the burning compound. He slid into the passenger's seat of Wog Carlotto's HQ Monaro, a thousand horses under the hood now rumbling and ready to gallop.

"She let those bears in, Wog. I'm gonna catch that bitch, and I'm going to fuck her up."

"Sure thing boss," Wog Carlotto said quietly.

A dozen cars rolled out of the shattered front gates. Big guns chattered out of the open windows, driving off the handful of drop-bears that ran to investigate the noise.

As the convoy drove towards Adelaide, the tank-farm caught a spark. Port Stanvac erupted into a furious blaze of flame, the explosion visible for miles. A moment later, the flames danced down through the pipes and reached the oil in the tanker. The sides of the ship erupted into fire and smoke, and it flipped over like a toy boat, destroying the pier. It shuddered and sank in seconds.

"We're finished, boss," the Bursar said from the backseat, as dry as a man who'd lost nothing. The Foreman was silent, reloading his pistol with shaking fingers.

*

Gretel ran the car hard up the Lonsdale Highway, and the AC/DC blaring out of the stereo matched her mood. She got as far as Seacliff before the engine shuddered, coughed, and finally rattled into silence.

The Torana rolled to a stop, just near the ANZAC monument. Lugging out the fuel-can one-handed, Gretel trained her revolver on the shadows, listened for a rustle in the overgrown hedges.

What she heard was the fat thunderclap from the south, a ball of flame and smoke marking where Port Stanvac had once stood. She watched, gob-smacked as her former home went up in a series of brilliant explosions.

"Holy shit," she said. Gretel felt a flood of relief, followed quickly by shame and guilt. She was safe now, and not a moment too soon. Place had always been a death-trap, run by incompetent junkies. She'd escaped the clutches of the Foreman, all evidence of her crime burnt to ash—but her friends were most likely all dead.

Aiming the jerry-can at the funnel, she cursed herself when she spilled half a cup of fuel onto the road. The sweet liquid poured into the Torana's belly, and by the light of the burning oil refinery, Gretel wondered if she would ever fuel up again.

Definitely going north, she decided. *Up to Port Wakefield, and sell the car before they hear about this disaster. Buy passage on a boat to Port Lincoln, and keep running.*

Still, I get to drive the old girl one last time.

A stick snapped behind her. Gretel dropped the jerry-can to the ground, more precious fuel sloshing out over the sides, gun up and tracking for a drop-bear. She watched the hedges by the memorial statue, big heart hammering. By the time you heard one, you usually had about two seconds before it tore your head off.

The bushes parted, and Gretel zeroed in on the threat, applying pressure to the trigger. When Mog emerged with a twitching pigeon clamped in his mouth, she almost considered shooting him anyway.

— 232 —

"Stupid bloody cat. You scared the shit out of me! Well go on. You can take your revolting dinner into the car."

Smiling, she lifted the jerry-can to finish fuelling up, and that's when she heard the engines, saw the glow of headlights. Someone flicked on a bank of spotlights, and she blinked at the sudden glare on the pitch-dark road.

Snapping the lid shut, she heaved the jerry-can into the back seat. It was still half full. Gretel threw herself behind the driver's wheel, swearing. Booting the car into life, she saw that she'd only filled up one-third of the tank.

Gretel looked over to Mog, who was steadily ignoring her as he tore feathers out of the dead bird. Throwing the stick into second gear, she punched the accelerator pedal to the floor, and when she dropped the clutch the Torana leapt forward like a greyhound from the starting box.

Bare seconds later, she had the big LJ up in fourth, pushing 90km/hr. She took the last bend onto Brighton Road at speed, drifting almost sideways with a squeal of rubber echoed by the horrified Mog, who almost slid out of the open window, pigeon and all.

Weaving through the artfully placed wrecks, Gretel glanced at the rear-view mirror. At least ten cars were following her through the reef of dead vehicles, all making for her with great speed. She realised then that she wasn't the greyhound. She was the rabbit.

She reached for the CB radio under the dash, flicked it into life. The American radios had still been unauthorised for use when the bears came, and found mainly in trucks and the homes of ham enthusiasts. The rovers had found a few, treated them like gold.

The rovers had a standing arrangement to talk on Channel 3 when on the road, and when Gretel flicked over she heard familiar voices, speculating on where she was going. Three cars were heading over to South Road, in case she tried to slip through the side-streets.

They'd shared a meal only a couple of hours ago. Now, her former comrades were rounding her up, doing their best to cut her off from a clear escape. Worst of all, she heard the nasal strine of the Foreman, dominating the airwaves as he directed the fleet of cars, urged the rovers to run her off the road.

"Get her!" he shouted. "Make her pay for what she did."

"You're all idiots," she said, thumbing the mic. "I can hear everything you're saying."

"You're gonna die, Gretel," the Foreman shouted. "I'm gonna break you apart, I'm—"

"What a dickhead," Gretel said to Mog, switching off the squawking radio. She put a Foghat cartridge into the 8-track, and focussed on the dangerous road.

The first strains of "Drivin' Wheel" blasted out of the speakers. Gretel saw the flicker of headlights closing in fast in her mirror, someone driving with suicidal abandon. It was Mick in his XB Falcon, and the battered old tank bounced from wreck to wreck. He clipped a wing mirror, and wiped out a stop-sign without missing a beat.

Soon he was nipping at her heels, tapping at her rear bumper almost playfully. Gretel veered left, putting an overturned cement mixer between them. Her car was faster on the straight, but Mick was ploughing through debris, heedless of the damage to his own machine.

Something struck her side panels like a sledgehammer. Again, and then she saw the man leaning out of the passenger window, working the slide action on a shotgun. A council thug, face wild with speed and howling for her blood. He unleashed another round of buckshot into the side of the Torana, and she winced at the sound.

The other cars were closer now. She could make out Wog's HQ, Percy's panel-van, the whole pack of Cadillacs and muscle-cars. Mick was tying her up with evasive manoeuvres, robbing her of speed. Another flash of the shotgun, and her rear window shattered in a spray of glass. A few of the glass slivers sliced at her neck, wasp stings that made her swear and grit her teeth.

"Hang on, Mog," she gasped, yanking up the handbrake. The Torana shuddered, swung away from the main road. Downshifting, she punched through an overgrown front yard, obliterating two picket fences and bypassing the truck parked across the mouth of the side-street.

She flicked off her headlights, took care to never touch her brakes. Gretel stole through the backstreets, navigating by moonlight alone. From time to time she saw headlights pass by. They were hunting her on the side-streets, roaring down the old alleyways the shit-carts used to take, knocking over bins gone long rotten for want of a garbo. Their rolling lights painted the dead houses, cast the shadows of wild trees across iron fences.

It was Mick who kept the closest. Something in his drunkard's logic kept him close to her heels, and blind luck would have him onto her if she didn't slip away soon. Gretel looked for a shed to pull into, but even as she cast around, she saw shapes moving against the moonlight, a quick silhouette on a rooftop and then gone. Dropbears, stirred up by all the noise. She couldn't stop.

Then she rolled past the corner store, saw the familiar billboard advertising Chiko Rolls. She saw the shapes crouching there, waiting for her to pass underneath, and she smiled. She stopped just shy of the ambush point, could feel dozens of hungry eyes on her. Once she left the middle of the street, the moment she was close to an eave or fence, they'd make their move.

Gretel revved the shit out of the 3300 engine, and leaned on the airhorn for all she was worth. *La Cucaracha* blared across the dead suburb, over and over again.

They came around the corner like over-eager dogs. Two cars. Mick in his XB, almost colliding with one of the Cadillac boys and at the last moment punching through a mail-box like it was made of tissue paper.

Gretel had the car in a slow reverse, now flicking her headlights in time with the garish mariachi tune. Then the two cars passed beneath the billboard, and she saw the dark shapes tumble from above, drop-bears by the dozen. Fat muscled shapes that smashed at glass, buckling roofs and shearing through the tin in seconds.

The Cadillac was covered with wriggling drop-bears, and in his panic to shake them loose the driver ploughed straight into the corner-store. The American car went up in a fireball, roasting bear and man alike.

Mick got closer, keeping his car aimed straight at her. Ford raced towards Holden, and not even a coat of monsters could persuade the drunken Irishman away from his final assault.

Gretel punched it then, reversing in a panic. The XB nudged her bumper, and even as she fought to stay on the road, she look forward, straight into Mick's eyes.

He was already dead. A bear had his head almost free of his neck, and the hands that clenched the steering wheel were no longer attached to the rest of him. The drop-bears were efficiently stripping the carcasses of all meat, before the car had even stopped rolling.

The camber of the road took the XB over the curb, and into someone's front yard. Gretel took no pleasure from that final sight, and long after she left the scene she could still see the car rocking back and forth, the headlights painting an abandoned swing-set, the shadows of the drop-bears as they ate their fill.

✳

They got her on the way through Adelaide.

Each road she tried the other rovers had already been to, hauling wrecks with winches to block off the main roads. She heard them on the CB radio, goading her, barking misdirections and threats. They'd blocked all the roads north, all the sneaky ways she might take to get to Port Wakefield. She could see bright headlights in the parklands to the south. Cars watching the ways out of Colonel Light's square mile, daring her to double-back, to make a run for Victor Harbour after all.

Teeth gritted, she played their game. All through the little side streets and alleys she raced them, but there were just too many cars to shake. One bloke with a rusty old Charger stuck to her like glue, nipping at her bumper. He was joined by a souped-up T-Bucket, which belched flames and herded her as sure as a kelpie drove the sheep to the knacker-truck.

Rundle Mall.

Fishtailing through the rubbish and rubble, Gretel could barely spare the ruins a glance. Behind her, the Foreman's men were leaning out of the car windows, spraying her Torana with gun-fire. They were aiming low, and it sounded like a symphony of hammers on the boot and bumper. They were trying to wreck the tires and force her to a halt.

There was no way to get out of the shopping strip, and she knew what was waiting for her a moment before the lights came on, blinding her. Four cars, spotlights on, and a rank of outlines in silhouette, guns out and blazing.

The volley of bullets made a mess of her radiator, shattered her headlights. Two bullets starred her windshield, but the glass held. Gretel felt the front-right tyre burst, and fought the slide, the rim sending up a shower of sparks as it ground against the flagstones.

A long-dry water fountain loomed in front of her. Even as Gretel jumped on the brake she knew she'd hit it at speed. The Torana met the masonry. Gretel flew forward, steering wheel breaking at least one rib, and her head flipped forward and down, slamming her face against the dashboard.

Groggy, nose leaking blood, Gretel had no fight in her as they levered her door open. The Torana was absolutely fucked. Everything was buckled, and it took three men to get her out of the car. She looked up through one half-closed eye to see the Foreman reach into her car, pulling out the mangled corpse of Mog.

"Look! It's a broken pussy!" he shouted, shaking the dead cat in his hand. Gretel screamed at the sight, swearing and trying to fight her way out of the huddle of men it took to hold her down.

The Foreman turned and punted Mog's body into the darkness. The men cheered, and a few moments later came the snarls of the dropbears, the ripping sounds as they made short work of the cat. *Her* cat.

Next they dragged her across the pavement, whooping, spitting on her, kicking her in the ribs and gut like she was a big slab of wriggling pork. As her broken bones grated against each other she cried out, and this just drove them on even more.

Soon they had her on top of a car bonnet, heavy men leaning on her arms and legs, pinning her down like a big butterfly on a board. Gretel fought them, fought like a mongrel, but it didn't matter. They had her.

She noticed that she was on top of Wog's beautiful HQ. Wog Carlotto and Percy were at the edges of this slavering pack, she noticed, but they were in the pack nonetheless. They didn't say a word, didn't raise a hand to help her.

"You burned down our town, ya fucking mole," the Foreman grunted in her ear.

"Let those fucking bears in, too," someone else said.

"I . . . don't know what you're talking about," she said, and a moment later she was sucking for air, winded as the Bursar drove the butt of a rifle into her guts. Hard.

"We had a good thing going. A real home," the Foreman said, dripping sweat and spit down into her face. "We were rich! Good looking birds, anything we wanted. Now we got nothing."

Someone started tugging on her boots, trying to pull them off her big feet. The Foreman grinned down at her, and all at once several hands were yanking at her shirt buttons, trying to undo her belt and zip.

Even as Gretel went someplace else in her mind, determined to blank out what was about to happen, she heard the first scream, the stutter of a semi-automatic. The noise broke the group-lust like a bucket of cold water, and in seconds they were snatching up their guns. One bloke already had his pants down to his knees, and tried to hitch them up and load his shotgun all at the same time.

Coughing up blood and snot, Gretel sat up, and in numb horror she saw them coming. Dozens, hundreds of drop-bears, spilling out of the ruined store-fronts and swarming towards them like flies to a meat-tray. The men did a messy approximation of a fighting withdrawal, guns barking out into that hungry mass as they backed towards the cars.

Rifle cracking, Louis wandered too close to the eaves out the front of John Martins. More drop-bears fell on him from above, a waterfall of fur and claws that came pouring out of the windows, dropping from the roof. Louis screamed for one long terrible moment, and then there was nothing but the ripping of meat, the grunting and squabbling of animals over a carcase.

In the face of that starved advance, the rovers tossed down their guns and ran for their muscle-cars and hot-rods. The motors roared defiance, chewing through the last of the petrol they were likely to ever see. In seconds, they'd laid down rubber, abandoning what was left of the Fuel Council.

"You pack of fucking cunts!" the Foreman screamed at their tail lights. He was almost surrounded by drop-bears, and in a mad panic he sprayed an M16 in all directions, emptying the clip to little effect. He shot one of his own men by mistake, and peeled a shotgun out of the dying man's hands.

Gretel leaned into the wreck of her Torana, wincing at the pain in her side. She emerged with the big .303 rifle. Climbing onto the roof of the LJ, she picked off drop-bears with a calmness that she didn't feel. There were so many it was almost impossible to miss.

Then the tide of flesh and fur had reached her car, and she was cut off from escape. Two men climbed up on the roof to join her. The Foreman, blood-spattered, working the empty slide of the pump action. The Bursar, his pinch-faced little lackey to the bitter end.

"Gimme your gun," the Foreman demanded, waving his hand at her. He was so preoccupied with the advancing bears that he barely noticed when Gretel levelled the big rifle in his direction.

"It's all yours," she said, and with one pull of the trigger the Foreman gained a fist-sized hole in his guts. White-faced with shock, he clutched at the wound, and slid down from the roof in a mess of guts and blood.

The bears went berserk with this latest offering, and Gretel jumped down from the roof, pushing through the feeding frenzy with her boots and her rifle butt. Those that weren't feasting on the dead man tried to nip at her, and she let the revolver blaze a path to freedom. Six roaring bullets and she was clear and running.

She looked back only once, to see the Bursar still standing on the roof of her car. *He could have run too*, Gretel thought. Very calmly, the man put his pistol against the roof of his mouth, and he blew his own brains out.

Gretel took the opportunity to run like fucking Phar Lap.

❋

Drop-bears weren't very fast on the ground; they were ambush predators, built for surprise attacks, the quick pounce. Their limb proportions and muscle mass slowed them down. It was possible to outrun them, but the squat little killers had stamina. People had to stop running sooner or later, and on land the drop-bears relied on tiring out their prey.

Gretel barrelled through the night streets of Adelaide like a fridge on skates, pausing only once to jam another bullet into the .303 and get her bearings. It seemed like the noise of the gunfight had brought all of the starving critters out of hiding.

They lumbered awkwardly out of the storefronts, out of the pubs and even Parliament House. Hang-faced killers watched her from balconies and broken windows, willing her to come just that little bit closer.

There.

She headed for the horse statue commemorating the Boer War, with a wary eye to the overgrown gardens of Government House. She was within stone's throw of the River Torrens, and once she had the water between her and Adelaide, the horde should find it harder to get to her. Wearily she considered her options. Without a car or a horse, it would take her days to trudge up the highway to Port Wakefield.

Her ribs gave a painful twinge then, and Gretel stopped by the base of the statue, leaning against the plinth and trying to catch her breath. By that point she was huffing like a horse herself—she didn't get to that size by running around a lot.

Past the barrier of wrecks, King William Street was broad and empty. Gretel considered the hulk of the Festival Centre, the rotunda long rotten and crumbling. Behind that, a gentle slope of overgrown grass, and boats drawn up to a dock.

Even as she smiled and shuffled towards the river, a shadow fell across her. Gretel had the barest moment to realise that a bear was dropping from the top of the horse statue, and cried out in terror.

It fell on her like a stone with teeth, clawing at her, biting. Even as they rolled around on the road, she had the presence of mind to jam her rifle stock into the drop-bear's snapping jaws. She held it at bay, crying out as the creature tore her arms to ribbons with its claws.

In one horrifying moment, the drop-bear crunched down on her big .303 with relish, shearing through stock, iron barrel and all. Spitting out all that metal and wood, the monster lunged at the woman, only to find itself spitted on a sharp blade. It looked at Gretel with its piggie eyes, bleeding and gurgling and confused to its last breath.

She rolled the creature to one side, pulling Purdie's big Bowie knife out of its throat. Slowly rising to her feet, she shuffled forward, bloody knife held limp and dripping in one hand.

Everything was pain. The riverbank seemed an impossible distance. Even as Gretel leaked blood from a dozen deep wounds, she staggered forward, unable to even muster a fast walk. Behind her she could hear them, a pack of starved killers hooting in delight, about to run her down in the middle of the road.

Then she saw it. Behind the Rotunda, parked neatly along the banks, she could now see the strangest machine. Something like a cross between a tractor and a steam-train, a big-bellied machine with a fat smoke-stack. It was draped with carnival lights, and behind it was a string of cars and trailers.

"Hey," she called out, waving her arms above her head. "Hey! Help me!"

The motion of her arms sent a wave of dizziness through her, and she wondered how much blood she'd lost. She shouted again, a wordless cry, and continued with the left foot, right foot, repeat, gasp.

She heard the machine cough into life, the hiss and roar of a big steam-engine. She was close enough now to see two figures hauling water pipes out of the river, and then they doused all the lights. Groggily she saw the road-train rolling forward, the reflection as it passed alongside the moonlit Torrens. They were leaving.

Gretel was on her knees now, and didn't even notice the transition. She stared at nothing in particular, and went somewhere beyond fear, past the pack of monsters that crept towards her. This was where she'd fallen, and she knew she wouldn't be getting up.

I die now, she thought, and that was when the machine crested the grassy banks, spot-lights suddenly ablaze, steam-whistle shrill and defiant. It was a juggernaut of metal, complete with iron cow-catcher. She saw the shape of a man in the cabin, and a boy scrambling onto the roof.

A seat up there. A turret, and above it the biggest crossbow she'd ever seen. The lad worked it with a set of levers, and it fired enormous spears just over her head. *Ka-chunk*, and then next big bolt was loaded into the crossbow, the string already drawn back and ready to fire.

"That's a steam-powered bow," she mumbled. She watched numbly as the machine slipped past her, didn't turn when she heard the crunching sounds, the squeals of pain. When the steam-engine returned and pulled up alongside her, she was still kneeling in the road, surrounded by a growing puddle of her own blood.

"Get up love," she heard a gruff voice say. "Please. I don't think I can lift you."

She felt a hand slide into hers, a rough calloused grip. Bleary-eyed, she rose to her feet, and in a weak daze she found herself remembering her father, remembered being scooped up on Christmas Eve, carried past a street of lit-up houses. Being safe, and warm, and on her way home.

"No room in the cab for you," the voice said. "You'll have to ride in back with my dad."

More movement, and somehow she hauled herself up a set of

steps. Then there was a flat surface under her back. Gretel let go, let the darkness come in.

*

"Hold still. Stop wriggling around!"

Gretel woke up fighting, thrashing around and yelling. It took her a long moment to realise that she was safe, and that a strange man was trying to stitch up her wounds.

She lay back down, blinking as the man fed a needle through her skin, sewing her up with something that looked suspiciously like fishing line. The man was aboriginal, his lined face buried in an enormous white beard. He wore an outfit of worn denim, and a greasy old Akubra on his head.

He whistled cheerfully as he worked, and in minutes he'd sealed up the worst of the damage. Her shirt was in shreds now, and Gretel felt a little embarrassed as the man poked around her ribs, pulling the wounds together.

She was in a type of trailer, stacked with crates and hessian sacks. Around her was a mess of bloody cloth, and the floor was damp beneath her. Sitting up made her feel woozy, and she wondered just how much blood she'd lost during the night.

It was dawn. Somewhere a pair of magpies were trading insults, and she could see trees, a crest of hill. They'd made it out of the city.

"Got an old shirt you can have," the man said, wiping his bloody hands on a rag. "Not much left of that one."

Gretel nodded. She saw a tousled head appear at the top of the steps, and under the mop of hair a pair of gentle brown eyes watched her warily.

"Boy," the man barked without turning. "Get water."

The lad disappeared like a skink.

"He doesn't talk," the man said. "Not to me, anyways."

Gretel finally managed to sit up, and rested her back against the wall of the trailer. That was when she saw the dead body. It was neatly packed up, like everything else back there. Canvas wrapped from head to toe, a coil of rope holding everything in place. But there was no mistaking that shape for anything but a corpse.

"That's my dad," the man offered. "Sorry. Don't have anywhere else for you to ride."

"That's okay," Gretel croaked. The quiet boy reappeared with water, and she sucked greedily from the canteen. The man gave her a shirt, a tent of flannel made for a big man. They gave her the privacy to change, and she gingerly removed the ruined shirt, let the bloody rag fall to the floor. It was all she could do to button up the new shirt, and then she was drifting back into asleep.

She woke to the movement of the steam-car. It was jolting around, and gripping the side of the trailer, Gretel peered over the side. She recognised the Princes Highway, and knew they were well into the Adelaide Hills. Her rescuer had taken the peculiar vehicle onto the shoulder of the Highway, and was passing a snarl of abandoned cars and trucks.

Up front, the road locomotive coughed and chugged. It looked like an old showman's machine, all decked out in lights and trim. PELICAN AND SON TRAVELLING SHOW—PERTH'S BEST!, the bunting declared. She could see the man in the cab, working the mass of levers and switches. Next to him the boy worked at shovelling, flicking coals from the tender and down into the furnace.

An enormous water tanker was attached behind the trailer she was in, and it was clear that the pair were equipped to travel a long distance in the old-fashioned machine.

Gretel was dozing off again, lulled by the motion of the road train. She woke with a start to find the boy sitting across from her, cross-legged from where he'd been watching her sleep.

"Got any food?" she asked, and the boy nodded shyly. He rummaged through the stack of supplies, emerging with a can of beans and finally a tin opener. She smiled her thanks. From a sack he pulled out a tile of oat biscuit, almost rock solid.

"Someone cooked this to last," she said, breaking the biscuit up with a dribble of water from her canteen. The boy kept his vigil, watching as she cracked open the baked beans.

"He your dad?" she said around a mouthful of food, indicating the man in the cab. The boy shook his head, and drew his knees up around his chin. He was months away from his last hair-cut, and it was impossible to tell if he was pink or black underneath all the coal-dust on his face and hands.

His shoes were a couple of sizes too big for him, ancient workboots held together with duct-tape and string. He wore an old school blazer over a t-shirt, and grimy slacks that needed taking up.

She did her best to scrape the cold beans out of the tin with the biscuit, and in the end she resorted to scooping them out with her fingers. She licked her fingers clean, and tossing the can onto the roadside she wondered if the boy would give her something else to eat. Even though her stomach rumbled and twinged, she did her best to keep to her manners, ignoring the big stockpiles of food around her.

"You got a name?" she ventured. "I'm Gretel."

He didn't offer a name in return, but leaned forward when she offered her hand, giving her a quick hand shake before returning to his side of the trailer. Gretel smiled, and they spent many miles in a companionable silence.

Soon they were looking down over the broad sweep of the Murray River, a brown ribbon winding to the horizon and beyond. The road led downwards, to a long bridge and a township on the far side. Either side, the trees grew thick, many sprouting from the water itself.

The man eased the road locomotive to a stop, climbed back over the tender to join his passengers. He sat next to the boy, tousling his hair affectionately.

"We're not stopping in Murray Bridge, but I can let you off there if you want," the man said. "Safer than Adelaide."

"Where are you going?"

"Lake Alexandrina," he said. "Gotta bury my dad there."

"Long drive just to bury a man," Gretel said. "Look around you. Everything is a graveyard."

"My dad was Ngarrindjeri," the man said, eyes suddenly bright and passionate. "He was born *here*, told me he wanted to come home before he died. Said he was strong enough to make the trip, but he died on the Nullarbor."

She looked at the body, now noticing the care which the man had wrapped it. She mumbled her apologies, and the man waved them away.

"Don't expect you to understand. Used to be our land, all around here. Then you white fellas took it, then the bears took it. Now it's no-one's."

When the road-train left Murray Bridge, Gretel rode with it.

✳

Gretel and the boy kept the fire going for three days, while the man kept vigil at the edge of the great lake. He buried his father by the water's edge, scooping out the sand and grit with his own hands. He didn't bother with a marker, and Gretel thought she understood.

She gave the boy a haircut, washed months of filth from his skin. His body was covered with scars, old jagged marks from a bear attack, silvered lines from a whip or belt. Someone had put a lit cigarette to his tiny little chest, over and over. Whatever horrors had brought him to this man had robbed him of all of his words.

Gretel did her best to care for the boy. She told him stories, sang silly songs her mother had taught her. Once, the boy laughed, and it was the most beautiful sound she could remember hearing.

When the man had finished mourning, he came back to their camp and slept like he was dead himself. By some sort of unspoken agreement the boy unpacked the trailer, erecting canvas shades and setting up a camp. After their journey of almost three thousand kilometres, she supposed the pair were entitled to a little break.

She learned the man's name was William Pelican, and he was the "Son" spoken of on the bunting on the steam-engine. Pelican Senior had been a boiler-maker over in Western Australia, and built the steam-tractor himself shortly after the Depression.

"We ran rides in the country fairs. Hurdy-gurdies, powered by the engine. Quiet times, he'd get the out-of-work circus folk, do little shows in towns. Cost us nothing to move from town to town. Just water, a little wood. Caught what food we needed."

They had fishing lines in the lake, and as the sun set they cooked a big mulloway over the coals of their fire. Pelican Senior had told stories of bad fishing, of a river in decline. It was rare to land such a big fish so far from the river mouth.

"Fish are coming back to the lakes," William said. "People gone away long enough, everything else starts to come back. Once the bears die out, the land will recover."

"What are you going to do now, William?" Gretel asked. She juggled hot fish meat in her hands, gobbling it down when it was cool enough to bear. The boy was wrapped up in a nest of blankets by the fire, watching them with dark eyes.

"I'm the first one to come back from the west," he said. "Figured I might stay now. Put in a claim."

"Claim?"

"Might not be tomorrow, might not even be next year, but they'll be coming over from Perth soon enough. When I left, they were getting a steam-train up and running. Once they've got the tracks fixed and the supply depots set up, people will come. Water here, good land."

"How many people?"

"There must be ten thousand now," William said, and Gretel nearly choked on her fish. Since the bears came, at most she'd seen two or three hundred people in one place.

"And I got here first," he said with some satisfaction. "They'll see the wreckage of Adelaide and keep on going. It'll be water drives the new world, not oil. Steam. And when they get to the Murray River, I'll be waiting for them. With a town. My town."

"An old bloke and a mute boy. You won't last five minutes out here. If the enclaves don't roll over you, a band of rovers will. There's some bad folks out on the road."

"Heh. They're all finished, just like the bears. Them out west have got a *government* now, and a train soon. Next comes the laws, and the money."

"Laws are just words," Gretel said. "And government didn't stop the bears here. Sabretooths in America, dinosaurs in Europe. All of our laws and money didn't do a damn thing. Humanity is on its knees, and we deserve to be here."

"Are you one of those believe we got punished? By God, or a mad scientist at Woomera?" William Pelican said, looking at her in mock seriousness.

"Yes. You give a better reason. Millions of monsters don't just happen."

"Here a reason—it doesn't matter why it happened." He spat a fish bone into the flames. "That's done. What matters is what we do now."

The lad watched him closely, and Gretel realised that the troubled boy worshipped William Pelican. He'd followed him across a dead continent, and would follow him in this new ambition. So would others.

"We live within our means. We let the land heal. The world has given us a second chance, and we'd best not fuck it up."

*

Two men trudged up the dusty road, bothered by flies and the sheer distance of their walk. They'd passed skeletons on the way, folks who died within a day of water. They passed by cars long gone to rust, and didn't even bother to tap at the petrol tanks these days.

A rumour drove their trudging feet onward. A prosperous new place, a town that had succeeded in opening up the Murray River to trade and settlement. Towns were springing up, right through into Victoria and New South Wales. Government was spreading from west to east, squashing out the looting enclaves wherever they resisted the rule of law.

Good manners were back in fashion.

When they heard the hissing and whomping of a steam-engine, the men stood their ground. Nowhere to hide here. One of the men held a revolver by his side, but his companion snatched it away, dropped it into the ditch for all the good it could do them.

A dust cloud approached, and the men waited patiently, only using their energy to flag the driver down when the vehicle got close. When the dust cleared, it revealed a refurbished LJ Torana, cherry-red.

The engine bay had been gutted to fit a bespoke steam engine, and water lines fed from a water tank in the boot to the boiler up front. From the depths of the car, a stereo was playing "Jump in My Car" by the Ted Mulry Gang.

"Well look at you two idiots," someone said, and the door opened to reveal a big woman, kitted out in animal hides. Dumbfounded, a man named Wog and a man named Percy watched as a dead woman stepped onto the road, as large as life.

"Gretel," Percy said. "We thought the bears got you."

"There were too many for us," Wog ventured after an awkward moment. "We had to run. You understand, right?"

"Well, as long as you boys can sleep at night," Gretel said. "So, where's your car?"

"No fuel left," Wog said. Percy said nothing, choosing to look down at his shoes.

"Oh hell, Gretel. You know what it was like. You'd have done the same if you were us. Bossman says you get someone, you get them."

"Hmm. So how's that world working out for you both?"

The men stood in the road, unable to frame anything worth saying. Gretel reached into the car, pulling out a loaded crossbow.

"Now Gretel, wait a minute—" Wog Carlotto said. She raised the weapon in their direction, and Percy gave a strangled cry as she pulled the trigger.

From a tree just behind them, an emaciated drop-bear fell to the ground, a fat crossbow bolt piercing it through the skull. The two men looked at each other, realising how close they'd been to death.

"Stupid things," Gretel said. "I've dropped shits scarier than that."

"Gretel, are you—are you going to the new town?" Percy ventured. "Pomberuk, or Murray Bridge or whatever they call it now?"

"Yep," she said. "About thirty kilometres that way."

The two men made to move forward, to get into her new car, but the big woman shook her head.

"Have a nice walk boys."

She climbed back into the car, and booted the home-made engine into hissing life. Throwing a lever, the steam-car lurched forward at a terrifying speed, the spinning tyres showering the men in sheep-shit and small stones.

Gretel left them in the dust, her music blaring, and gave a solid middle-finger salute out of the car window.

AFTERWORD

It's no mistake that when I approached Russell Farr with the idea for this collection, I suggested an emphasis on the post-apocalyptic. Since I've been tinkering away on short stories, time and time again I've returned to these scenarios.

The destruction of civilisation, of safety and comfort, the removal of the thousands of conveniences that we take for granted. I'm not sure whether it's a latent streak of misanthropy, or a fanboy's love of the subgenre, but post-apocalypses are a long-standing obsession of mine. It started with *Mad Max 2*, everything Romero ever looked at, and the clocking of countless hours on *Resident Evil*. For some reason I love to mash these obsessions together, which is why so much ozploitation gets into my short fiction.

It should be noted that I'm not a fan of apocalypses as such—the initial moments when everyone is running around, freaking out, and trying to figure out what to do ("We need to aim for the head!") bore me silly. "What happens next?" is the question I always ask myself. "What the hell are they going to do when the dust settles?"

So whenever I delve into a post-apocalypse, these are the questions that I'm trying to answer for myself. Like some sociopathic child with a magnifying glass, I like to watch my fictional worlds burn. All to see the people run around like ants afterwards, trying to build things up to something like they were. That to me is the meat of the sub-genre.

As for zombies, they are the sub-genre's rotten meat.

L'HOMBRE

This began life as my 24-hour challenge story at Writers of the Future. I had to combine three things—an interview with a stranger (house-painter from Guatemala), a token (5 peso coin), and an element researched in the Hollywood Public Library (supposed methods for the enchantment of weapons from folklore). I ended up with some sort of mongrel child of *Highlander* and your nanna's bridge game, if she was playing it at the end of the world. Dedicated to the late and great K.D. Wentworth, giver of tokens and soft-spoken teacher of many.

THE SCHOOL BUS

One of my ozploitation zombie tales, complete with zombie kangaroos, barricaded outback town full of hick cannibals, bus-full of idiot townies, and a quadruple amputee sex slave who is a thinly veiled Nicole Kidman. Oh, and the whole thing is told through the eyes of an innocent child.

UNDEAD CAMELS ATE THEIR FLESH

"Undead Camels" started life as a critique piece during the Clarion South workshop, where Gardner Dozois sang 'Undead Camels Ate My Flesh' to the tune of 'Camptown Ladies Sing This Song'. Jack Dann also sang this song, at the book-launch of *Dreaming Again*, where tonnes of folks joined in. As for the story . . . it's exactly what it says on the tin.

PIGROOT FLAT

Another foray into an Aussie zombie apocalypse. Here, I've written a reverse Wolf-Creek, added autistic zombies, and let a frustrated serial killer do the rest. Good times!

THE HOUSE OF NAMELESS

This is the story that won Writers of the Future, and led onto all sorts of cool things, including a draft opera libretto at the time of writing. Here I present a surreal post-apocalypse, the aftermath of a godly revolution. Intelligent city-ships, a randy minotaur, a man whose name has been erased from the universe, and a sassy teen caught up in the whole mess.

GOODNIGHTS TO HEAVEN

I wrote this as a Christmas present for fellow zombie aficionado Chuck McKenzie. It's kind of an homage to my Tamsyn Webb stories (zombies in Old Blighty), and a little nod to Cormac McCarthy's *The Road* as well. This has apparently made a few people cry, which means I've done my job properly.

FOR WANT OF A JESUSMAN

A true labour of love. This is the first story to feature Lanyard Everett, scum-bag, failed knight-errant and last of his order. Pseudo-Australian landscape, echidna men, and dimension hopping witches. Many violent and nasty doings ensue.

HUNTING RUFUS

This is one of my earliest science fiction pieces, where I unleashed an wave of carnivorous megafauna against an Outback town. It set the tone for much of my short fiction career.

GUNNING FOR A TINKERMAN

The sequel to "for want of a jesusman." "Tinkerman" follows Lanyard Everett on a fool's quest, and expands on his own murky past. Some of this material influenced *Papa Lucy and the Boneman*, a novel I wrote set in the same world.

ROLLING FOR FETCH

My first close call with the Writers of the Future contest. This is a steampunk dystopian love story, where gangs of scum chop off their feet to fit wheels on their legs. They race, roll for fetch (couriering) and generally terrify everyone. For love, our hero gives up the wheels he loves, and once more takes up the feet that he hates.

BUSKING

Inspired by the buskers of Rundle Mall. I posit a horrible event where everybody instantly vanishes, except for the confused buskers in a shopping strip. The only thing keeping them alive are their performances, which they don't dare stop . . . but how long *can* you juggle for?

WHEN THE CHEERFUL MISOGYNIST CAME TO TRUE TOWN

The sequel to my Writers of the Future winning story, in print for the first time. A minotaur and his foster-daughter find themselves under siege in a faux Algiers, and must travel to the last moments of the universe. There, Raoul and Imogen find themselves pitted against the minotaur's future self . . . who knows full well that he's coming to kill him.

GOGGY

A nasty, nasty piece of flash fiction. I cut my teeth writing short-short stories, and it seemed appropriate to add at least one. This particular story won me the Australian Horror Writers Association Flash Fiction contest one year, and has caused a few people to actually say "what is wrong with you?"

EVERYTHING IS A GRAVEYARD

This was great fun to write, and ticks all the boxes I need to tick. Post-apocalypse, check. Bogans scheming and double-crossing each other, check. 1970s cars pumping the music of the era, while scavengers pick over the corpse of Adelaide. A heroine who is built like a brick shithouse, taking on hordes of drop-bears with her cherry-red Torana. Check, check and check. I built the whole novella around the cover-art for this volume, which existed before the story. I love a good challenge, and like to think that I've delivered the goods.

Jason Fischer
Adelaide, September 2013

ACKNOWLEDGEMENTS

"L'Hombre" © Jason Fischer 2013. Appears here for the first time.

"The School Bus" © Jason Fischer 2010. First published in *Andromeda Spaceways Inflight Magazine #46*.

"Undead Camels Ate their Flesh" © Jason Fischer 2008. First published in *Dreaming Again*, edited by Jack Dann, Harper Voyager.

"Pigroot Flat" © Jason Fischer 2012. First published in *Midnight Echo #8*, Australian Horror Writers Association.

"The House of Nameless" © Jason Fischer 2009. First published in *L. Ron Hubbard Presents Writers of the Future Vol. 26*.

"Goodnights to Heaven" © Jason Fischer 2010. First published in *Necroscope—The Australian Zombie Review Blog*.

"for want of a jesusman" © Jason Fischer 2009. First published in *Aurealis Magazine #42*.

"Hunting Rufus" © Jason Fischer 2011. First appeared in *Midnight Echo #5*.

"gunning for a tinkerman" © Jason Fischer 2010. First appeared in *Aurealis Magazine #44*.

"Rolling for Fetch" © Jason Fischer 2012. First appeared in *Aurealis Magazine #49*.

"Busking" © Jason Fischer 2008. First appeared in *Midnight Echo #3*.

"When the Cheerful Misogynist Came to True-Town" © Jason Fischer 2013. Appears here for the first time.

"Goggy" © Jason Fischer 2011. First appeared in *Midnight Echo #5*.

"Everything is a Graveyard" © Jason Fischer 2013. Appears here for the first time.

TICONDEROGA PUBLICATIONS LIMITED HARDCOVER EDITIONS

978-0-9586856-9-6	Love in Vain BY Lewis Shiner
978-0-9803531-1-2	Belong ED Russell B. Farr
978-0-9803531-9-8	Basic Black BY Terry Dowling
978-0-9806288-0-7	Make Believe BY Terry Dowling
978-0-9806288-1-4	The Infernal BY Kim Wilkins
978-0-9806288-5-2	Dead Sea Fruit BY Kaaron Warren
978-0-9806288-7-6	The Girl With No Hands BY Angela Slatter
978-0-9807813-0-4	Dead Red Heart ED Russell B. Farr
978-0-9807813-3-5	Heliotrope BY Justina Robson
978-0-9807813-6-6	Matilda Told Such Dreadful Lies BY Lucy Sussex
978-1-921857-00-3	Bluegrass Symphony BY Lisa L. Hannett
978-1-921857-07-2	Bread and Circuses BY Felicity Dowker
978-1-921857-23-2	Wild Chrome BY Greg Mellor
978-1-921857-27-0	Midnight and Moonshine BY Lisa L. Hannett & Angela Slatter
978-1-921857-37-9	Prickle Moon BY Juliet Marillier
978-1-921857-41-6	The Bride Price BY Cat Sparks
978-1-921857-45-4	The Year of Ancient Ghosts BY Kim Wilkins
978-1-921857-68-3	Havenstar BY Glenda Larke

TICONDEROGA PUBLICATIONS EBOOKS

978-0-9803531-5-0	Ghost Seas BY Steven Utley
978-1-921857-93-5	The Girl With No Hands BY Angela Slatter
978-1-921857-99-7	Dead Red Heart ED Russell B. Farr
978-1-921857-94-2	More Scary Kisses ED Liz Grzyb
978-0-9807813-5-9	Heliotrope BY Justina Robson
978-1-921857-98-0	Year's Best Australian F&H EDS Grzyb & Helene
978-1-921857-36-2	Dreaming of Djinn ED Liz Grzyb
978-1-921857-40-9	Prickle Moon BY Juliet Marillier
978-1-921857-92-8	The Year of Ancient Ghosts BY Kim Wilkins
978-1-921857-28-7	Bloodstones ED Amanda Pillar (tpb)

THE YEAR'S BEST AUSTRALIAN FANTASY & HORROR SERIES
EDITED BY LIZ GRZYB & TALIE HELENE

978-0-9807813-8-0	Year's Best Australian Fantasy & Horror 2010 (hc)
978-0-9807813-9-7	Year's Best Australian Fantasy & Horror 2010 (tpb)
978-0-921057-13-3	Year's Best Australian Fantasy & Horror 2011 (hc)
978-0-921057-14-0	Year's Best Australian Fantasy & Horror 2011 (tpb)
978-0-921057-48-5	Year's Best Australian Fantasy & Horror 2012 (hc)
978-0-921057-49-2	Year's Best Australian Fantasy & Horror 2012 (tpb)

WWW.TICONDEROGAPUBLICATIONS.COM

THANK YOU

The publisher would sincerely like to thank:

Elizabeth Grzyb, Jason Fischer, Jason Paulos, Robert Hood,
Jonathan Strahan, Peter McNamara, Ellen Datlow, Grant Stone,
Sean Williams, Simon Brown, Garth Nix, David Cake,
Simon Oxwell, Grant Watson, Sue Manning, Steven Utley,
Lewis Shiner, Lezli Robyn, Talie Helene, Isobelle Carmody,
Stephen Dedman, Felicity Dowker, Terry Dowling, Dirk
Flinthart, Lisa L. Hannett, Kathleen Jennings, Martin Livings,
Penelope Love, Jason Nahrung, Angela Slatter, Anna Tambour,
Kaaron Warren, Cat Sparks, Donna Maree Hanson, Pete
Kempshall, Karen Brooks, Jeremy G. Byrne, Kim Wilkins,
Marianne de Pierres, Bill Congreve, Jack Dann, Janeen Webb,
Lucy Sussex, the Mt Lawley Mafia, the Nedlands Yakuza,
Shane Jiraiya Cummings, Angela Challis, Kate Williams,
Andrew Williams, Kathryn Linge, Al Chan, Alisa and Tehani,
Mel & Phil, Jennifer Sudbury, Paul Pryztula, Helen Grzyb,
Hayley Lane, Georgina Walpole, Rushelle Lister, Nerida
Fearnley-Gill, everyone we've missed . . .

. . . and you.

IN MEMORY OF
Eve Johnson (1945–2011)
Sara Douglass (1957–2011)
Steven Utley (1948–2013)